The History

of Us

The History of Us

Philip Leslie

Legend Press

Independent Book Publisher

Legend Press Ltd, 3rd Floor, Unicorn House,
221-222 Shoreditch High Street, London E1 6PJ
info@legend-paperbooks.co.uk
www.legendpress.co.uk

British Library Cataloguing in Publication Data available.

ISBN 978-1-9065581-0-9

Set in Times
Printed in the UK by J F Print Ltd., Sparkford.

Cover designed by Gudrun Jobst
www.yellowoftheegg.co.uk

Legend **Press**

Independent Book Publisher

Editor's Introduction

As the well-known epigram[1] reminds us, Geography is about maps, Biography about chaps. *The History of Us*, a biographical fancy, is about three chaps: our popular actor and national treasure James Rudd[2]; his friend the libidinous genius[3] Wilson who, behind all the mischief and fanfaronade, is a much-admired painter; and Alison Dury, *sine qua non*, of whom you will not have heard, and whose diary[4] forms a substantial portion of this book.

A brief word on structure. In the catalogue to his 2004 retrospective[5] Wilson describes how, during his time as an art college lecturer, he would drive to work not by the most direct route, but circuitously, along narrow lanes, through out-of-the-way villages and around a tortuous suburban maze. His reason? Because, Wilson being Wilson, he needed to ogle the beautiful women he knew would be waiting at various bus stops[6]. A waste of petrol perhaps, but his round-the-houses commute provides a useful analogy for the structure of this book. Put simply, do not expect to be taking the most direct route. At times you will even find yourself heading backwards[7]. Furthermore, inspired by parallel narratives in Faulkner[8], Golding[9] and Kaye-Smith[10], this editor has decided to keep each biography self-contained rather than blend them into an homogenous, chronological whole, thus better preserving their individual voices.

Notes:

[1] More accurately, a clerihew, named after the inventor of that species of humorous verse, Edmund Clerihew Bentley.

[2] It is requested that all correspondence regarding Inspector Poole should be directed to the various appreciation societies and internet fan sites, not this editor or his publisher, vita being so brevis, and ars, beautiful ars, being so much longa.

[3] '[Wilson's] moulding of the female nude is sheer genius.' Michael Hunt, *The Twenty-First Century Nude. Erotic Arts Review*, Summer 2004.

'In his nudes explicitness transcends mere concupiscence. It is not difficult to see why *Bonjour Louise!* – bold, brash, intellectually uncompromising – is his masterpiece, and possibly one of the greatest British paintings of the early 90s. Genius!' Chris Davies, *The Independent*, May 1994.

Or, if you prefer: 'Genius he is most definitely not. He's no more than a hard-on with a lavatory brush attached to it.' Jessica Toll, *Dirty Old Man: The Sordid World of Wilson. ArtSmack*, Winter 2000.

[4] Privately owned. Used with permission.

[5] *Private Parts, Public Places: Forty recent oils by Wilson.* Green and Smart Gallery, London 2004. Wilson's prolixity is counterbalanced by a short yet generous appreciation of the artist's work by James Rudd. 'Nothing escapes this painter's eye. He could solve a murder simply by setting up his easel next to where the body was found.'

[6] Not strictly true. Wilson neglects to mention that his daily journey was achieved in defiance of a three-year total ban resulting from drink-related driving offences. The various detours were necessitated by fear of arrest rather than voyeurism.

[7] According to the artist, the figurative works in *Private Parts, Public Places* were hung so as to offer the viewer 'a striptease in reverse'; an attempt to demonstrate how eroticism increases with concealment. The artist's thoughts on this subject are explored in conversation with Nicola Potter: *Christine Keeler's Chair*, Contemporary Art Studies, Spring 1999. W: 'You've watched porn, right?' NP: 'In the name of research, yes.' W: 'Same here. [Laughs] The point is, wouldn't you agree that the opening scene, when everyone's fully clothed, is powerfully erotic? It's the expectation, isn't it. I mean, here I am, sitting here with you, and the main thing that's running through my mind is: are those stockings or tights...?' [Winks and laughs]

[8] William Faulkner, *The Sound and the Fury*. New York, Jonathan Cape and Harrison Smith, 1931. Regarding Caddy, Faulkner said: 'To me she was the beautiful one, she was my heart's darling. That's what I wrote the book about and I used the tools which seemed to me the proper tools to try to tell, try to draw the picture of Caddy.' (Quoted on p97 in *The Achievement of William Faulkner*. Michael Millgate. Constable, London 1966.)

[9] William Golding, *Rites of Passage*. London, Faber 1980. While it is possible to close Golding's novel at the point when Talbot's narrative ends, true understanding comes only through reading Colley's letter. Similarly, the James and Alison sections of *The History of Us*, though independent, are the two halves of one whole.

[10] Sheila Kaye-Smith, *The Lardners and the Laurelwoods*. London, Cassell 1948. Out of print but well worth the effort of tracking down. Similar to the Faulkner in that four different

narratives – here, all third-person – when added together solve a puzzle.

JAMES

ONE

Look what I've found, Alison.

This photograph. It's us at sixteen play-wrestling in my nephew's sandpit. I'd not seen it for years, had I. And do you know where it was? It was caught in the pages of my first *Inspector Poole* script, which I discovered jammed behind the radiator in my study. Instantly: the jangling sunlight, the hair-drier breeze laden with thrips and dandelion fluff, the clamour of next door's kids, my brother hurrying into the garden with his instamatic pressed to his face, paparazzi-style.

How was I to have known Martin coveted you? Unwittingly I gave you to him. I grabbed you around the middle and lifted you, and you kicked out and bicycled and managed to overbalance me onto the hot sand, just as the camera clicked and he got your famous legs.

'Famous? Show me that. Now remind me about me. This girl I'm looking at.'

That's easy. Build: essentially lissom with the standard issue squidgy places. Height: above average. Hair: dark, shoulder-length, always perfectly sleekly groomed as if you were in an ongoing shampoo advert. Face: deadpan pale, ineffably pretty. Eyes: aluminium grey, huge. Voice: you'd been raised to eschew the local accent and to *enunciate*. I loved your voice. I miss it tremendously.

'Appearance?'

Smart but casual. No great interest in fashion.

'Did this girl have any hobbies?'

Books, the cinema.

'The very solo pursuits they advise you not to put on a CV, along with chess and self-abuse.'

Books and cinema are on mine. My interest in *Who's Who* is 'staring out to sea while staring in to see'. Can't get more solitary than that.

'How long had we been friends at the time your brother snapped us?'

Oh, since for ever. I can still remember when I met you. Our mothers were chatting outside your house. They used to do that at one time. I spotted you in your front garden and strayed in to see who you were and what you were doing. After that, mainly because of our proximity as near neighbours, we were rarely apart. You were invited on holidays with us and I accompanied your family to the cottage you rented in Dorset. We were glued together, even through the trials of puberty. People often wrongly assumed we were a couple.

'Describe the you I'm looking at.'

He's a fraction taller than the girl, slim, with a mousy mop. Not particularly smart, definitely casual. As for his voice, his parents had no preference as to how he spoke, only that he spoke sense. Although his local accent had vanished, undermined by elocution lessons and years of parroting other accents. His interests included amateur theatre and staring at the sea – or into blank space, whichever happened to be handy at the time. He was something of an artist too; a draughtsman rather than a painter. Mainly stage designs which his mother sometimes used, although he drew you once.

'And the stamping ground of these good friends –?'

– was Gorleston-on-Sea, a sprawling accumulation of housing estates to the south of Great Yarmouth on the Norfolk coast. We lived at the southern end of the town, on an enclave of 1960s bungalows a short stroll from the seafront. Our nearest pub was a 1930s Art Deco former hotel situated halfway along Marine Parade within beer-mat-frisbeeing distance of the sea. In spite of its attractive curved-brick central bay, its assorted projections and period asymmetry, its once-fashionable strata of brick, painted concrete transoms and Crittall, *The Links* was incomprehensibly bulldozed in the late nineties to make room for five architecturally unremarkable executive-style dwellings. I added my voice and household name to the protests, but the decision to raze it had already been passed. I shed a few tears. I know a lot of people who did.

Back at the start of the eighties, just before those Reagan-Thatcher argy-bargy years, you and I could be found in *The Links* most evenings.

'"Pint of bitter, please." That was you as the narrator in *Return Journey*. Surely there can't be many people who learnt to order beer from reading Dylan Thomas.'

Except we could usually only afford half pints, taking miniscule sips to make each one last an hour. When we were so destitute that even an eighteen-pence cordial was beyond our combined means, we'd exile ourselves to the seafront, loitering with no intent, or waging guerrilla attacks on the sea with stones. Or else we'd take your celebrated timorous taupe terrier for long walks.

'*Oliver*. I loved my boy Oliver.'

When the weather was bad we'd sit in one of the concrete shelters, as snug as a pair of OAPs. We'd sit there in the dark, too, waiting for navigation lights to pass across the blackness. We pretended they were sprites, lost souls, inconceivably far-off stars. But the prosaic mercantile truth was equally inspiring. Our game was imagining how far those ships had travelled or where they were bound.

'Nantucket perhaps. I often wondered if the place was as lovely as the name. Your favourite destination was Archangel.'

Relentless snow and colossal stone buildings crowding

around an ice-locked harbour. That's how I've always pictured it, anyway. I never want to know what it's really like. I suspect in reality it's as mundane as Hull or Harwich.

'Much of our river traffic was from mundane-sounding places. Amsterdam. Rotterdam.'

I was invited to Amsterdam once to meet Poole's Dutch fans and the actor who dubbed my voice, but I really couldn't face the journey. Shortly afterwards the fans disbanded their club and started the Morse Appreciation Society in a fit of pique.

'Your favourite memory, please.'

That's difficult.

'Pick one favourite memory, then.'

Southwold, December 1980.

'Apart from when we... Apart from that.'

Christmas Day 1980. You called on me first thing with Oliver. I'd only just ripped open my presents: socks and Toblerone from you, a pile of paperbacks, a new pen, a couple of LPs, and I'd treated our lungs and my vocal chords to a black plastic cylinder of fifty John Player Special.

'Our parents would have gone ballistic. My other present to you was a diary, which you never used. I stayed for toast and coffee while you got dressed. You were hard work that morning: could hardly bring yourself to talk to me. As soon as we arrived at the beach you pulled away from me and played with Oliver. I leaned against one of the sea defences, watching the waves swipe half-moon shapes out of the sand. For ten minutes you seemed to forget I existed. You gave Oliver so much attention that he had no need for me. Then suddenly you turned and stared, and *stared*, as if you'd been hypnotised, and walked slowly towards me, and we noticed we were both crying, and I put my arms out and we hugged.'

I told you things you closed your ears to, and you stopped my mouth with a limpet kiss. We drew apart when Oliver was being threatened by a bully Alsatian.

Afterwards we sat in dazzling sunlight in our favourite glazed shelter on the upper esplanade, smoking the ciggies, reciting chunks of *Under Milk Wood* from memory. It had been my school production in December, and I'd read the part of the first narrator. You, typically, knew the play better than I did. I wasn't thick, I just wasn't perspicacious. You and I could read the same book or watch the same movie and you'd see all sorts of things that I'd miss. I really have to work hard to understand the characters I play. Saying that, Poole is a doddle. He's simply the superhero version of me.

'Acting was your thing. Right from the start.'

If I managed to get the required grades, I intended to train to be an *ack*-tor at drama school.

'Your mother was right behind you.'

I've never known anyone so passionate about theatre. She directed three, four plays a year.

'Finding roles for you in most of them.'

I'd run the gamut, from an urchin in *Oliver* to murdered child in the Scottish play to football hooligan in *Zigger-Zagger*. I think I was probably quite good.

'Although you were far too modest to admit you were.'

Are you implying I was conceited?

'Sometimes you were. If you were high on applause and curtain-calls you could be insufferable. Or when your poem was in the *Yarmouth Mercury*. Or when you did that big drawing of me.'

That was a good attempt, for a novice. Half life size, charcoal and white chalk and more than a drop of spit. I had you reading a book, prone, with your legs in those bottle-green nuclear-blast-proof tights, raised up and crossed at the ankles. Your hair was spilling over your shoulders and onto the page you were studying. Took me hours.

'Three hours, to be precise. You refused me more than one break an hour, even when I was in agony. I'm sure there's a law to prevent exploitation of life models. Poole would have come to my rescue.'

It paid off, though, didn't it. Mum reckoned I was a genius and showed the finished picture to a local painter.

'Who got it framed and exhibited in Yarmouth Central Library. *Local Art 1981*. Success went straight to your head. You even phoned the *Mercury* to do a feature on you.'

And sent them a snotty letter when they didn't.

'Such a bighead.'

That was nothing. You should've been around when I landed my first sizeable TV role six years later (bi-sexual drug-dealing ice-cream seller fleeing Hastings, pursued by the Triad). The day after it was shown I walked along Oxford Street anticipating a rugby scrum for autographs. I'd even bought a pen. I was disappointingly ignored. And insanely jealous when I heard that my co-star had been mobbed by appreciative students while his taxi was stuck at traffic lights.

'Jealousy was your Achilles' heel. You really hated it when I posed for Wilson.'

I'll tell you what really rankled about all that business. You were my model and you posed for him. It felt treacherous, especially when I saw you'd given him the same pose with the book, your face turned to the artist, watching him watching you watching him.

'He was at Yarmouth art college. It was all above-board.'

Wilson was a notorious lech.

'Unfounded. He behaved himself perfectly with me.'

Ogling your body.

'James, James, I got ogled by builders when I cycled to school. When I sat in *The Links* I got ogled. Even Anne's dad used to look at me strangely. At least when an artist ogles you it's for an artistic end. It's the equivalent of your stage-kissing an actress on camera. You wouldn't call that a real kiss, would you. I'll tell you what annoyed you so much: his drawing was miles better than yours. As it should've been.'

I was livid when it was chosen for his college's exhibition in the library less than one month after my picture was shown. And it ended up on your bedroom wall, didn't it; pride of place next to posters of *Japan* and *Le Genou de Claire*, the film by Eric Rohmer our twin-town visitors projected at a meeting of the Rambouillet Society. You refused the offer of mine.

'a) it was far too big, and b) your parents wanted it. I was happy having a photo of it. That went on my wall.'

For about a week. Then it disappeared. You claimed you'd taken it to Lowestoft to show to your grandmother. Really you'd consigned it to a shoebox of odds-and-sods under your bed.

' – !'

Archived along with such treasures as a punk-style collaged invitation to Anne's fifteenth birthday party (at which I observed you snogging with Simon, and an hour later with Darren) and a wristband thrown to you at Wimbledon by Sue Barker.

' – ?!'

I looked once.

'When?'

When we were reading in your room and you went to answer the phone. I was poking about hoping to discover your diary. I wanted to find out what you'd written about Southwold.

'I didn't keep it under my bed, Mr Nose. It was wrong of you to look.'

You looked under mine!

'In case you'd acquired any interesting perusal-material without telling me. There was no diary. If there had been, I wouldn't have read it.'

I've always been too lazy to keep a diary. If something's worth remembering, I make a point of remembering it. Poole's lines, for example, or the history of you and me. Only trouble is, I find myself remembering lots of useless stuff as well. I wouldn't say that Christmas 1981 is worth remembering, but I have photographic recall.

'It wasn't the best of reunions, was it.'

Disastrous. Utterly. Especially when you think how symbiotic we'd once been. That time when I suffered all day from stomach pains and I called on you in the evening to discover you tucked up on the sofa with a hot water bottle, debilitated by a painful period. Uncanny, that. Or that time we skived off for the afternoon and met in the concrete shelter without having pre-arranged it. Pure symbiosis.

'Symbiosis my foot! Maybe if you'd kept a proper written diary you'd see, yes, how much in love we were, but also how separate our lives were. I probably spent as much time with Anne as I did with you. And I went out with Wilson for almost a month that last summer before we left Gorleston.'

Pathetic gangling flick-fringed drunken art college layabout waster. I remember the first time I saw him, when he was drawing a giant sexually aroused man (sort of David Hockney meets the Cerne Abbas giant) on the sand at low tide. It was twenty, thirty yards long, so that the further you were from it, the easier it became to read. A woman with two kids in a buggy swooped down from the upper esplanade to tell him if he didn't erase it she'd do so herself because it was crude and disgusting. Wilson smirkily explained it was quite the opposite, it was a celebration of blah-blah-blah – some twaddle he'd read in a book on Celtic mythology and was now regurgitating to make the woman feel intellectually inferior. He was such an arrogant piece of work.

'He needed to grow up, that's all. Did he erase it?'

What do you think? He leaned on the handrail, laughing, while the woman obliterated the cock and balls with a length of driftwood. When he saw me watching, he said, 'I wish I had a cine camera. Project the film backwards and it'd look as though she's drawing.'

A few weeks later he turned up in *The Links*, but he didn't recognise me. There were more interesting things for him to swivel his eyes at or observe indirectly in the distorting Claude glass of his Guinness-and-bitter.

I remember a lot about him; much more than I care to. I remember the weasel face with that congenital supercilious sneer. I remember the occluding fringe which pointlessly rendered him monocular until tossed or swept aside. I remember the cigarette-kippered contrived slovenliness; the caricature-toff demeanour which developed over the course of an evening from braggart to boor with each additional excessive beer. When sober he could be a lurker, I remember, sidelining himself to the periphery in order to watch and measure us and furtively jot his observations in a notebook none of us was ever permitted to see. Most of all, I remember that in spite of these and other shortcomings, he managed to captivate and eventually pull the darling of Grove Grammar. Quite how, I'll never understand.

'We got talking down the pub one night.'

Where was I?

'In the pub too. It was Darren's birthday. Your rival for my affections was in the saloon with Anne and her boyfriend and me. You were in the lounge next door playing snooker with the gang. You were very drunk, and no less boorish than Wilson. We kept hearing you. "Sink the pink!" Funny, but funnier was knowing you were unaware that it meant something rude.'

Never mind that. Fraternising. Behind my back. With Wilson of all people. Why couldn't you content yourself with Darren? You two got on. He was likeable. He liked you.

'Because the art student was a novelty. He told us about art. The man who kicked off modern art when he exhibited a urinal. What the Tate pile of bricks was about. He got us debating if graffiti is art. Then he asked me if he could draw me. I struck a pose but he explained not here, in his studio. I thought it was wonderful he had a studio. He was using the upstairs of his cousin Sharon's recently acquired chip shop while it was closed for renovation.'

My Plaice. Goes by a different name these days. We bought some chips from there when it was *Upon My Sole* and there was sand on them. You had a go at the owner when he refused to give us a refund. You turned into Barbara Woodhouse.

'Bogus bluster, that's all. Method acting. You should know all about that. Got us our twenty pences back, didn't it? And probably speeded up its demise.'

Tell me about this so-called studio of Wilson's. I never saw it.

'There was no 'so-called' about it. It was the genuine article. He'd turned the bedsit into a place of work. I liked it up there. You had virtually a ringside view of the harbour mouth from the east window, so you could see ships coming and going. I used to watch them while Wilson painted.'

I'd be interested to know how many other girls that Don Juan of the palette knife enticed into his lair.

'Since when has Don Juan had a lair?'

Don't be picky. You know what I mean. How many others?

'Two or three. He was an artist, James. They paint people. That's what they're supposed to do. Do you think he still paints?'

In the early nineties I was doing a play at the *Hexagon* in Reading. One afternoon, to unwind after the matinee, I went for a stroll. I saw a poster advertising an exhibition of his. His name was in big letters, as if he was famous, or trying to be. He'd called the exhibition *Tracts and Figures*. I went along for a gander. Just to see what he was up to. How good he was. Or how bad. There were twenty large oil portraits and twenty touristy-type watercolour landscapes. The landscapes were all very competently done, reasonably priced and red dotted, but I found them soulless. The oils, on the other hand, were the real McCoy. They were amazing. Half of them showed curvy or lanky lovelies lolling about on draperies, semi-clothed or starkers; while half were more sober portraits painted about ten years earlier. I recognised Julie at twenty paces. He'd caught her to a T.

'Were the ones of me there?'

I was coming to those. There were three of you. A zigzag composition depicting you in a flowery frock draped sideways across an armchair –

'Wilson devised the pose, but it was my idea to pull up the frock to show my legs. Famous legs.'

Which were luminous creamy white while the rest of you and the background was in shade.

'Chiaroscuro.'

It was very effective. Then there was the painted version of the drawing of you reading –

'Bottle-green tights, red and black dress, on a daffodil-yellow throw. The throw smelt fusty. What was the third picture?'

You on a bed reading. White drape on the bed. Lit from above somehow –

'Because there was a skylight over the kitchen area. He'd hung blankets at the main windows so the top light dominated my form.'

Oh, very posh. Top light. Form.

'They're words, James. Monosyllables, at that. What would you prefer: zenithal illumination of my reclining position?'

I just prefer you to sound like you when you speak, not like Wilson.

You're top lit, stretched full out on your right side with your back to the viewer; the artist. Your face is turned to look over your shoulder.

'I got such a crick in my neck. I remember the pose evolved as we went along. I was wearing a man's baggy shirt.'

Sort of fell off, did it? Or did he rip it off with his teeth?

'Grow up, James.'

How could you have posed for him like that? With nothing on. Imagine my surprise.

'It was no big deal. Didn't you think he did my feet really well? He even got the sore bits on my heels where my new shoes had been chafing.'

Nude, though! You'd have refused point blank to pose nude for me if I'd asked.

'Too right. If anyone was going to be staring at my squidgy places, they'd have to be a serious artist.'

Wilson was just a student.

'A serious student, though. You'd be hard pressed to find anyone else with his dedication. He worked on that particular picture eight hours a day for a fortnight. I posed for it an hour each day. Always between one and two in the afternoon, when the sun was blazing straight down through the skylight. We listened to music. And we chatted.'

You two always were good at chatting. Books, art, music. I never could do the old conversation thing. I'm the dour silent type unless I'm being paid to act otherwise. Maybe that's why I've never found anyone who'd marry me.

'Cue violin.'

Not that I've been looking.

'Cue an entire string section.'

I've only ever wanted you.

TWO

Cue Wilson, summer 1981, unlocking the Windolene-smeared front door of his cousin's out-of-action shop.

'You're early,' he says, swiping his overlong fringe out of his eyes. The trademark cigarette smoulders between trademark ochre fingers. He stands aside to let you in, then locks the door again. You know the routine. You squeeze past the fryers, which have been draped in dustsheets, and ascend the narrow wooden stairs to the bedsit.

The one spacious room, with windows to the east and the south and a skylight, is filled with clamorous summer light. You like it up here, in spite of the neglect, the ancient damp stains on ceiling and walls, the unshiftable smell of mildew and cold chip fat and sun-rotted curtains. You like the view of the harbour mouth and the utilitarian pier with its boxy coastguard station at the end. You like the view from the south window too: the *Pier Hotel*, the discus-shaped dance hall called *Ocean Room*, and the beach bustle glimpsed in the gap between buildings. But most of all, you like this room because he is up here being *obsessed* with you. Drawing you, painting you. Initially he was obsessed by your face. He confessed that your face was the magnet that attracted him back to *The Links* after his January recce. He is too shy to admit to now being obsessed with your famous legs as well.

You help him peg a heavy brown blanket over each window. He offers you a cigarette and readies himself for the afternoon's session. With the care of a surgeon preparing to operate, he lines up his brushes and palette knife on a table beside the easel on which your picture rests. There is no shortage of paint. Any dribble of money that is not spent on cigarettes or alcohol is used to buy paint.

'One is a right royal lazy cow today,' you tell him, using the Queen's nasal tone. 'One stayed in one's bed until twelve. One has only just had one's breakfast.'

'Late night?' Wilson inquires, searching though his cassettes for suitable music.

'Half two,' you tell him in your usual voice. 'I went round Anne's and we had a good old rant about boys.'

'Oh.'

'Not *you*. Darren's been shitting her about. And James is being a complete pain.'

'In what way?'

'The usual.' You stub out your cigarette and start unbuttoning your blouse. 'The green-eyed monster.'

'Dr David Banner?' he says in what's supposed to be an American accent. "You won't like me when I'm angry."'

'He's jealous. Of you. And me. Up here. And him not knowing exactly what we get up to. His imagination has been busy.'

'You're welcome to bring him here.'

You throw your blouse over the back of a chair and unzip your skirt. 'I don't want him here. This is private. You'd prefer not to have people nosing about in your studio, wouldn't you?'

Wilson nods. 'Even Sharon doesn't come up here without asking.'

Turning your back to him, you unhook your bra and pull on the man's shirt, which is already buttoned; then you step out of your knickers and throw these, along with the bra, on top of the skirt. (When you first began posing for this particular picture you would take great pains to conceal them.) You hug yourself, awaiting instructions while Wilson ignites a cigarette with his Zippo. He's the boss.

You climb onto the bed. Using the painting as a guide he directs you into position. He fine tunes, tweaking the shirt, taking extreme care not to touch you; arranging your hair; directing you to move your upper foot first this way then back as it was. You enjoy this formal intimacy, fanning out your toes as a measure of your delight.

'*The Planets Suite*?' he inquires.

'Not today. I feel in the mood for some jazz, Daddy-O.'

Wilson's taste in jazz is relatively conservative at this stage. Later he will prefer the way-out, but in 1981 the formative period of Miles Davis is to his taste. He chooses the Miles Davis Quintet *Live in Europe*, which he has taped from an LP. It is an exciting record, raw, energetic. Good to work to.

'Herbie Hancock's playing brilliantly,' Wilson remarks, swaying his hips to the beat. 'Listen to that. Proper jazz. Not like his recent electronic crap.' Wilson is strong on opinions. He knows what's what. He knows which artists are good, which are crap. He knows which novels are worth reading, and which authors ought to be pulped. But these days he is always careful to check who is sitting nearby before mouthing off. Once he was in a café in Norwich, giving his ill-considered opinions on the state of the contemporary novel to a girl he'd known from school, when who should be overhearing this tirade from an adjacent table but a lecturer in the Contemporary Novel from the University of East Anglia. She leaned across and asked, 'Ah, but have you read so-and-so's last novel?' Wilson admitted that he'd not. 'Then have you read such-and-such's novels?' 'Never heard of them.' Stripped of his authority, Wilson resorted to sarcasm. 'Never heard of 'em, and I expect they're overrated.' To which the woman replied, 'Overrated? I wouldn't say my novels are *overrated*.' I wish I'd been there to see Wilson's cheeks turn the colour of the rose madder he is now squeezing from the tube to mix with a blob of zinc white.

'Got to get those heels right,' he says. 'God, I love this sax solo.' He dikkadums tunelessly along.

'It is good,' you say. But what do you know? Why is it a good solo? Simply because it is loud and breakneck? Perhaps you agree with Wilson because you don't want him to think you are thick. You are in awe of him. You accept whatever claptrap he comes out with not because you believe he is more intelligent than you, but because he is a year older and the King of Bullshitters. This offering up of your backside for scrutiny is as instinctive as Oliver submitting to the investigations of a Doberman.

'Apparently they have good jazz at the *Royal Oak* in Ormsby,' you tell him.

'Then we'll have to go,' he replies quickly. Now he will be able to brag to his chums down *The Links* that Alison has asked him out. Like the time your best friend Anne bumped into him in Great Yarmouth and they'd spent the afternoon together, and Wilson had turned truth into a rubber band when he reported to his chums how Anne had *invited* him shopping. Girls enjoy his company, but they only want him as a pal, not for a mate. He gets too drunk too often; he smokes too much. You couldn't take him home to meet the parents.

Except you had. You wanted your mum to meet the artist you were posing for (fully clothed you'd said, of course, although there were nervous jokey remarks made about nudes). Admittedly he had behaved impeccably, saying please and thankyou and resisting the need to light up. The only controversial moment was when he grabbed your sixth-form photo from the top of the TV and admired it a little too ardently. Apart from that, he managed to rein himself in, talking sensibly about books with your mother. She was a voracious reader, although her taste was for detective fiction, which Wilson did not rate unless it had been critically acclaimed as literary. Not that he told her this.

'Dikkadah – dikkadikkadah –' He conducts the quintet with his brush. 'You okay?'

'Uh huh.' You think again. 'Actually I'm getting pins and needles in my foot.'

'Take five, then. Fancy a coffee?'

You slowly roll onto your back. Having poked the shirt between your legs, you cup your hand there in the interests of propriety. Wilson fills the kettle and busies around you searching for the least stained mugs. All the while his eyes are surreptitiously flitting across your body, perhaps hoping for a glimpse of that downed cranny you conceal like a pet shop owner reassuring a timid hamster that has strayed near the reptile tank.

You sit upright to accept the mug. He passes you a lit cigarette, fitting it neatly into your pout. You enjoy the intimacy of the gesture. You fix your eyes on his for a few seconds longer than would be seemly, experiencing a low-voltage tingle of excitement. He is fully clothed and you are not. And now you notice his attention is drawn below your chin, to the vee of your inadequately buttoned shirt.

To close the vee would mean you are bothered. You're not. You say, 'God, if my mum walked in now.'

This breaks the spell. Wilson sniggers. 'Or James.'

'Or my dad.'

'Or Sharon.' Wilson reconsiders. 'Actually, she wouldn't say a thing. This is what artists and models are supposed to do together. You could be nude and it would be perfectly normal.'

'I don't think I could go nude.'

Wilson shrugs. 'There's nothing more natural than nudity. It's not erotic at all. Clothes make a person erotic. What's sexier, you stark naked or you in a flattering bikini?'

Seeing the picture of the two yous he has put in your head, you slowly nod.

'Sexy is imagining what you can't see,' Wilson continues. 'I mean, look at those two paintings.' He nods towards the previous clothed compositions. 'They're miles sexier than if you'd had your kit-off. The one in the frock works because I've deliberately fetished your legs while keeping the rest of you under wraps. The same with the one of you reading. And both pictures are sexy because the person looking at them imagines the body under the clothes.'

'Since when have bottle green tights been sexy?'

'It's what's in them that's sexy.' Wilson, becoming increasingly animated, waves the cigarette about. 'Have you ever seen any porn on film – or video?'

'Might have done. Why?' You find yourself blushing.

'Well, don't you agree that the sexiest part of the show is when the actors are all fully clothed at the start, idly chatting and pretending to be getting to know one another? As soon as the clothes start flying off all sense of mystery evaporates. Naked people are boring.'

'So where have you been watching all this porn?'

Now it's Wilson's turn to blush. 'Someone brought a tape to one of Darren's parties. How about you?'

You delay replying by holding the mug to your lips. 'You mustn't tell anyone this.'

'I won't. I've told no one about this latest picture we're doing, have I.'

'Well, James and I were round Anne's one night.'

'Anne's into rude films?'

'No!' You take a long drag on the cigarette. Your smoke curls and eddies below the skylight like a ghostly eel. 'Her dad has got a tape hidden in a box on top of the wardrobe. And the tape's further hidden inside a nondescript box marked *Electrical Bits*.'

'And Anne just happened to find it.'

'Something like that. Anyway, one night when her parents were out, Anne fetched it down and she, James and I watched

it. Anne and I thought it was pretty yukky and silly. But James...
It got James so hot and bothered he had to nip to the bathroom.'
You laugh, remembering my stooping, chimpanzee gait, and
Anne's crude remark about minding where I aimed.

At this mention of my name Wilson says, 'How come you
two have never been an item?'

'Because he's my best friend.'

'And best friends never hook up as lovers?'

'Definitely not.' You stab the dog end into a *We Had a Lovely
Time in Gorleston-on-Sea* ashtray.

Thinking he has irritated you, Wilson says, 'I'll change the
tape,' using an amusing voice to conceal his embarrassment.

'No more jazz. Something calm.' You lie on your back,
moving your toes, staring at the sky through skylight grime.
While Wilson calls out suggestions for music, you
experiment with the hem of the shirt, raising your arms to
reveal the paler tops of your thighs. You realise what he
means about clothes. There is nothing stopping you from
tearing the shirt open and showing him everything. But this is
far more interesting and delectable for both of you, to suggest
rather than reveal.

'Delius, *Japan* or Kate –' he glances round suddenly.
' – Bush?'

'Delius,' you decide. 'No, let's have a drop of old Katie:
Lionheart.' You roll into the pose, your heart pounding in your
throat. Bush. Had he seen? What if you'd inflamed his desire
and he climbed onto the mattress with you? Would you evict
him?

The record starts. *Symphony in Blue*. Wilson has a liking for
this odd, melancholy music. You have chosen it because he
likes it. You want him to feel comfortable. You feel him
approach. If he wants you, he can have you. You wait for his
touch.

'I'm just going to, ah –' He lifts the shirt past your bum,

taking scientific care not to touch you. Surely by now he was feeling the urge to ravish you. He'd ravished Julie, hadn't he? Snogged her? Felt her up?

'The light's already beginning to change,' he informs you. 'We won't be able to paint for much longer.'

'Draw me afterwards, if you like.'

'If you feel up to it.'

'Short poses. I like those.'

Wilson concentrates on getting weight into the top leg, to make it look as though it's pressing down. Something's wrong, however. The leg is starting to lose its shape. He consults a postcard illustration of the *Rokeby Venus*, an inspiration for his own painting.

'It's not going right,' he confesses, scowling at his paintbrush. 'You might as well get up and have another stretch.' He switches off the music, scowling at the cassette player as if he suspects a conspiracy is going on. 'What we need is a coffee.'

Wilson's exasperation concerns you. You want him to be happy. Having volunteered to make the coffee, you flit and flirt around him, gathering cups and spoons and jars, wearing the shirt like a miniskirt, exaggeratedly stretching and bending. He doesn't appear to notice this peek-a-boo game, however. Unless he's an expert at play-acting self-absorption. Not that you care. You're finding this modest and intermittent exposure stimulating. On tippytoe you reach up to help him take down the blankets. He has to have seen something by now. Bottom. Bush. Was he this boring with all his models?

For there have been others. They feature in several large oils and acrylics leaned faces to the wall. He showed them to you a month ago, when you first came to pose.

'I want to look at these again.' You reverse the stretchers while Wilson throws the windows open to cool the room.

'This is so like Julie,' you tell him. Wilson has posed her in jumper and jeans on an upright chair glowering into space. Her legs are straight out and overlapped at the ankles, her arms crossed as if bored. Julie is famous for being bored. She was once bored at a Red Arrows air display off Lowestoft, when everyone else was rigid with excitement.

A different model. 'What's this girl's name again?' You sit on your haunches to inspect the painting.

'Claire.'

'Did you ask her, or did she offer?' Claire is nude, on her back with her arms behind her head and her defiant face withering the viewer.

'Fifty-fifty.'

The painting dates from immediately after the Julie ones and shows an advance in technique. It is more tightly controlled, more realistic, better observed.

'It's very good,' you tell him.

Wilson closely regards his handiwork, oblivious to the now extreme décolletage you are presenting.

'It's okay. They liked it at my interview. I think it works so well because I'd run out of paint and only had three or four colours to use. Less is more.'

'You liked Claire a lot.'

'You reckon? Why?'

'Well, for a start –' You break off to enjoy the frisson caused by him towering above you. 'For a start she's starkers.'

'So? It's a life painting. Nothing unusual about that.'

'No, but you've made her more than just flesh and bones. She's got personality. Like a proper painting.'

'Proper painting,' he mocks.

'As in Norwich Castle Museum proper painting.'

'Interesting.'

Is it? Perhaps you can think of some other interesting comment. You scrutinise the fifteen square feet of canvas, corner to corner, edge to edge. 'I think...' You point to the eyes, one of which is partly obscured by a lock of brown hair. 'That's why she's a bit raunchy.'

'It is?'

'Watch.' You show your face to him, first without, then with a veil of hair. 'It's the same as your theory about clothes being erotic.'

He's nodding. 'You're right. She's starkers, and yet she's still hiding something from us. You're brilliant.' Wilson swipes his own fringe out of his eyes and rewards you with a cigarette and a digestive biscuit. 'I've been wondering for ages why it's not completely objective. That's what's wrong about the one I'm doing of you now. There's no come-hither. Someone's going to stand in front of it and think so what?' He's on his feet and thinking aloud at the easel. You remain on the worn carpet, cross-legged and wide-eyed like some awed novice.

'I mean, I could have the shirt hiding more bum.' He draws a line with his cigarette: 'The less you see, the more you have to imagine. Or... You might not like this, but if you're up to it, you could do away with the shirt altogether and try the hair-thing.'

'I could do that.'

Wilson pulls on an invisible old master's goatee. 'Except then you'd be looking the wrong way –'

'You want me facing you?' Your lower abdomen grinds with nervous pleasure.

'How about you just look back at me. Want to try? There's no pressure.'

You finish your cigarette and coffee first. Then you disappear into the grimy lavatory for a pee, afterwards gazing dreamily for a long while through the mossy skylight, idly touching yourself. It would take little effort to come, but you've been in here too long already, and you can hear Wilson moving about, no doubt impatient to continue. You pull off the shirt and stride confidently towards him across the room.

'You've got to say hello,' you demand.

'Who to?'

'All me bits.'

Wilson is clearly torn between averting his eyes and gawping. He chooses to gawp.

You rub a tiny bruise below your collarbone he has noticed. 'Oliver jumped up,' you explain, in case he's wondering. A trifle too coolly you announce, 'I'm ready. How do you want me?'

Wilson has to swallow twice before he can reply. 'On the – on the – ah – bed.'

A back with a slight twist in it is clearly not the easiest of shapes to describe. He draws you for thirty slow minutes, pausing intermittently to assess his work, huffing out his cheeks like a jazzman, mumbling admonishments and instructions to his wayward hand. You watch him in your peripheral sight.

'Any good?'

'So-so.'

'I'm getting a crick.'

'Take five, then.'

Unseen by Wilson, you've just spent the half hour working your fingers between your legs. Consequently, you're ready to come. You could achieve it without him knowing, turning it into a yawn. But this being on the verge feels exquisite, and you prefer to sustain the arousal. With your judgement thus impaired, you sit on the edge of the bed, uncricking your neck, making sure your knees are pointing straight at him. You fix your eyes on him and give him your best smile.

Wilson usually knows a come-on when he sees one. But this prurient display might simply be you at your ease and negligent. Until things are clearer he thinks aloud about Art. He thinks of Munch's *Puberty*, the anxious-looking nude girl who sits on the edge of a bed, arms crossed defensively across her body; and he thinks too of Egon Schiele's openly erotic watercolours in which models wantonly display their pink-edged genitals. 'Would you mind staying like that. Just for five minutes.' He is amazed when you acquiesce. 'Keep those toes still,' he mock-barks. His hand is trembling as he scratches a hasty outline and sloshes watercolour onto the page. 'Look straight at me. Oh wow. That's – wow.' You wonder if Schiele had encouraged his models this way, like some flamboyant 1960s fashion photographer.

You've started something now. As soon as the picture is as finished as it can be, he wants another. *Demands* another. He leaves the pose up to you. You sprawl, one foot on the bed, the other leg hanging. The top light washes down over your shoulders, chest and thighs. You stare at him through a veil, ravished by his attention, by his excited movements. Your abdomen boils, sending plumes of heat into your chest and bowels.

'Do you ever –? Did you –?'

'Go on.' Wilson is too inspired to halt. He daubs like Hollywood's idea of a great artist.

'Did you like Claire?'

'Yes. I liked old Claire. I had a postcard from her the other day. She's sorted out a flat in Hull. She's starting Graphic Design in September.'

'She's beautiful.'

'Definitely.'

'So did you – you know – like her?'

'Fancy her, you mean?'

'Uh-huh.'

'Uh-huh.'

'A lot?'

'I did, yes.'

'Did you –? Help me out here.'

'Did I have it off with her?'

'You must have done.'

'Why?'

'The way she was looking at you.'

'She was posing. Just like you are now. Well, sort of. This is more – Expressionist.'

You don't care what it is or might be. All you know is the boiling is growing ever more persistent. Instinctively you reach down and rake your hand along the folds Wilson has been giving his close attention to.

He assumes you have an itch. 'What happens in a Henry Moore sculpture,' he says, 'is you have all these huge blocky shapes, and then something small and detailed to give your eye something to fix on.' He means he is drawing your labia and pubes in sharp focus, in case you feel uncomfortable with him staring immovably between your legs. It's all above-board. It's what artists are trained to do.

You have another itch, and you rake it twice this time with two expert fingers. Wilson looks away. Pretends to be locating his cigarettes.

'Did you – you and Claire – have it off?'

Wilson is suddenly at an audition for a play. Ah, here they are, on the paint table. *Note how surprised I am at finding them. Now which pocket is that Zippo in?* He searches himself as if cop and felon are sharing the same body. He's hammier than a sandwich. My mother wouldn't even consider him for a corpse.

There is genuine pain in your voice as you repeat your question.

Wilson looks at you, grinning because you have made him nervous. 'Do you feel like calling it a day, Ally?'

You haven't felt as shameless as this for some time. You throw yourself onto your back, then settle onto your side facing him, the exact mirror image of the painting. You let Wilson see what you are doing. He watches but doesn't have the courage

to approach. Until you reach out for him with your free arm.
And then he stands and moves slowly towards you.

THREE

Was that how it was?

'Who's asking? James Rudd or Inspector Poole?'

Sorry. Well, was it?

'Pretty much. You've certainly done your research.'

The painting was not for sale in Reading. In fact, none of your poses were for sale. (However, Julie looking bored: to you, Guv, nine hundred quid.) They were displayed to show the line of development. But of course anything can be purchased if you have money.

'I wonder why he'd hung on to them.'

Sentimental reasons. One of my regrets is trashing all my artwork: the stage designs, the picture of you.

'He was sentimental. He snipped a lock of my hair towards the end of the summer. He wanted to kiss it in my absence.'

To kiss kissable sable, you might say.

'What were those watercolours like?'

I didn't think much of them. They were whopping great things. Boring colour-drained CinemaScope landscapes. You couldn't see any people in them. He'd revisited his favourite haunts in Norfolk and Suffolk and celebrated them in a set of remarkably precise but ultimately touristy pictures. Any reasonably competent artist could have painted them. To tell you the truth, he needed money for drink. He was going through a particularly thirsty phase round about then.

'Pretty girls were what he was best at.'

You.

'Me, yes. And Julie, and Claire.'

Claire was extraordinary, but she was a Hitchcock blonde. You were a Godard Karina and far more alluring.

'You have to say that really.'

But it's true. I ache whenever I look at the few photos I have of you.

'Something you do often?'

Now and again.

'A rainy day ritual?'

Rainy-sunny-snowy-windy day ritual. I wish I had more photos. I wish I had the ones taken in Fritton Country Park. Your face ran the gamut of expressions that day.

'Where are those photos?'

Long gone. Martin thought it best they were destroyed. Wish I'd stopped him.

'They wouldn't be me as I'd be now. That's what you really ought to have instead of pictures from the past.'

I try to imagine you at forty. I don't think you'd have changed much.

'Come off it. Everyone changes. Were we to meet, I doubt if you'd recognise me. Necks get lined and inelastic. Eyes get wrinkles around them like towns get bypasses. Look at you with your receding hair and your paunch.'

I saw Julie not so long back. Only knew it was her from her voice and smile. Charming woman, but she really had been overdoing it with the sunbed and the peroxide.

'The glamorous Julie. I never saw the appeal, myself. She was too girlie.'

That's what blokes liked. They all took turns going out with her. Except Wilson. He wasn't involved in those shenanigans (one quick snog and a feel of a breast through a jumper doesn't exactly count). When Wilson got drunk he became deliberately obscure, even surreal. It was a pose. Inadvertently it put the girls off. Would you want to date a person whose idea of a chat-up was to quote the Dada manifesto at you?

'Or someone who thinks he's the next Jeremy Irons quoting *Endgame*.'

"One! Silence!..." I'm an *ack*-tor, love.

'Julie just thought you were a weirdo.'

"It's finished, we're finished." She did?

'She was this close to asking you out once, but apparently you switched into Beckett mode and scared her off.'

This close, you say? Wilson was this close as well. He was a jumper and a bra away from bare boob. Five millimetres in my estimation.

'What did he have to say about Julie?'

Nice tits.

'Is that all? "Nice tits?"'

Nice tits. Magnificent arse. *Legs*. Beautiful smile. Gorgeous eyes. In fact, all the credentials a girl needed to compete for Miss World. He regretted that she became a bit silly when drunk (he could talk) and had abysmal taste in guys, but ultimately he found her alluring.

'What did he have to say about me?'

FOUR

'Alison Dury. She's amazingly pretty.'

We are sitting at a table outside *The Links*. It is a mild mid-evening in May. The rest of the gang are patronising the *Cliff Hotel* so as to be better positioned for a disco at the *Ocean Room*. I'm not keen on either venue. The *Cliff* I find overly formal, while the *Ocean Room* is too loud for conversation. Wilson doesn't like crowds. Had the others been here our communication would have been restricted to the usual cursory nod and hollow hello. But tonight we are obliged to talk. And after a few beers, he is borderline drunk.

'I'd love to paint her,' he drawls. 'Especially the face. Especially those eyes.' He flourishes an imaginary brush. Splodge, splodge. I presume these are your irises.

'I've sketched her,' I tell him. 'Charcoal and white chalk.' I exhale my smoke vertically and brusquely, copying the style of Wilson. I suspect he has acquired his mannerisms by watching famous writers and artists on TV. In his mind he probably thinks he's sitting in some Parisian café honing Existentialism with Sartre.

He doesn't believe my picture will be any good. 'Charcoal's shit. One sneeze and you've erased it. Paint is what you should use. Oil on canvas. There's nothing to compare with it. Once you've taken the plunge, there's no looking back.'

Wilson is irredeemably plebeian in spite of his professed love of bourgeois culture and his systematic, untutored ironing-out

39

of the local accent. A few flat vowels regularly escape his attention: Great Yah-mouth instead of Yar-mouth; and toob, rather than tyoob for what his oil paint comes in. A would-be famous actor, I'm sensitive to these things. My talent for regional accents goes back to our first Dorset holiday, when we were nine, and I did a more than creditable impersonation of a local café owner. "Foyve cream teas furr table foyve, midear."

'I enjoyed using charcoal,' I say. 'I fixed it with hair spray as I went along. I managed to build up a really black layer.'

'Conté crayon gives a better black.' He's determined to have the last word on art materials. 'A velvety black.' I hate him. I wish I'd stayed inside. Or at home. 'I can give you some Conté if you like. Black, sepia and white. I've loads to spare. Shop near the college sells it.' I still hate him. 'Do you reckon whatserface'll let me draw her?'

He can't even remember your name. 'Al,' I prompt. 'Ally. Alison.'

'Will she?'

'She doesn't enjoy sitting still for long. She fidgets.' A lie.

'Good for action poses, then,' he says, undeterred. 'She's got a beautiful face.'

Beautiful now, is it? A moment ago it was just pretty. 'Hmm.' I want to pour his beer over his head. He wouldn't do anything to retaliate, he'd more likely just sit there and laugh, with the beer running into every crevice. Anything to fuel anecdotes about his recklessness, his Bohemianism.

'The secret's in the eyes,' he mumbles, sipping his drink.

'Alison is a lovely person,' I say. It sounds forced, but he's too drunk to notice.

'Ask her if she wouldn't –' He pokes a Peter Stuyvesant filter-last into his mouth, reversing his error only as he raises the Zippo flame. He has been smoking like a laboratory bunny all evening. ' – wouldn't mind, ah, posing for a portrait.'

'Ask her yourself.'

'Maybe...' He looks dreamily away. For a brief moment he appears to have been struck silent by some profound thought, but really he has switched off, and is staring blankly towards the empty horizon. I don't interrupt. I'd switch off too, if I wasn't so worried about you and him getting better acquainted.

A movement in the corner of my eye. Nuclear Scott in his TA uniform. I watch him march leftrightleft and right into the saloon bar of *The Links*. My heart sinks. The bar is dead tonight. Chances are he will be coming outside to join us. That guy gives me nightmares. Literally. And his macho army-speak has made you wary of talking to him anymore.

'When are we going to see your portraits of Julie?' I inquire.

'Eventually,' Wilson says. 'They're in college at the moment.' He sips his beer contemplatively. 'Now *she* is a good-looking girl.' As if there's now some dispute over your beauty. 'Didn't you go out with Julie once?'

'No,' I say bluntly. 'Nearly.' Inwardly I stare in cinematic close-up at Julie's worried–looking frown, brought on by my drunkenly garbled recitation of Hamm's long speech from *Endgame* beginning, 'One! Silence!' I'd committed it to memory for interview, and I was spouting it to impress her with my cleverness. But that frown had indicated she thought otherwise. It was as if she'd been cornered by a gibbering psychopath. She'd bolted at the first opportunity. And yet when Wilson had quoted Dada at her on another occasion, she'd merely laughed at his twattish nonsense-talk.

'She's got amazing eyes,' he says. 'And yummy lips. And proper curves.' He makes his eyebrows dance. 'We... Did you know we had a bit of a snog?'

I don't care. Correction, I do care, but only because you're to be his next model and he may try and snog you. I feign lack of interest by overacting the observation of a gull.

'Nice tits,' Wilson murmurs. 'Really nice pert firm tits. She let me feel them.' He mimes this. I shudder, picturing his hand moving in slow motion towards a generalised bare breast. Above it, not Julie's face, but yours.

'We had a lovely cuddle.'

I refuse to sound interested. Instead I try to remember the poem about a gull I once wrote. *Fine gauze cloud about the sea. No breakers. Only water folding gently upon water upon water.*

'Jules and me. Lovely long cuddle.'

Above me a gull – No. *A gull rises above me and* – Something about it wheeling behind me like gulls do. Not one of my best efforts.

'But in the end we decided to –' Wilson breaks off. 'Oh bugger.' He's seen Nuclear Scott marching towards us carrying a glass of lager. He grins at him. 'Gugger.'

'Can't stay long, chaps. Just enough time for a quick flagon.' Scott flings his beret onto the table. He sits and consults his watch, which is some special sort of watch with inset dials and extra numbers and winders, and a rotatable circumference. 'We're on a special operation tonight. We're tracking Soviet spy planes.' He nods in the direction Wilson has been staring. 'There's this one plane, every night it's been getting closer and closer by precisely six feet. Of course, we know exactly what they're up to, and they know we know, and we know they know we know, but that's the sort of game they like to play.'

Scott Spencer is older than us by five years. He is short and stocky and so luminously ginger-haired that camouflage is rendered useless. One tuft would be more than enough to give his position away. Turned down by the police force because of his height, and the regular army because of his eyesight and feet, he has ended up working in his dad's butcher's shop in Gorleston High Street, serving customers or delivering to local businesses in the van.

'Are you tracking them from the usual place?' I inquire.

'Usual place.' Scott looks over each shoulder. 'But I haven't told you about it, right?' Hollow words. A catchphrase. Every

Links regular knows the precise location of this oubliette beside an electricity substation in a meagre spinney of dirty-boled birches by the A12. He glances about before reaching inside his camouflage jacket. 'The latest Protect and Survive leaflet FYA: for your attention.' He slides one to each of us as if dealing cards.

Wilson pounces on it. 'Same nonsense as last time, I suppose.'

'As it's yet to be distributed to the masses, it's still all hush-hush, so whatever you do, don't show it to anyone, otherwise –' He mimed the slicing-open of his windpipe; military-sponsored, presumably.

Wilson has a skim-read. 'Yup. Same old bollocks. What a waste of wood pulp. Again, what they've failed to mention is that when the bomb drops, we've had it. It's common knowledge.'

I agree with him, although I'll not say so out loud. I'll show I'm more open-minded. I peruse the leaflet. 'I've never understood having to paint Windolene on our windows.'

'The less you see of the initial flash, the better,' Scott explains. 'I've got two bottles standing by, one upstairs, one down. Mum's not allowed to touch them.'

Wilson scans the text. 'Take internal doors off hinges... tum-ti-tum... lean doors against wall and pile cushions against them... How long have we got to do all this?'

'Well, say a big one drops on London, say the centre of London.' Scott slides the ashtray to the middle of the table. 'Say this is five miles across. All this will be vaporised, right? Instant vaporisation. Woof!' He finds an appropriate gesture for annihilation in jazz hands. 'Five miles outside of that, serious blast damage, ten miles further, minor blast damage and serious fire damage. Twenty miles outside of that, sporadic fire damage. Fifty miles, nothing, depending on the weather.'

'The weather,' Wilson says.

'Specifically the wind.'

'Ah.'

'Strong southerly wind, say force six, and we'd have the radiation driven up here within a few hours. Then we'd need to keep ourselves under cover until it's dispersed.'

'Under some cushions,' Wilson confirms.

'Lots of cushions.'

'Is that what they use at Sizewell and Windscale, when the people are handling the fuel rods?' Wilson says. Windscale being the former name of Sellafield. It was renamed after a chain of accidents made it a dirty word; and the Irish Sea even dirtier. 'Do they strap cushions to themselves? I'll have to nip down to *Arnold's* and buy a selection. The question is, though: floral or plain? Or doesn't it matter, so long as it's a cushion? I suppose chintzy material deflects the radiation better than cotton.'

Scott adjusts the rotatable ring of his watch. 'There're different sorts of nuclear radiation,' he says. 'It's like the difference between orange juice and orange squash. What you get in a power station is concentrated. It's orange juice. What you get after a bomb explodes is orange squash. You can cope with occasional exposure to squash, but it's only through prolonged contact that you come a cropper. Same as if you drink, say, four pints of orange squash, you've had the equivalent amount of orange as if you'd drunk half a pint of juice.'

'So if a bomb drops, chances are we'll survive,' Wilson says. 'Provided we have enough cushions. And there I was thinking we'd be flying up to the pearly gates.'

'Supplies. You'll need food and water.'

'What about the toilet, though? I use that quite a lot.'

'You'll be able to nip to the toilet,' Scott assures.

'Are the sewage farms still working, then?'

Scott nods. 'We've been trained to keep things running

smoothly.' We being the TA. 'Sewage, water, power. It's all remaining as it is now. Continuity to Avert Crisis,' he says in quotation marks. 'Cee ay cee,'

'Or, more accurately, CAC,' Wilson says, chuckling to himself.

Scott wafts this remark, and the smoke accompanying it, aside. 'The main thing is not to panic. When you hear the siren, stay calm and prepare your safe area. As the man says, there will be casualties as a result of a Soviet missile attack, but chances are that it won't be you.'

When Wilson has finished guffawing into his beer he says: 'Where will our illustrious government be during an attack? Under the stairs at Downing Street?'

'Deep underground,' Scott assures, hearing concern not irony. 'Mrs T will be able to direct operations safely from there.'

'Will she be letting the Opposition join her? After all, she says she wants to get rid of Socialism. A nuclear war will be her big chance. Lock everyone out she doesn't like.'

Scott shakes his head at such irreverence.

'Where will you lot be when the missiles rain down?' Wilson says.

'That's classified, I'm afraid.'

'Go on. We won't tell.'

'Sorry. Top Secret.'

Wilson persists. 'I hear there's a nuclear bunker underneath Gorleston police station.'

Scott becomes guarded. 'I've been trained to keep shtum about that in case the Soviets are listening. They can listen in on conversations like ours from spy satellites.'

'Bollocks.'

'I assure you it's not. They can probably tell what colour underpants we're all wearing.'

'You're telling me there's someone listening to us?' Wilson

looks up towards my wheeling gull. 'Greetings, Comrades!' He waves. 'Come on, Jim. Wave at Ivan and Olga and the rest of the KGB.'

'If you think it's funny...' Scott says.

'Oh, it's hilarious. Coo-ee!' He waves at a different gull.

'It's not improbable,' Scott says, eyeing the bird suspiciously.

'But pretty unlikely.'

'Nothing's unlikely in the world of espionage.'

'Yes, but...' Realising he cannot topple Scott's wall of programmed caution, Wilson returns to the subject of the bunker. 'Not for use by the likes of us, is it,' he goads.

'There is a list of who's entitled, but it's classified. Anyway, the people on the list will know who they are.'

'That'd really piss you off, wouldn't it,' Wilson says, 'if you're on the list and then you change jobs and no longer qualify to be preserved.'

'I don't know if it works like that –'

'The important thing is for the Unchosen Ones to invest in much Windolene and many cushions.' Scott nods and Wilson smirks that he has once again duped the pachyderm with sarcasm. He stubs his smouldering filter into the centre of the ashtray and lights a fresh cigarette.

Scott regards this and shakes his head like a disappointed parent. 'If you could see inside your lungs.'

'At least smoke's not invisible,' Wilson says. 'Like radiation. Imagine if radiation was like this.' He blows a cloud of fallout towards Scott. 'People would see it coming to get them, and realise you need twenty-foot-thick steel reinforced concrete cushions to keep it at bay. I don't think they sell those in *Arnold's*.'

'You won't be laughing when the balloon goes up.'

'Why, is that how we aim to defend our country: with massive Pink Floyd pigs to bounce the missiles back?'

Scott is not inclined to joke about such matters. 'As soon as we spot incoming missiles, we send off a shed-load of CMs: counter-missiles.'

Wilson groans. 'Causing the Soviets to reply with counter-counter missiles, which we attempt to intercept with counter-counter-counter missiles. This could go on forever, like one of Zeno's paradoxes. You realise World War Three might never actually start if both sides have an infinite supply of counter-weapons.'

'If only,' Scott says. 'The terrible truth is both sides are pretty evenly matched. Whoever goes first wins. Simple as that, I'm afraid, gents.'

I am starting to feel decidedly gloomy. 'What's the point of doing anything when the world is poised on the brink of destruction? How can some people just carry on as if nothing is wrong?'

'*Winter Light*,' Wilson says. 'The Bergman film. In it some guy has become so depressed by the prospect of world war that he commits suicide.'

'I've seen *Winter Light*,' I say. Wilson doesn't have the monopoly on culture.

'Defeatist attitude,' Scott says. 'You've got to think positive thoughts. In the end the good guys will win. If you really want to do something positive, why not join the TA?'

'I'm a pacifist,' Wilson says.

'That's not very patriotic.'

'Neither's the government. Right bunch of unpatriotic bastards they are. All they're doing is dismantling the country, bit by bit, flogging it off and buggering off with the proceeds.'

'I wouldn't know about that,' Scott says.

'I hate all that flag-waving bollocks.' Wilson looks at me. 'Don't you?'

I've never given much thought to the matter. I shrug.

'I wouldn't lift a finger to defend this country, not while our own government is having a dump on us.'

'That's just sounds like you're a coward,' Scott retorts. 'Say the enemy invaded and put a gun to your loved-one's head. What would you do?'

'That argument's so ancient, it's not worth bothering with.'

'What would you do, though?'

'I'd defuse the situation by performing a pirouette.'

'You what?'

'In a pink tutu. And while the enemy are working out what's going on, my loved-one will scarper. It always works for Bugs Bunny.'

'*Seriously*.' Scott's brow is a ploughed field of frustration.

'Surely there's bugger all you can do in a situation like that.'

'You could try and overpower the enemy,' Scott suggests.

'Go on the offensive with a letter opener?'

'Are you saying you'd just standby and watch your loved one getting raped?'

'You didn't say anything about her being raped.'

'They're raping your girlfriend at gunpoint.'

Wilson thinks about this. 'I don't have a girlfriend.'

'But say you do. Say it's – who do you fancy? – say it's Julie. Would you save Julie, or stand there and watch like a coward?'

Wilson makes a noise like a chicken.

'Pathetic, absolutely pathetic.'

'Okay,' says Wilson. 'He points a gun at Julie and starts to rape her. I ask him to desist. He points his gun at me and kills me. It doesn't save Julie, does it? What's the correct answer?'

'It's not a quiz.'

'Okay, then. What would you do?'

'I'd blow his sodding brains out before he got anywhere near her.' He mimes using an invisible firearm, with Wilson his foe.

'Typical. Wouldn't you try and find out why he's your enemy in the first place? All conflicts must start somewhere.'

'If my fellow citizen has a gun pointed to their head, I'm going to defend them.'

'Even me?' Wilson asks.

'Even you,' Scott says. 'It's what I do.'

'Because you're a disposable fighting unit. With the emphasis on: you nit.'

'Less of the disposable, if you wouldn't mind.'

'It's true, though. Look at World War One.'

Scott looks at his watch instead, expresses panic and stands. 'Got to skedaddle, guys.' He finishes his drink in one giant swallow. '*Skywatch*,' he mutters, adding, 'You didn't hear me say that, did you.'

'What, *Skywatch*?' Wilson blurts.

Scott holds up his palms. 'You are to forget that word. Evening, gents.' He is suddenly marching off, glancing up occasionally as if Soviet agents are mapping his path.

'Bully,' I say to Wilson, half meaning it. 'You scared him off.'

'Skywatch!' Wilson scrunches up the leaflet. 'This is such shit. This is to make us proles believe that if we take the necessary precautions, we can survive a nuclear attack. The reality is we're all going to cop it, especially living in East Anglia, where the Yanks have got all their air bases. East Anglia will cease to exist after the four-minute warning. And if the blast doesn't kill us, the radiation certainly will, only more slowly. Either way, there won't be many survivors in a nuclear war. The only reason they want the general population under piles of cushions is so we don't go on the rampage and stop the Chosen Ones from going to earth.'

I ask him how he knows so much.

'I read some copies of *Sanity*, the CND magazine.'

'Propaganda,' I tell him.

'No. *This* is propaganda. Lies.' He places the ball of paper in the ashtray and holds his Zippo to it. His weasel phizog is waxy orange from the resulting bonfire. 'Have you ever been in Scott's house?' I shake my head. 'I have. Upstairs there's a spare room, but all that's in it is piles and piles of this sort of propaganda. For distribution to the moronic masses.'

'Is it a TA project?'

'Hardly. He's volunteered to deliver them on behalf of the local council. Of course, Scott makes out it's part of some secret operation, but Julie's mum has volunteered to deliver them as well, and she's nothing to do with the TA. She works in a newsagent in Yarmouth.'

Yah-mouth. Hear that? Dead giveaway.

'Sky flaming watch.' He shakes his head. 'Load of bollocks. He's gone home to watch the telly with his mum. Where's Alison tonight?'

This question throws me. I'm not sure where you are; you have spent the day with Anne. To admit that I don't know, however, would mean we aren't as symbiotic as we think. 'Girls' day out,' I say vaguely.

'I might call on her tomorrow.'

'Bad idea,' I say.

'You think? Why?'

'It just is.' I hope the cryptic tone will shut him up.

It doesn't. 'I'll risk it. Nothing ventured, nothing gained. Fancy a refill, old chap?' He hauls himself to his feet and clangs his glass against mine.

Old chap, like he's some posh gent.

'No thanks,' I tell him.

'Just a half. Go on, Jim. Just a half.'

'Oh, all right. Same as yours.'

He toddles inside and I hurry off home to watch TV.

FIVE

'Nasty trick.'

Well, I figured he'd drink it himself.

'He called round the next day. I remember I was feeling somewhat fragile after Anne and I had ended a pub crawl at the *Ocean Room* disco. Is that place still there?'

Still there. The open-air swimming pool that was next to it has gone, though, demolished in the nineties and replaced by a flower garden like the one there in Edwardian times.

'I never wanted another gin as long as I lived. I was spewing into the toilet at three in the morning.'

Wine's the alcohol I can't face. The merest whiff. It has bad associations.

'I was in bed. Mum answered the door. She wasn't sure whether to let him in at first. She didn't know anything about Bohemianism; she thought he was underprivileged. He was wearing that old 1960s sheepskin car coat of his dad's, and his jeans and trainers were daubed with oil paint. And she said he reeked of cigarettes. She made him wait in the kitchen in case he ruined the furniture. She soon warmed to him, though.'

He brings out the maternal in females. They want to fuss over him.

'By the time I'd got downstairs she'd made him coffee and served him a giant slice of fruit cake, and they were discussing the difference between gouache and watercolour, because Mum was telling him she'd always wanted to paint. A lie. "*Would you like another slice? Ally, why don't you take your young man through to the lounge?"* '

Young man? Jumping the gun, wasn't she? Wasn't I your young man? Not this trespasser, this mediocre morphometrist, this wolf in weasel's clothing.

'I'd not spoken to him properly before, although we'd often chatted briefly down the pub. He asked me straight out if I'd like to pose for him. He said he had a studio above his cousin's chip shop, and that he'd already painted Julie, who'd been perfectly happy just to lounge about for an hour or two a day while he drew and painted her.

'I said, "Why me?"

'He said, "Because you've got a really interesting face." "Interesting?" I said. "Ahm, attractive," he said, and blushed. No girl can refuse such a compliment. I sort of knew I was attractive, but to have an artist want to paint you was the ultimate flattery.'

I'd drawn you. Wasn't that flattering?

'But I knew you. This offer had come from someone outside of our immediate circle.'

He'd appealed to your vanity.

'"All is vanity." Quiz: who said that?'

I don't do quizzes. Poole, on the other hand –

'You're no fun. It's in the bible and the heroine of a famous novel quotes it, but I'm thinking of the movie. Tess. As in *Tess of the D'Urbervilles*. I went with Wilson to see it in Yarmouth shortly before I left for Oxford, and Wilson fell head over heels in lust with Nastassja Kinski and pilfered a poster from the cinema foyer. After Tess runs away from the dairy, she beds down in a wood and touches her face. "All is vanity." It is too.'

Wilson called again soon after, didn't he?

'The next day, in fact, wearing clean and ironed jeans this time, and he'd swapped the suede for a regular coat. He had a long chat with Mum about detective fiction.'

Which he wouldn't have been able to do on the initial visit, because he wouldn't have had time to gen up. It's so obvious, Alison.

'Then he took me to his studio.'

SIX

Bluebeard's Castle. Except it's called *My Plaice*. His cousin has
generously suspended work on the bedsit until he goes away to
college, although his brother-in-law and a builder friend are
busy retiling and decorating the downstairs. The two men assess
Wilson's latest choice of model and warn you (humorously) that
they'll be upstairs to watch the strip-tease in ten minutes. You
laugh, but they have unsettled you. What if Wilson expects you
to be as professional as he is? Could you bare everything if he
were to demand it? Did the other models?

You follow him up a steep flight of uncarpeted stairs,
knowing the builder is grabbing a serendipitous look up your
skirt. Wilson flings a door open. You anticipated some
cobwebbed hovel. Instead, there is this bright but dust-moted
room. You are greeted by the delectable odour of oil paint and
turps, redolent of earnestness and industry. It is as welcoming as
new bread in a bakery. Everywhere there is art.

He has been busy. There are innumerable drawings, faces
mostly, and hastily-executed full-length poses. Drawings are
piled up on dust-clothed furniture, or masking-taped to the
peeling 1960s wallpaper. Faces. Girls' faces. Straight-on, three-
quarters view or profiles. The chimney breast is a shrine to the
female face. And there are paintings. Huge paintings. None
smaller than three feet by five.

'Help yourself,' he says, seeing you are eager to inspect
them.

'It's Julie. Wow, that's so lifelike.'

There are further ones of Julie. The one with folded arms.

'Amazing,' you say. 'That's her exactly. Who's this?' Your chest tightens.

'Girl called Claire. She's at the art college with me.'

'Can't she afford clothes?'

'It's a nude. Nudes are supposed to be... nude.'

'Did you make it up?'

'Make it up? *Make it up*?' He overacts being offended. 'Madam, I'll have you know this was painted from life... You're not shocked, are you?'

'I wasn't expecting you to be doing nude stuff up here.'

'It's hardly a Page Three, though, is it.'

You find yourself wondering why it isn't. Where exactly does the difference lie?

Wilson can tell you. He says, 'Life painting's not about titillation. It's more scientific than that. It's about muscles and tendons and bony bits'

'Where was she posing?' You look about the room.

'On the floor in front of that south window. That's why the light's so intense. I blocked out that other window and the skylight with blankets. Do you like it?'

'It's wonderful.' And far more erotic than perhaps the artist realises. 'Was there – anyone else here?'

He smiles at your question. 'What, like her mum to chaperone us?' He finds the thought of this amusing. 'No, it was just her and me.'

He liked Claire, that's obvious. And she liked him. The preparatory drawings he made for the paintings are informal like snapshots. Close to, they are little more than bundles of lines, squiggles, cross-hatchings. Hold them at arm's-length and they make arms, hips, skeins of hair, buttocks, ankles. A living person emerges. Not stiff or formally posed, but caught on her way from A to B. Even with your modest appreciation of art, you can tell a great deal of thought and effort has gone into these drawings.

'James draws me now and again. One of his pictures is going to be exhibited in Yarmouth library soon. Local artists have submitted the best work.

'Our exhibition's the one following that,' Wilson says. 'The best work from the Foundation Course. Nothing's been chosen yet.'

'How about showing one of these?'

'Perhaps,' Wilson says, as if his tutors have no say in the matter. 'Claire won't mind people staring at her body. She's modelled for the class in the evenings. To tell the truth, I think she's an exhibitionist.'

'How about one of me, then?'

'A nude?'

You bite your lower lip and glance away. 'Just a painting.'

'There may not be time for a painting,' Wilson says, lifting his fringe away from his eyes. 'I've got two canvases of Claire to finish, and I want to draw the countryside before I leave Norfolk. I'll draw you, though. I'll try to paint you during the summer holiday. Deal?'

You have already worked out a pose for the drawing. It's the pose you gave to me. With a variation: the sideways look. You offer it to him now, on a mattress on the floor. Wilson approves. He finds you a book, the fat paperback of James Joyce's novel *Ulysses*, opened halfway through. He arranges your hair, and with your permission pulls your skirt into a more pleasing shape. He sits cross-legged a few feet away to draw, the large drawing board propped against a chair. He works vigorously. Black Conté, white Conté. You are able to watch him watching you. Where his eyes look you feel a corresponding tingle: the top of your head, your shoulder, your heel, your elbow. Holding out the Conté crayon as a crude measuring stick, he fixes your proportions onto the blank page. You want to see, but it is too soon. How long will he take? How long is the proverbial piece of polypropylene twine? James took twenty minutes. How long will a real artist take with you?

'You okay?' he inquires. 'You're smiling at something.'

'Feeling self-conscious, that's all.' You suppress a giggle. 'Who's your favourite artist?'

'Oh, that's tricky. I like Munch.'

'You'll have to spell that one.'

'Edvard em-you-en-see-aitch – Munch. He was Norwegian. You must know *The Scream*.' He pulls a face.

'Oh, that.'

'My favourite of his is called *Puberty*. Young girl sitting on a bed, kit off, with her arms folded across herself, her shadow behind her on the wall like a huge grey cock...' He stops himself and apologises. 'I mean, willy. Very unsettling, it is... I'm a great fan of Stanley Spencer's work too. Know it?'

'*Willy*? Why don't you just use the words you mean? I'm not a nun. I say cock, and prick, or knob. I do know what a cock is; and the earliest recorded use of it to mean penis. I have the shorter OED.'

He's blushing. 'There are some books over there. You're welcome to borrow them. What sort of art do you like?'

You have been hoping he wouldn't ask this. Your knowledge of art is scant. 'Klimt,' you hazard. 'Nothing too way-out. You've got to be able to see what it's supposed to be. That's why I like your stuff. Work, I mean. I wish I could draw.'

'Anyone can draw if they put their mind to it. It's simply a matter of wanting to. If you like something, you'll do it more, and the more you do it, the better you'll get at it.'

You find this funny. The suppressed laughter sends an earthquake through your pose. You legs wave about uncontrollably like saplings in a breeze. 'Sorry.'

'You want to take five?'

'No, I'll be all right. It's just that...'

'Come on, let's take five. It wasn't going too well.' He scrunches the drawing into a ball and serves it across the room at an overflowing wastepaper basket.

You sit up. 'Was I okay? Apart from just then.'

'You're perfect. Do you fancy a biccy and a smoke?'

He flings the south window wide and you both kneel at it, hanging over the sill. Squinting into the sun, you observe dog walkers, retired couples, dissolute youth, the shift workers and unemployed carrying fishing rods and tackle to the pier. 'What wasted lives,' he observes.

'Wasted?'

'What are they actually doing with their three score and ten?'

'They're being alive,' you say. 'Same as us.'

'Ah, but they're not like us at all. We're going places.'

'Snob!'

'No, listen. They could go places too, if they wanted. See that guy with the wicker fishing basket? He was in the upper sixth when I was in the first year. He was in the school play, he had a band, he twanged his electric guitar in assembly, he did stuff. He's now twenty-five, twenty-six, and what's on the menu today? Dangling a lugworm into the North Sea. Don't you think that's a waste? He could've gone to college; broadened his horizons, even a bit. Instead, he took a crappily paid part-time job in a mini-market. He's still living at home. His mum cooks for him and cleans up after him, like he's still a helpless kid. His guitar's probably disappeared under a layer of dust. All he probably does is watch TV in the evenings, and nips down the *Tramway* for a couple of pints on Saturday night.'

'So?'

'So: what a waste. Like in your namesake's song.'

'Not everyone wants their horizons broadened,' you tell him, sidetracked by a memory of bog graffiti: ALISON (BLOCK)HEAD GIRL. WHAT A WAIST. Red permanent marker, possibly lower school cursive, although the parentheses and paronomasia suggested GSE and above. Not malicious, you decided, merely the spin-off of constipation or sluggish menses. 'For all you know, he might be perfectly happy dangling a lugworm off the pier. I've got you sussed. You're scared that you might turn out to be him.'

Wilson considers this for a moment. 'Maybe.'

'Told you I had you sussed. You want to be a famous artist, and are terrified you'll end up being one of the herd. Ordinary.'

'Maybe.' Wilson considers this; eventually nods. 'The thing is, I almost ended up like that guy,' he says. 'If I hadn't bumped into Rocky one morning on my way to the sixth form block.'

'You're going to have to explain that. Rocky?'

'I went into the sixth form because I hadn't a clue what I wanted to do with my life. I started off doing O-level retakes – maths and physics – and A-level art, but I ended up skiving the lot. For thirty-five periods a week I hid myself away in the sixth form block, reading. No one noticed. Until one day I was skulking to the coffee machine when I bumped into old Rocky – Mr Stones, the art teacher, good bloke – and he persuaded me to join the art room fraternity again. Which I did. Thanks to him, I got hooked on drawing and painting big-time, although I never believed I could be much cop. It was his wacky idea I should apply to the art college. He phoned up and arranged the interview at the eleventh hour and then helped me sort out some work to take along. Fortunately I got in, otherwise...' You regard the unwanted of Gorleston together. '.....what the heck would have happened to me? I can't do much else apart from art, and I hate fishing. At least now I'll be able to delay joining the real world by at least three more years.'

'Where are you off to?'

'Where do you think I am going to, Boyo?' Wilson says.

'Hyderabad?'

'South Wales.'

'Oh. Right. Boyo. Nogood Boyo. If I were you, I'd steer

clear of impressions.'

Wilson is undeterred. '"To begin at the beginning..."' He hams it up more than it needs to be. 'I enjoyed that stage version James was in. He was really good. He was brilliant in *Salad Days*.'

'James is definitely going to be famous,' you assert.

Wilson says, 'I always thought you and James were an item.'

'A lot of people do. We did – get close. Once – in Southwold. But not many people know about it. You mustn't say. Promise.'

'Southwold, eh. Is that the place to go for romance?'

'We caught the bus there from Lowestoft before Christmas. Just for something to do.'

Lowering his voice, Wilson confides: 'Julie and I got close. Once.'

'You did? Where?'

'Up here.'

'Oh.'

'I thought I'd better mention it, in case you heard it from someone and thought...'

'Right.'

'It was only a quick snog. No how's-your-father.'

You imagine them gnawing at one another, chastely then less so, and wonder how long it will be before he makes his move on you. Given his reputation as a lech, seduction is inevitable and all the more likely to suceed now that you know him better and like him.

Wilson fillips his dog end to the tarmac below. A gull immediately swoops to investigate.

You reach over the sill and crush your dog end against the bricks and watch the ash and filter disperse.

Wilson has already lit a fresh cigarette. 'Here's a crazy idea: why don't you just go out with James and be done with it?'

'Because he's my best friend. We've known one another since we were so high. You don't get romantically involved with friends who go back that far.'

'You said you did in Southwold.'

'That was a very pleasant mistake. And you've got to forget I mentioned it. Now, are you ready to draw me again? I'm ready.'

You return to *Ulysses*. Wilson tweaks your hair and skirt. 'Ever read it?'

'Attempted.'

'How far did you get?'

You rummage to about half way through. 'Here.' You quote from the page with a suitable Oirish accent. If you could see his face, you would know Wilson fails to recognise the quote, not having read half as far as you. 'Yeah. Excellent,' he says, straining to understand it. 'Leopold Bloom is one of the great characters in literature.'

The passage you've just read may have sounded like Double Dutch to Wilson, but to you it is quite straightforward. 'He certainly is.'

'*A Portrait of the Artist as a Young Man* is amazing,' he says before you can quiz him on *Ulysses*. The secret of successful bluffing is to establish the parameters. Find out what the other person knows and then sidestep those topics as you would a landmine.

'It is,' you agree. 'It's probably my favourite of his books. The wading girl sequence!'

'I'm a *Dubliners* fan myself.'

'Me too. Do you know *The Dead*?'

'Mm.' Wilson accelerates away from the subject. 'Fancy a drop of music? What do you like?'

'*Japan*.'

'No *Japan*, I'm afraid. I've got *The Planets*, Miles Davis, Bowie and Kate Bush.' He is proud of his eclectic taste.

You choose Bowie. *Heroes*. The music stops you from becoming self-conscious and giggling. You watch Wilson's hand, the path it takes across the page, dragging the arm after it, like Oliver straining at his leash.

'I'll be taking my dog along the beach later,' you say. Then, after a pause: 'Fancy joining me?'

Wilson nods. 'What about Jim?'

'I'm not asking James.'

'Okay then. What time?'

'As soon as we've done here.'

'And you don't think Jim will mind if he finds out.'

'James and I are just good friends,' you state with finality.

' – Only I don't want any aggro between him and me.'

'Just mates. Okay?' You stare at him until he nods.

The drawing is declared finished fifteen minutes after *Heroes* clicks off. Wilson fixes the drawing to a blank patch of wall and lights two cigarettes to assist joint contemplation.

'It's brilliant,' you decide. 'Look at how you've done my hair. And my legs.'

'The shape of the legs echoes the angle of the arm,' the artist explains. 'As soon as I trim an inch off the right-hand side of the paper, the composition will work better. It's all about diagonals.' An ochre forefinger demonstrates the substructure of angles.

'It's much better than James's drawing.' Although you have reservations about the likeness. He has drawn the twin sister you've never had. It's in the eyes. He has made the eyes too dark. You'd like to mention this flaw, but it's not your place to. He is the artist, after all. While you are merely his raw inspiration.

SEVEN

You do not know this, but I see you and Wilson with Oliver later that afternoon.

I am bored. I've been revising for my A-levels for several hours and need fresh air and company. I call round for you. Your mum tells me you are out with Oliver, tactfully not mentioning you are also with *him*. I take myself down to the seafront and scan the beach from a vantage point on the upper esplanade. There are a few dogs nosing their way between the first flush of holidaymakers, but none resembling Oliver. I predict you are taking our usual route, south along the sand to Hopton village and then back towards Gorleston using the path by the golf course. I decide to walk along this path and meet you at some point along it. I imagine you spotting me from far off and waving madly, Oliver tearing towards me off the lead and you running after him.

"Alison, my darling!" I yell.

"Oh, my darling Jim."

There is music. Soaring violins. A dozen harps. In extreme slow motion we collide and combine and collapse into a tussock of soughing, bee-jewelled grass and –

– you bicycle your legs and –

– and we strip away our clothes and –

What exactly would I see if you were naked? Properly naked. Beyond the bikini.

Gurning at this flight of the imagination, I walk slap-bang

into Julie, who's waiting at the bus stop where Marine Parade ends and Yallop Avenue begins.

'What was that in aid of?' she says.

'What was what?'

'That pig-ugly face. Hello, by the way.' She is wearing a sensible dress and flattie sandals instead of her more usual tight jeans and trainers, and her hair is tightly woven into a dark blonde plait that swings between her shoulder-blades like a ship's rope.

I shrug. Easier than having to explain. 'Off to work?'

''Fraid so.' She is working with her mum until September, hence the uncharacteristic appearance. 'I'd rather be sunning myself on the beach. So what are you up to, you lazy sod?'

'Off to find Alison.'

'Your other half.' She wrinkles her nose. 'Not for much longer, I should think.'

'Meaning?'

'She's got a new admirer.'

'Wilson.'

Julie nods.

'Has she said anything to you?'

Julie grins. 'That's got you worried, hasn't it.'

'What's she been saying?'

'First, what's Wilson been saying about me?'

'Only that you two had an intimate moment,' I say.

'You what?'

'A snog.'

'Is that what he's going around saying?' Her eyes widen, silent cinema-style.

'Isn't it true?'

'He tried to kiss me, but I wouldn't let him.'

'He's also saying he felt your – erm –' I nod towards her chest.

'The lying sod. Why would he want to say that?'

'Didn't he?'

'No.' Outrage colours her cheeks. 'No!'

'He's saying you let him kiss you and feel you up,' I summarise. Oh, it was lovely making enemies of my enemy.

'Who's he been saying this to?'

'*The Links*,' I tell her.

She does a curtsey of irritation. 'I'm going to give him what for tonight.'

'And you reckon Ally likes him?'

'God knows why.'

'I thought you liked him.'

It's her turn to shrug in order to save words.

'He wants to paint her,' I say. Julie appears indifferent. 'Like he painted you.' I want her to feel betrayed by him. Used then discarded, like a vampire's top-up. I want her to hate him.

'Maybe he's lonely,' she comes out with suddenly. 'Maybe that's why he's been going round saying we had a snog.'

No. No.

'He is a nice bloke,' she says, clearly no longer annoyed with him.

But he's not a nice bloke. He lies. He steals people's soulmates from them.

'Maybe,' she says, 'he didn't mean anything nasty.'

My plot is all burnt out. The ashes of it trickle through my fingers. 'You'll still tick him off, though?'

'I'll see.'

She'll see? And why is she now smiling? Pathetic.

'Here's my bus.' She fishes in her shoulder bag for her purse.

'He's such a creep,' I say as she's climbing up, hoping to rekindle her mistrust of Wilson.

She looks back. 'If I were you, I'd go and find Alison.' The door hisses shut and the bus pulls away, belching hot fumes at me.

*

'Did Julie tick him off?'

What do you think? He made out he'd exaggerated while under the influence of alcohol. And she believed him too. Forgave him and challenged him to a game of darts. Pathetic.

'You were saying you saw me that afternoon.'

I did. And our shared life flashed before my eyes.

EIGHT

'Hello.'

'Hello.'

My mother stands at the gate. 'Behave yourself now, James,' she warns.

I feel very grown-up, despite being three years of age. I have performed in panto. I was Dick Whittington's cat's kitten. 'I'm James.'

'Alison,' you sing-song say. 'Ally Pally.' You are busy searching the heads of chrysanthemums for earwigs. I have a mortal fear of them getting inside my brain via my ears, but you are built of sturdier stuff. When you find one you poke it gently with a cocktail stick until its pincers lock on it, then you transfer the creature to a jam jar. I count one-and-one-and-one-and-one earwigs circling the base of the jar.

'What're you going to do with them?'

'Don't know.' You grin. 'We could –' you look around for inspiration. 'We could put water on them.'

This sounds fun then sad. 'No. We have to let them go.'

Amazingly you agree, and we pour them through a hole in the fence into your neighbours' garden. We hope they will devour everything that grows there. We take turns looking through the hole.

I follow you into the back garden. You have a swing and a slide, and also a playhouse with two teddies, a knitted rabbit and a Christmas fairy in residence.

'Push me, please,' you say, sitting on the hard wooden seat of the swing.

We take turns at pushing and swinging until it is time for my mother to take me away.

'Do you like Alison?' she inquires.

'She's my friend,' I tell her.

'Good,' my mother says. 'Her mother's my friend too.'

*

You are being bullied by the girl whose thumbs are missing. Every time she sees you by yourself she scoops up a clump of soil and throws it at you. She is a good shot. Her preferred target is your skinny legs, because if she throws hard enough there is a good chance she will topple you. You tell your parents. Your parents approach and tick-off the girl. The girl fetches her dad. He is furious. He says how could anyone in their right mind believe that this sweet-natured child would do anything wrong. You were a liar and a bully and you had to stop picking on her.

A few days later I see her targeting you again. She might as well be throwing clumps at my legs, for your hurt is my hurt. War. I choose a suitably heavy clod and lob it straight at her face. I am a good shot. The clod hits her on her open mouth and explodes before she can scream. Her pink tongue curls through the soil like a worm. No matter how hard she spits, she cannot completely empty her mouth. She runs off and promptly returns with her dad. He is livid. I hare off home and the pair follow. I hide in the bathroom, quaking with fear, while they report to my mother. I hear snippets: '...bloody dangerous...', 'could've blinded her...', '...it's not as if she did anything to provoke...'

My mother laughs at this. A proper panto laugh. 'Don't give me any of that butter-wouldn't-melt rubbish. I've watched her. She terrorises the children round here.' She reels off some of the girl's crimes. The man mutters something and Mum tells him to: 'Jolly well bugger off, then, and if I see your daughter within a hundred yards of my house or the Dury's, I'll send for the police, and which one of us do you think they'll have the most sympathy for, you pathetic little man?'

As soon as they leave Mum comes to fetch me. We go over to your house for food. And that is the end of the bullying.

*

'No, this is sex.' We are in your Nan's bedroom. She is downstairs chatting with your dad. You are lying on your back on her bed with her ancient double bolster, a heavy feather-filled stripy sausage, on top of you. You are not sure what to do with your knees, though. 'I reckon I have to keep them together, than I can support my lover better.'

'Where does he put his willy?' I have been occupied helping my Action Man and your Barbie to have sex with the aid of modelling clay prosthetics. I throw them down and come over to the bed.

'It grows like a snake,' you tell me confidently. 'As soon as he's lying on top it grows down into my crack to plant the baby.'

'Yuk.'

'Don't worry,' you assure. 'We won't even know it's happening. The worst part is when the baby wants to come out.'

I jump on top of the bolster and we wrestle until I am underneath the bolster and you are on top of that.

'Darling,' you say, when the giggling has diminished, 'let's make a baby girl.'

'I'd prefer a boy, *darling*.'

'I hate boys.'

'I'm a boy.'

'I hate you.'

'No you don't.'

'I want a baby girl called...' You form your hair into a paintbrush and gently tickle my eyelids, mouth and chin. 'Hilary.' There is a Hilary in our class.

'I'm going to have a baby boy called...Oliver.' Oliver was the boy who wet himself and the floor during assembly because he was too shy to put up his hand.

You laugh at this. 'Silly. You can't have a baby. Only girls can.'

I'd forgotten this. 'Then you'll have to give me a spare one of yours.'

We yes and no and tussle, me on top, then you on top. The bolster ends up on the floor and I end up on top of you.

'We're doing sex,' you tell me, just as your father comes into the bedroom.

He chokes on his anger as if it's a fishbone. Next thing, I'm Peter Pan flying towards the door, suspended by my collar and shorts. My feet do not touch the ground until I am dropped at the front door. I am propelled outside with a violent shove, like Jerry being evicted from Tom's house, and ordered to wait in the car. When you come out a few minutes later your face looks as though a typhoon has passed across it. You sit in the back with me until your dad tells you to get into the front. Not one word is exchanged during the short ride back to Gorleston.

I tell my dad what happened. He laughs at first, then becomes serious while he sits down with me and calmly explains what sex actually is and why Mr Dury was so irate. I wait with a jam sandwich, meditating on what I have just learned, while he goes to have a chat with your dad.

I make a mental note to ask him, when he comes back, what the lady who is having sex should do with her knees.

. *

We have attended the same infant and junior schools, but now we go to different secondary schools. We are able to cycle together for part of the morning journey, however, and when school is finished we wait at an agreed place in order to share the last mile. We make up for being apart during the day by spending evenings and weekends glued together. Martin goes through a phase of calling me a big girl because I never play football with him, but really he is jealous I have a close friend who happens to be a girl. His best friend is a hairy, stooping, chimpanzee of a boy called Carl, with whom he has formed a rock group. All their songs are about not being able to get girlfriends and are in the same key because Carl only knows four chords in E-major. They invite you to sing with them as soon as your breasts have started showing. When you inform them you can't sing, they tell you it doesn't matter because no one will be interested in your voice. You tell them what they can do with their rock group.

*

Your body fills out and your legs grow and grow some more, and men start whistling from moving cars at the sight of you. At this time I have no erotic interest in you, and do not appreciate just how pleasing to the male eye you are becoming. In Dorset we paddle and swim off Weymouth. I get cramp and panic and flail wildly while you rescue me. You have saved my life. The man from the coastguard says you deserve a medal. When we are walking back up the beach I look round and see he is standing with his hands on his hips staring at you, shaking his head in wonder.

*

We get invited to parties together. One invite between us as if we're married. We even get joint Christmas cards. When he's not quite nineteen, my brother gets married for real and moves into a flat above Nuclear Scott's dad's shop and promptly turns vegetarian.

*

We begin to travel beyond the boundaries of our enclave. By ourselves. We don't need anyone else. We use bicycles to explore the seafront and utilitarian pier. We catch buses. We walk, along the beach, into the countryside; sometimes even as far as Lound Waterworks, the deserted woods and lakes of which we trespass and explore, Ransome-style.

*

Symbiosis.

Example: I hurt my ankle during Games. Yours starts to hurt during French.

Example: I write a story for English about a robot girl who is created by a mad scientist. You don't know about my story (I lifted the idea straight out of *The Tales of Hoffmann*, not that anyone noticed), but when I see you later, you approach me, for no reason, like a robot.

Example: We buy each other the same Christmas present.

Example: One night I am awakened, from a dream in which I feel intensely alone, by the sound of you tapping on my window. I let you in. You explain that you woke up feeling intensely lonely and needed to see me. We squeeze into my bed and fall asleep.

*

'A story, please. Tell me a story.' You ask me this first thing the following morning.

'What, make one up?'

'You have to entertain your guest. It's the Law.'

The robot girl story was still fresh in my mind.

'"Once upon a time, there was a scientist who was brilliant but very lonely, so one day he –?"'

'Why was he lonely?'

'You're not supposed to interrupt.'

'You didn't say why he was lonely.'

'Because –' I think for a moment. I'd neglected to explain this in the written version. 'He lived on an island, because he was afraid of spies who would want to steal his brilliant ideas. Satisfied?'

'Uh-huh.' You snuggle further down. 'Carry on.'

'Okay, then. "One day, as he was eating his supper all by himself and feeling lonelier than ever, he had a brainwave. He would invent a robot friend to keep him company. Straight away he began designing the robot. It was to be a girl robot, because this would solve the problem of him not having a girlfriend as well. For a year and a day he laboured to make her. He built an outer shell from a new type of metal that was as soft as skin. He shaped the metal and filled the insides with electrical components, the likes of which no one had ever seen before, they were so advanced." Ouch! Cold feet.'

'Don't you love my tootsies?'

'Keep them away from me or I won't carry on with the story... "One night, when all the internal wiring was complete, the scientist carried his robot to the top of the laboratory tower and plugged her into a giant transformer that was connected to the lightning conductor. Then he waited. Waited for an almighty storm to brew. A storm so powerful that the lightning would strike the tower and jolt the robot to life. While he waited, he made a beautiful white dress for the robot with cloth from spare lab coats, and a wig of sleek dark hair woven from a secret mixture of chemicals."'

'Sleek. Dark. Hair,' you echo. 'I like that. Sleekdark hair. Sleek, darkhair. Sleekdarkhair.'

'When you've quite finished…'

'Just like mine.'

'Sort of, yes.'

'Are you the scientist? If I'm the robot girl, are you the scientist?'

'Look. Do you want me to tell this story?' I huff. You settle to listen. I pause to remember the original plot. '"The robot is brought to life and they live happily ever after. Until one terrible day when the scientist spills dangerous chemicals over himself and becomes very ill. Death is hours away. While he lies groaning in agony on the floor, the robot, who is capable of original thought, has a brainwave. She springs into action and brings a pile of her spare body parts to the laboratory and hastily assembles them into a whole new robot. Then, after putting the scientist to sleep with drugs, she snips out his brain and wires it into the robot, and the two of them go on to live an eternal life of bliss on their island..." The end. Now it's your turn.'

'You rushed it. You could've strung it out more.'

'You do better, then.'

'I mean, you could have described their happy-ever-after in greater detail. What did they do on this island? Did they ever get bored?'

'Never.'

'So what did they do?'

'I don't know. They just hung out together, enjoying each other's company. Went on long walks.'

'How big is this island?'

'I don't know. Does is matter?'

'Is it as big as, say, Brownsea Island?' We'd taken the boat there while we were in Dorset, hoping to glimpse a red squirrel.

'Bigger. And the laboratory looks a bit like Corfe Castle before it was a ruin. It's on a hill at one end of the island.'

'I reckon in real life they'd have got very bored, stuck there.'

'Scientists are never bored,' I state. 'They're too busy thinking to get bored. That's why he got on so well with the robot, because she could help him with his thinking. She did all his calculations for him, and suggested improvements to his experiments. They were a perfect team.'

'Did he love her?'

'Yes. He made her to fit his requirements.'

'Sleek dark hair.'

'That's right.'

'Gripping hands, like Action Man?'

'She was so lifelike you could hardly tell that she wasn't a real live girl.'

You roll to face me. 'I take it she could talk. Where did her voice come from?'

'It was synthesised.'

'From what? The scientist's own voice?'

I don't like the idea of this. I think for a moment. 'The scientist took a boat ashore one night and went to the local inn. In his pocket –'

'Hold on. If he had a boat, why didn't he go ashore more often? He wouldn't have been lonely then.'

'The locals thought he was mad. They wanted nothing to do with him, although,' I add, anticipating a possible next question, 'they did sell food to him once a week at the market.' The nitty-gritty of the scientist's life was beginning to have a detrimental effect on the story. '*Anyway*, he went to the inn, one moonless, star-bright night.' I pause, hoping you'll relish this combination of words. You don't. You are busy sealing the sheets to prevent a fart from escaping. 'He put on a disguise and sat by himself (the locals were suspicious of strangers) listening for the voice he would most like the robot to have. It belonged to the barmaid.'

'Serving wench. If this is an inn, then you'd expect to find a wench serving the ale.'

'Fine. So he hangs around the inn until closing time, and when all the villagers have gone, and there's just him and the serving wench, and she comes over to wipe his table, he switches on a secret tape recorder he has in his pocket and captures her voice. As soon as he's back at the lab he transfers the voice to the robot's speech system.'

'So when she says "I love you", it's as if the barmaid's saying it.'

'The voice is synthesised from her voice. All you're doing now is trying to catch me out. Why don't you tell me a story and let me rip it to shreds?'

'One last point. Just answer yes or no. Does she have a whatsit?'

'She's virtually indistinguishable from a real girl,' I reply.

'So they bonk.'

'When the mood takes them.'

'Final question: does she enjoy bonking, or does she provide a service for the scientist? I'm thinking of those pleasure robots in *Westworld*.' We have watched this sci-fi movie recently on TV.

'She enjoys it just like a real girl would.' Seeing your brow is furrowed with puzzlement, I say: 'Go on, then. Last question.'

'I was only wondering, if you really could make a robot, would you give her free will, or would you ensure that she only ever loves you? Because if you rigged it so that she loves you, wouldn't you just be as lonely as before?'

We consider this in silence for a while. It is too much for my brain to cope with at seven o'clock in the morning.

'I'm never going to tell you another story,' I say.

*

We get a key cut for you so that Saturday and Sunday and holiday mornings you can let yourself in. You climb into bed with me and finish snoozing, or else we read, or chat. Your parents would freak out if they knew, but mine think it's rather sweet. It's cosiest in winter, before the heating comes on, when you are so cold from having walked down the road that you hurt me until you have finished stealing my heat. Door creak. Creak of floorboards. I raise my head from the pillow and ungum my eyes to see you silhouetted against the curtains, pulling your clothes off down to your knickers and t-shirt. Then the torturing wake-up of your cold feet and knees and hands.

This goes on for years. Until your presence tortures me in another way.

*

At Anne's fifteenth birthday party I experience jealousy for the first time. We both drink too much (you cider, I wine), and while I grow dizzy and sleepy, you become lascivious. You strike out on your own and start flirting. First with Simon, then with Darren. Long, muscular snogs with each of them. The effect on me is a kind of slow poisoning, spreading from the pit of my stomach up into my throat and eyes. Anne finds me crying and brings you to me. I cannot tell you why I am upset, but you are not thick. We leave the party and head for the seafront. After we have vomited ourselves sober, we hug for an hour in a shelter and almost kiss several times.

*

Oxford is suggested to you. One of your teachers went to Oxford and raves about it. She reckons you stand an excellent chance of getting a place and will help you to cram. She can help you with the Latin. *Amo, amas, amat, bellum, bellum, bello.* And the Anglo-Saxon. And the extra French. And the Current Affairs. There is a lot of learning to do. I am enrolled as your quizmaster. I ask questions and weigh your answers. Dates, lots of dates. And lists. Lists of prime ministers, monarchs, battles. If I were able to retain this knowledge, I would apply with you. We resurrect the Sunday morning lie-in in order to get cracking at the crack of dawn, but within a few minutes of finding myself entwined in your hot legs, I'm broadswording you in the ribs and you get dressed and disappear into the kitchen while I writhe in the warmth you have left behind.

*

We go to the *Ocean Room* together. I hate it and the following weeks you go with your classmate Anne instead. You develop a taste for the place. Some weeks you go twice, three times. I begin to hear stories. Of boys who crowd you like dogs around a bitch on heat. Of the fights that erupt over you. Of you and Anne being chased along the lower esplanade by a gang of girls whose boyfriends have shown too much interest in you. Of the joints you toke on the beach. Of white knuckle rides in cars. Your hair reeks permanently of the night before. You have arguments with your parents over lateness. One night you arrange to stay with Anne, but after you see her heading off along the beach with some boy, you decide to spend the night with me. I am awakened by you stumbling across the room and dropping onto my bed. You are not drunk but merry, and worn out from your brisk solo walk. In the dark you strip to your knickers and forget to borrow a t-shirt. We entwine and while you noisily sleep, I cry silently into your neck.

*

In time you tire of the fast lane. The *Ocean Room* becomes boring. 'Not only that, I've been neglecting my work,' you announce. 'And I've been neglecting you.' We go to the cinema once, twice a week. Sometimes we even go to a cinema in Norwich dedicated to showing foreign language films. We see Bergman's *Winter Light* and strange, puzzling French thrillers that don't thrill, but do haunt me for days afterwards, although I am not exactly sure why. We attend concerts, and you help me rehearse for plays. You do not have the nerve to appear on stage yourself.

*

We collect the taupe terrier puppy from the dog rescue home where he was born. He is called Samson in the home, but you rename him Oliver, after a TV actor you have a crush on. He is like a wind-up toy that has been over-wound. He leaves teeth marks in chair legs as if they are sticks of rock. He rarely sleeps. He will not obey simple commands such as: for fuck's sake shut up. He consumes newspapers, socks, flex and cushions. He kills garden plants with his pee and leaves turds wherever he feels like leaving them, outdoors and in. Your dad arranges for him to attend obedience classes. I go along with you to keep you company. Oliver is slow to learn as he is terrified of the other dogs, but within a few weeks he will sit, stand, fetch (but not drop), stay, and even shut the fuck up.

*

('You were saying, you saw me that afternoon?')

*

'Mind where you aim,' Anne calls after me. The two of you

laugh dirtily.

When I return to the room the video is being snapped back into its case. Anne is wondering if her mother knows about *Electrical Bits*.

'Feeling better?' you inquire. I'm too embarrassed to speak. My face is burning. You put out your arms and wrap yourself around me. Anne leaves the room to return the video to its hiding place. 'It was my fault,' you say. 'I was the one who insisted we watch it. I'm sorry if I've corrupted you. Did you think about the pretty woman with the legwarmers?'

'Yes,' I lied, because I had thought about you.

*

When my nephew is old enough to be safely left with us, we babysit him, one Saturday night. He soon realises we are a soft touch. He runs rings around us. All we want to do is drink beer and watch TV, but the Boy will not settle. You draw on your dog training experience to control him. 'Bed! Now!' But it is a story he wants. I sit with him and read *Krapp's Last Tape*. He is asleep in minutes.

We babysit regularly after this. It gives Martin and Lizzie a break. We are well provided for. There is always a good supply of beer in the fridge for us, and crisps and biscuits in the cupboards. Martin hires a video of our choice from the local shop.

The Boy develops a liking for the writings of Samuel Becket and the Oirish accent I employ. The rhythms of *Malone Dies* rapidly induce sleep.

We have always been Jim'n'Ally, but now we are JimnAlly. We are a team. It is unthinkable for one of us to arrive without the other. Martin and Lizzie assume we are a couple. When their taxi returns them from their night out they grin at us lopsidedly, assuming we have been making love on the sofa. Their neighbours once heard us having it off in the garden, but really we were rolling about in the sandpit in the dark, silly through drink. Of course the harder we stifled our laughter, the more laughter there was, like trying to stopper a tap with your thumb. Martin refuses to believe my version of the story and calls me a lucky so-and-so.

*

('You were saying...')

*

Snap.

It is unnecessary to ask you to say cheese, or to pose. You do all this instinctively whenever a lens is pointed at you. Our families' albums are full of you posing beautifully by sandcastles, or on the battlements of real castles, in rowing boats, or dodgem cars. But until you are twelve or thirteen you are curiously nondescript, just another not-especially-pretty, skinny kid grinning out of the photo. And even then, as you grow and fill out and fill out some more and grow some more, there is no hint of what is to come, and so suddenly too. Seemingly overnight at the age of fourteen your legs arrive, and your facial features settle into their final proportions. Two years on, legs and face have the same power to interrupt a driver's concentration as a patch of black ice.

Snap.

Photos of you can no longer be merely perused, they demand study. I've seen it so many times, male relatives and visitors flicking through the albums in increasing slow motion until they can hardly bear to turn the page for fear of not finding you there.

Snap.

Your sixteenth birthday. There's a tea party in your house and garden and, with the consent of the local coastguard, a party on the beach in the evening. Thirty people attend. Martin has volunteered to be official photographer. He brings a pocketful of films with him and doggedly documents them: group shots, couples, individuals, the mirth and the mayhem, the cutting of the cake, the spilling of drinks, the smokers who queue for a place behind the greenhouse when your parents are occupied indoors, and you.

Snap.

You.

Lots and lots of you.

'Hold it there!' *Snap*. 'And again.' *Snap*. 'One more. Smile!' *Snap*. For every photo he takes of someone else he takes three of you. *Snap*. Trapping the photons that have bounced off you. Close-ups of your face, and low-angle shots to get your legs in. I do not know he covets your legs. *Snap*. 'Tell you what,' he says, 'I'll treat you'n'Jim to a day out at Fritton.' *Snap*. 'Yes?' *Snap*. 'One more!'

Snap.

There are twenty of us initially on the otherwise deserted beach, although many people come and go during the course of the evening. We build a bonfire from driftwood and sit around it boozing until we are either asleep or puking. My brother shows for a while. His flashbulbs are blast-bright, phantoms on our retinas for minutes afterwards.

You go off for a piss and fail to return. But when Martin snaps Wazzer puking I am able to catch a half second glimpse of you in the background snogging some nerd from the year above with your knickers not fully pulled up. A knife is driven into my heart. I feel my way to where you had been standing, but you have vanished. 'Ally?' I drift around the crackling bonfire examining couples. 'Anyone seen Ally?'

I find Anne. She is supine smoking a joint, seemingly oblivious to the guy who is mauling her chest. She says, 'I've not seen her for ages.' Then she bats the hand away and gets up, as unsteady as a newborn foal. She totters, dropping the joint and standing on it. She yelps, staggers, then lurches against me, knocking me over and collapsing on top. Automatically, as if a director has yelled 'action', we start kissing, and pretty soon she is grinding against me, urging us both on with rhythmic gasps of pleasure. My abdomen starts to boil.

Snap.

I hear Martin guffawing, then I hear you, exclaiming at what you have seen. Next thing I know, Anne is slithering down my body. 'Oops! Bye, Jim!'

Snap.

You are dragging her by her ankles.

Snap.

Separating us, like a playground monitor breaking up a fight.

Snap. Snap.

'Piss off,' you tell her. Anne simply laughs and crawls back towards her mauler. You fall beside me and put your arm across my chest as if to claim me. 'Sorry.'

'What've you been up to?' I demand.

'Not what you think. What were you up to with my friend?' You poke me hard on the breast bone.

'It just happened.'

'Not with Anne, please. It'll get all complicated. Want me to fix you up with someone?'

'Not really.'

'Go on. It's about time you got some use out of it.'

'No. I'm saving it.'

'For?'

'For the right person.'

Knowing I mean you, you smooth my cheek with the cool back of your hand. 'It'll ruin everything if we do.'

'We don't know that.'

'Trust me.'

'But –'

Your seal my lips with your fingers. 'Shush. Listen. I can legally do it, as from today, right? But I only intend to go down that road a) when I'm sober, and b) when I feel ready.'

'How will you know when you're ready?'

'I just will.'

'There's got to be more to it than that.'

Snap.

You sit up. 'Martin!' He is kneeling by your feet. The camera is directed up your skirt. 'I want the fucking negative of that one.'

'I was taking your feet,' he says, a shade too defensively. 'Anyway, that was the last shot.'

'Good,' you complain. 'You've half blinded everyone.'

He leaves. We fall asleep hugging, waking hours later to see the sun rising above a bruised horizon. We are chilled-to-the-bone stiff, and smutty from the fire, too hangoverish to speak. Fifteen bodies lay around us like battle casualties. You go over to Anne, whose dress is still rucked up from sex, and gently wake her, pulling her dress down for her. You scowl at me for not averting my eyes. 'Come on, sweetie,' you help her to sit up. 'If James can give me a hand here –' We pick her up and support her while she pukes between her feet.

Then it's my turn.

Then yours.

I remark that it's a good thing the tourist season doesn't begin for a while yet.

Anne focuses on the body she has slept beside. 'Him! Oh, my God. I'm such a slag when I drink.' She remembers more. Her eyes widen as she regards me. 'Oops.'

'Good thing I was around,' you tell her. 'Can't have my two best friends sleeping together.'

*

('You were saying, you saw me. Saw me that afternoon.')

*

'Now cross them at the ankles. That's right. And sweep you hair out of the way – I can't see the book. Are you sure you won't take your tights off?'

'*No!*'

'Purely in the name of art.'

'You're a pervert.'

'Just because I –'

'*Joke*. You're the least perverted boy I know.'

'Boring, in other words.'

'I was thinking dependable. I'd be able trust you with my life.'

*

'"Country matters",' I say. 'Why's that so funny?'

'It's a Shakespearean rude joke,' you say, fanning your cheeks with *Hamlet*. 'Good God, James, you're not thick.'

Oh, but I am, I am. I read aloud the dialogue we've been over-acting for our pleasure. '"Lady, shall I lie in your lap?" "No, my lord." "I mean, my head upon your lap." "Ay, my lord." "Do you think I meant country matters?"'

'*Et cetera, et cetera*, then Hamlet says to Ophelia: "That's a fair thought to lie between maids' legs"... Gettit?'

'Erm –'

'You're hopeless. Country matters means matters relating to Ophelia's –' She waves her hand like the Queen passing by and then limply points between her legs.

'I've just got it,' I say.

*

We are hanging out on the seafront, smoking in a shelter. We are bored and have resorted to I-Spy. It is my turn to think of something.

'S,' I say.

'Sea.'

'No.'

'Sky.'

'Nope.'

'Sulphuric acid. Shostakovitch. Six stout-hearted secretaries selling seashells on the seashore.'

'Wrong, wrong... wrong.'

'Shit?'

'We've done that already. D for dog shit.'

'Then I give up.'

'*Scott*,' I say. 'Nuclear Scott. Look.' I direct your attention towards the beach, along which Scott is briskly marching with the family Alsatian leading the way like a regimental mascot. 'I know names don't count, but ?'

Taking hold of my arm, you say: 'I detest him.'

'He's just a harmless twit. Deluded.'

You squeeze. 'He's a nasty piece of work.'

'Since when?'

Your lips are bloodless through compression. 'I don't agree with all that military crap he's so keen on.'

'I don't, but I wouldn't have said he was nasty.'

You don't say anything, but watch him until he is out of sight.

NINE

Yes, I see you that afternoon.

I glimpse you from three hundred yards away on the twisty path, through a serendipitous alignment of gaps in the foliage. There's someone mooching beside you. Male. Disappointment paralyses me. Why is he with you? A chance encounter? I invent a story. You are out on a stroll, he sees you, pursues you, foists himself upon you and you are now obliged to endure his company, although you intend to shake him off at the first opportunity.

More likely the truth is he called on you as he threatened he would and you willingly went with him. Fool.

This is horrible. I'm compelled to find out what is going on. But how? Calmly stroll towards you until we meet? 'Tra-la-la. Oh, hello, you two! Gosh, isn't it a lovely day for it? Mind if one joins one?' My posh *Salad Days* voice. Better to conceal myself and spy on you.

There's no one about to notice me crawl into the path-side leafage and between the gnarled hobbity stems and roots of ancient hawthorns. I hunker down to wait.

I wait for several minutes before I hear animated chatter approaching. And laughter. The irksome laughter of two people perfectly at ease with one another. Don't we laugh like that? Haven't we laughed like that for years? Is it Wilson's turn now?

Closer.

Holding my breath, I listen through the din my heart is

making.

Your voice. 'Sounds really good.' What does? What sounds not just good but really good?

'Oh, you have to see it. It's a marvellous film.' There was no trace left of the drink-exacerbated bolshieness.

'And you have to see *Le Genou de Claire*.'

Why? Why does he? That's our film. The film we enjoyed together at a Rambouillet Society meeting. Enjoyed, even though it was out of focus much of the time and barely watchable through a locust plague of dust; even though the action was halted twice for the spools to be changed; even though it was several minutes before anyone noticed the last spools were in the wrong order.

'Le what?'

Ignoramus. Mono-lingual moron.

You enunciate and translate. '*Claire's Knee*.'

'A film about a knee?'

'It's about a man's obsessive desire to put his hand on this girl's knee.'

'And does he?'

'That'll spoil the plot.'

'Obsession is a good thing,' Wilson says as he lights a cigarette. I hear the ker-ching of his Zippo. He has lit one for you too. 'I mean, to produce great art you have to be obsessed. Haystacks, bowls of fruit, Tahitian maidens.'

'You're obsessed by Gorleston maidens.'

Wilson scoffs. 'Only particular ones.'

You pause for Oliver to sniff the ground. What if he sniffs out a trail leading straight to me? How will I be able to explain my hiding in the bushes? Looking for lost golf balls? 'Spot of bird watching, darling. Glimpsed a Lesser Wozzlewit and simply had to follow it to its nest.'

'I used to come along here a lot, sketching,' Wilson says. 'These old roots fascinated me. They're so – sculptural.'

I peep and see his artist's hand describing shapes in mid-air, as if he's feeling-up a ghost.

'We had to draw something like that in Art once.' You are offering your past to him. 'It was really hard.' Your past is no one's but mine. Same as my past is yours alone. Perhaps if I were to leap out at you I could nip this friendship in the bud. 'I've never been any good at drawing. Not like you.' Ah, so you've seen his work, have you? My heart-thumps suddenly feel wrongly strong, like an engine about to blow. If it were to explode and I were to die here, how long will it be before my body is found? Before the flies and worms have stripped me of my flesh? Perhaps Wilson can somehow be implicated in my murder and be whisked away to prison. A fragment of a drawing found close by, a mislaid pencil with his fingerprints. Oliver would sniff him out for the jury.

You are continuing on your way.

He says: 'Before I started at the art college I turned my bedroom into a studio. Almost every day last summer I used to go out sketching in the morning and then paint indoors in the afternoon. The first proper thing I did was a couple embracing under a street lamp. I had this kind of vision as I was leaving Darren's late one night. The light was...' I miss the rest of the sentence when a breeze shakes the leaves and covers your words like a wave on shingle. I follow, hunchbacking silently through the bushes until I've caught up.

'Cairo-what?' you are saying.

'Chiaroscuro. The opposition between light and dark. I painted the couple brightly lit against the dark of the night. And I hid the light source behind silhouetted leaves.'

'Sounds really clever.'

Oh, put a sock in it, you stupid girl. If you could hear yourself. You've crammed for Oxford and here you are calling this dishevelled dimwit clever. It's almost as if you're telling him what he wants to hear. Massaging his ego. Flirting. Doing an Anne.

I shock myself with such traitorous thoughts. I shouldn't be angry with you. It is Wilson I ought to be hating, and I do hate him. But I find I hate you more. You're encouraging him. Flirt. Slag. *Whore*. If he were to shoulder you into these bushes and rape you, I'd not stop him. I'd watch. I'd make sure you saw me watching. I'd be grinning. I wouldn't lift a finger to help. I might even shout encouragement: 'Give it some welly, mate.'

'I didn't really know what I was doing, though,' Wilson drones on, as if he's being interviewed for a TV programme. I creep two yards further forwards. 'I was using far too many colours. I should have kept my palette simple. In the end I found a book on oil techniques in Yarmouth library. I picked up a lot from that. What I realised I needed to do was improve my figure work. My people looked really wooden.'

'They don't anymore,' you chime in, like some easel groupie. Have you been to his so-called studio, then? The only people who are permitted entry are girls willing to pose for weeks at a time.

'We had to do life drawing every Thursday at art college. All day. And we did extra sessions some evenings.'

'That's when Claire posed.'

Claire? As in *Le Genou de*? No, a real Claire. How do you know someone from his art college life, the set of friends he deliberately keeps away from his *Links* friends, almost as if he wants to live two separate lives?

'Did you ever go out with Claire?'

My hearing becomes a notch more sensitive. Perhaps he is still romantically attached to this Claire.

'We had a bit of an encounter at a party. You know: unpremeditated heavy snog and a cuddle. It didn't lead to anything, though we ended up mates. We used to walk round Yarmouth together at lunchtimes. Sometimes we'd hold hands to cross the road. I asked her out a few times, but she liked us as we were. She ended up with this guy called Joseph. He was heavily into ceramics.'

I can proceed no further. Several narrow trunks are barring my way. Your voices diminuendo to quieter than the bees and flies and eventually to nothing. I wait a full five minutes before bushwhacking my way out of the scratchy foliage into the afternoon sunlight. I am in time to see the two of you reach the end of the lane and haul Oliver in the wrong direction towards Wilson's house.

TEN

'He invited me in, but I couldn't, not with Oliver.'

But you did call round eventually.

'Guilty as charged!'

Your growing friendship with Wilson was a secret you were keeping from me, although I noticed you talked to him more in *The Links*. Proper two-way talking, not you listening to him lecturing. I felt powerless to stop it.

'Your old Achilles' heel, you see. I'm surprised you allowed me to talk unchaperoned with other blokes. Like Darren.'

Darren I was fine with. And Nuclear Scott, when you went through a phase of two-way talking with him.

'It wasn't intimate talking.'

No, Scott didn't do intimate. He could do comradely. ("Yes sah! No sah!") He could do retail affability ("How about this lovely piece of brisket, missus? Do you know, you're looking younger every time you come in here?") But intimacy was quite beyond him.

It certainly wasn't beyond Wilson.

'We went to see your picture in the library. He thought it showed real ability. He reckoned you could get into the art college.'

But I didn't want to be an artist. I wanted to be an *ack*-tor, ducky. The winter of our discontent, and all that. The National. Stratford. A horse! A horse! The dogs of war! I can't picture myself poncing about at an easel. Can you imagine Inspector

Poole played by anyone else? According to a recent readers' poll in *Hello!* the answer's a resounding no.

'After the library, we came back to Gorleston and he asked me in for a coffee. This time I said yes. I met his mum, and it turned out she knew my mum from somewhere. Then I went upstairs to his room.'

The lair of the lickerish Lothario. I expect there was a good deal of porn on show; posters, discarded magazines.

'Books, actually. One wall was covered in books. The room smelt like a second-hand bookshop. Mainly fiction, but there were also titles on every subject you could think of.'

The bluffer's armoury. He'd have only consulted them when he needed to impress someone.

'He had a lot of books about Dylan Thomas. He particularly liked *Under Milk Wood*. He could do the entire first speech from memory.'

But could he do the Richard Burton accent? The trick is to give it a slight nasal quality and play down the Welshiness. Dylan was posher than a lot of people imagine. He had elocution lessons early on. Like me.

'He could also do several of the poems from memory as well.'

Amazing what those council house kids can do. One whiff of high culture and they're away. Did you get the impression he was an aberration? A traitor to his class?

'Now you're just being a berk. A house is a house. Doesn't matter if you rent it or own it. If you ask me, you're just inventing feeble excuses for why you hated him. You wouldn't consider yourself a snob, would you?'

No I wouldn't. Of course I wouldn't. I'm Inspector Poole, not King Lear.

'Well then. Stop knocking his background. I loved his parents.'

I met them on a recent jaunt to Gorleston, on Marine Parade

where *The Links* used to be. Nattered with them about the old days, and what Wilson was up to. I took them to lunch at the *Cliff Hotel* and we talked about Alison Dury. They have very fond memories of her. Said she was nice and normal.

'Claire had been too art-school weird for them, asking profound questions about the ornaments.'

They'd seen you as a potential daughter-in-law.

'Me. Married. To him. Imagine. Alison Wilson. Mrs Alison Wilson. The rhythm's dandy, but I don't like all those esses.'

What else did you do on this first visit, apart from listen to him read poems?

'He showed me his favourite books, and read from them. Then we looked at his photos.'

This sounds ominous. Photos. Like etchings. Come-up-and-see-my. I can picture the two of you side by side on his bed. Makes me shudder.

'I was stretched out in my drawing pose while he was perched next to me explaining the photos. He only used an instamatic but the results were striking. He had a good eye for composition.'

Permission to yawn, sir?

'There were dozens of pictures of the gang: Darren gurning every time and Julie posing if she'd just been declared Miss Norfolk.

Which she very nearly was in the mid-eighties. My parents snipped her out of the *Mercury*: swimsuit, big hair, heels and a sash, clutching a consolation rosette. Her beauty was at its zenith. It was just unfortunate that the curves and countenances of the Misses Cromer and Norwich were more abundantly nymphaen. I felt for her. She was a trouper, however. The following week she was back in the public eye, promoting Gorleston seafront in cut-downs and a sombrero. *"I want you all to switch your tellies off, slip your flip-flops on and spend a day making sandcastles with me. The beach isn't just for tourists.*

It's yours too, so use it!" The Council's words, not hers, quoted verbatim in the *Mercury*, with no mention of how execrably acted they were for the TV cameras, or the crowd mockery, the umpteen takes and the dictionary's worth of expletives.

'Wilson liked the beach. He said it was life class, landscape and still life rolled into one.'

Let me just add that to my 'Aphorisms of The Master'.

'He was always down there, photographing, or sketching in that little book he carried. Christmas day, while we were trudging about, he was out taking pictures. I'm sure we're in one of them, two little dots and an even littler dot ascending the slope to the upper esplanade. In fact, I know it's us. He must have walked across our footprints. It's almost as if our paths were meant to cross.'

Or else it means there were so few things to occupy us back then we were virtually queuing up to walk on the same bit of beach, or along the one lane by the golf course. You have to remember that there were only three TV channels then, which rarely broadcast much later than midnight; hardly any shops were allowed to open on Sunday; video games were in their infancy; pubs were open less. And there we were stuck at an end-of-the-line, out-of-season town on the Norfolk coast, with nothing to look at but what everyone else was looking at. Each other.

'You have to admit, you were happy at the time.'

Only because I didn't know any better. Only because we were all in it together.

'You missed the place.'

Take it from me, love, when you're stuck in a mouldy, colander-roofed, sash-rattling, wallpaper-sloughing, web-ruched student house on the outskirts of London with two feuding lesbians, an Anglophobic knuckle-cracking Scotsman and a one-bar electric fire, you do start to yearn for the more genteel existence, yes. At the time I envied those friends of ours who'd stayed behind. I was on the verge of rejoining them permanently when we all met up at Christmas. Drama school wasn't the easy ride I thought it would be. And by then I'd been told the statistics of how next to bloody impossible it would be for us to become successful; and I wasn't pleased at the prospect of a lifetime of one-line walk-ons, adverts for carpet warehouse sales (*"While stocks last, folks!"*), or guest appearances in cop shows as corpses. I changed my mind when I saw you and Wilson at Christmas, the very best of friends, I suddenly knew I had to succeed in order prove that without you to hold me down I could fly as high as I wanted.

'Since when had I held you down? That's just bullshit. You're rewriting history. The truth is we held ourselves down. I denied myself a regular love life for fear of upsetting you, while you were permanently on your guard against people who threatened to come between us.'

We should have been a proper couple. The friendship we were so scared of losing was lost anyway through denial and jealousy. We'd have been better off enjoying what we had, and then if it hadn't worked out, enjoying what we could've had with someone else. Maybe you didn't fancy me enough.

'Oh I fancied you alright.'

And Wilson?

'Him too. Eventually. He grew on me.'

I was hooked on you from the moment I clapped eyes on you. Thought you were incredible, catching those earwigs. Wasn't long before I was in love with you. Although I didn't recognise the symptoms until much later.

'Ah, but would you have loved me if I hadn't been attractive?'

You weren't attractive. You should check out your school photos. I doubt if you'd recognise yourself: cheeks puffed out as if you had sweets hidden in them, wonky little mouth you'd prised off a cherub and glued on wrong. You couldn't have been called pretty until you were about fifteen. The point is, I wouldn't have cared one jot *what* you looked like. I'd have fallen in love with you if I'd kept my eyes shut for all those years.

'Flattering, but not possible.'

Course it is. People fall madly in love in internet chat rooms without ever meeting.

'I'm amazed you know about such things. I mean, you've never even considered upgrading your manual typewriter.'

Out of the question. I've had that since college. I write all my letters on that. Replies to fan mail, mostly. Stop grimacing. You know how much fan mail I get. Lots of my admirers want to marry me.

'Sorry to burst your bubble, but it's Poole they want to marry. The lecherous detective. Not James Rudd who stares out to sea while staring in to see.'

Jealous.

'Of middle-aged women?'

Young ones too. But yes, mostly middle-aged women. What's wrong with middle-aged women? They're passionate and loyal. They're in love with me, a lot of them. They send me their photos. I get photos from all over the world. And I send them signed ones of me if their letter's not too raunchy. I had a stalker for a while. She used to wait outside the studio to ogle me, which I could tolerate, but then she started ogling me on holiday. She'd stare at me through binoculars. I wasn't doing anything, just sitting in my chair, sunning myself, staring into blank space like the people on either side of me. In the end I reckoned it was Poole she was in love with, not Jim Rudd, and that she would only take heed of Poole. So even though I was not particularly Poole-ish-looking without the sideburns, moustache and wig, I marched up to her and gave her a suitably Poole-ish talking to. I ordered her to go home at once and never to bother me again, or else she'd be in serious trouble. I borrowed lines from a telling-off Poole gave to an over-inquisitive journalist.

'And did she go home?'

I've not seen her since. But we're digressing. What did you do after Wilson shared his photos with you?

'We chatted.'

Naturally. What about?

'Various subjects. Books.'

What books?

'Just books. And a bit of politics. Maggie. The Royal Family.'

I suppose Royal Wedding fever was in the air at that time. Was he weighing-up your form? Was he obsessed by *les genoux d'Alison*? What were you wearing? One of your denim flirt skirts? Were you showing him *vos jambes*?

'*Tes jambes*, actually. *Ton, ta, tes*. Don't you remember testing my French?'

I've told you, there's little wrong with my memory.

'Until it comes to French grammar.'

Because I wasn't the one learning it. If I'd bothered to learn it, it would still be up here. "Dad, The Chester Mullins Quintet is playing at the Five Bells tonight. You fancy coming along?"

'You've lost me.'

Inspector Poole's first ever words, spoken into a telephone from his girlfriend's flat. I say girlfriend; she was a two-night stand, which in Poole's world counts as a serious relationship. I remember her first words, as she emerged from the bedroom dressed in nothing but her underwear and diamond-patterned stockings: "I suppose you're going to tell me I'm overdressed." They used this to advertise the Brand New Series, obviously because it was raunchy-looking. "Overdressed?" I reply. "Oh, definitely." At which point she removed her bra. I've got the entire scene still up here.

'Show off.'

Just proving a point. So were you showing him *tes jambes*?

'Guilty. His eyes seemed to be enjoying themselves. But it was all very innocent. After we'd finished looking at the photos, we had a cigarette, and then he went downstairs to fix another coffee. Which gave me the perfect opportunity to look under his bed and in his chest of drawers for secrets.'

What kind of secrets did you have in mind? Porn?

'Porn wouldn't have rattled me as much as love letters from that Claire person.'

She bothered you that much?

'I wasn't convinced they'd been mere mates. I needed to know. After a quick root around, I found his diary. It wasn't hidden, it was merely camouflaged. He'd bound a number of exercise books together and wrapped the cover in wallpaper. It was sitting on one of his bookshelves. I only noticed it because I was looking for it. It covered about a year and a half of his life.'

So you read it, then.

'I was shocked. It was like the diary of a twelve-year-old girl. All his crushes, his innumerable crushes, were painstakingly described. One entry went on for six sides, describing in tedious detail a typical Wilson day. He really ought to have got out more when he was at school. The highlight of this particular day was when he glanced up to find the slinky temptress Anita staring at him and smiling (and I quote, ladies and gentlemen of the jury) "as if she wanted me to peruse her book of love". I cringed.'

In Wilson's defence, bear in mind this diary was only meant for his eyes.

'I beg to differ, Inspector. He liked to quote: "Anita more terrible than an army with banners."'

What army with banners?

'It's from the *Old Testament*. *The Song of Solomon*. Terrible meaning terrifying... You don't fill private diaries with quotes unless you want to be regarded as clever. "Jerome K Jerome said about love that it was silly and soppy and as controllable as water from a tap."

'I found a few references to me which were all flattering (except he kept referring to my eyes as cold and expressionless. I didn't think they were). Claire got more column inches. How she'd teased him, rejected him, encouraged him: "Claire (Oh Claire de la loony) suggested I paint her nude. I'm bound to get erections galore and become a laughing stock. Still, it will be good for my career to paint her. And I *have* seen her without her clothes several times. She has a damn fine bottom but no breasts. The thighs are a trifle on the flabby side."

'I saw my name: "Alison, oh Alison! My heart is yours, should you wish to claim it." That set me fluttering with excitement. But flicking randomly through, I found I was just one filly from a stable-load. Alicia, Marina, Jenny, Kath, Claire. "Girls, girls, girls, girls – what else do I think of? I spend my life wishing, dreaming, hoping, failing."'

Such a fickle philogynist, that Wilson. So all his diary's about is girls, girls, girls? No politics? He seemed to have views. What did he have to say about the Royal Family? About the wedding?

'Royal Wedding Day, July 29th, he's mouthing off about the Queen not paying taxes, and wondering if the general public are footing the bill for the celebrations. "Everywhere the streets are empty and silent. Everyone is indoors worshipping at the shrine of the TV." He heads off to the seafront with a gang from *The Links* and they rustle up a makeshift protest against the royals. "I drew a giant caricature of Charles and Di on the beach and wrote the words 'You'll pay for this' in six-foot high letters alongside it. Meanwhile, Julie, gorgeous Julie, with a piece of net curtain secured round her head, and Darren in his dad's flasher mac, went up and down the seafront flashing at people. Julie! Julie! Oh, Julie!"'

Did he have any thoughts on art?

'Oh, loads. No discussion, though, just his likes and dislikes.' As you'd expect.

'And much patting himself on the back. "My finest work to date. After five hours of solid observation, I ended up with my best ever drawing. It was easily the best drawing in the room. Tutor Mike went and fetched his colleague Dan to come and admire it, although, typically, Dan was sparing with his praise. Kath came over and said I was a genius and that she was going to throw her drawing away after seeing mine. I love Kath so much. It is her birthday soon and I intend to buy her a present. Perhaps that copy of *The Thief's Journal* in Gorleston Trading Depot."

'Now that I knew what sort of a person he was, I knew how to behave with him. Those other girls had made the mistake of blowing hot and cold on him. They enjoyed his attentions, flirted with him, but wouldn't commit. It was a power thing. Like they had him on a leash. By posing for him, and spending time with him, I was showing him constancy.'

He was reluctant to make a pass, though.

'He liked painting me. He didn't want to scare me off. It was the strict adherence to modelling decorum that made the nude pose so erotic. It felt like the ultimate seduction.'

And you went out with that no good easel-weasel.

'Much to your disgust.'

Wilson the lech.

'That was a myth.'

You won't deny he was one of the biggest drunkards *The Links* had seen in years.

'Another myth. He hardly drank those few weeks we were going out. We stayed away from pubs. We took Oliver walkies most evenings, either to the beach, or into the countryside.'

Arrogant, then. You can't deny he was arrogant.

'Who's not at that age? You were.'

You reckon? Little ole me? I thought we agreed I was Mr Modest?

'Strutting your stuff on a theatre stage, you had to have had a touch of arrogance.'

Self-confidence, yes. But Wilson wasn't on any stage. Unless you count Gorleston and the surrounding district as one giant theatre. You're just making excuses for him. I admire your loyalty.

'Curmudgeon. You're jealous.'

With good reason to be. He'd pulled you.

'The darling of Grove Grammar, as you put it.'

Now you're laughing at me.

'I'm laughing at you still being jealous after all these years.'

Don't you admire my loyalty to you? Undiminished by time.

'James, you should have moved on. Found yourself a new girl to love.'

No one measures up. There was one girl. An actress. I saw her on TV. Glimpsed her. Couple of seconds. Some stupid advert for shampoo. Set my heart racing. She was – she was amazing. She was just – perfectly you. Your double. I videoed the adverts all evening until that one showed again, and I played her two seconds over and over, obsessively. She was shaking her sleek dark hair. Over and over. Smiling at me. *At me*. I knew I had to find her, so I used my influence and cast her in the one episode of Poole that I'd been permitted to write. I rewrote my first draft, in fact. Completely changed the plot in order to give her more screen time. More time with Poole. I put him in her bed. I had him making love with her, telling her how he couldn't live without her. You know. Obsessing. A man driven mad through obsession. I wanted her face in close up. I wanted to fill the screen with her face, to put her into eleven million homes. And I did all this rewriting without having met her. Kelly. Assigned the role to her without even testing her. Which wasn't easy to pull off, but I managed it.

I met her at a script workshop a few days before we were due to begin filming. I usually hate these meetings – they're interminable – and arrive late, but this time I was the first one there. I wanted to be there when Kelly arrived. I even bagsied a couple of chairs for us. I wanted to make sure I was sitting directly opposite so as to be able to study her.

I received a shock when she did step coyly into the room. She had short hair. Really short. Shorter than your bob. I panicked. I said, "In the advert..." And she explained she'd worn a wig for that and could easily do so again. She'd be in a blonde wig for two-thirds of the episode anyway. "Don't worry, Mr Rudd, they'll fix me up so that I look exactly the way you want."

Her voice was all wrong. Too Estuary. And the lips were too full. And the eyes, the eyes were hazel. And the top of her head only came level with my chin. She was all wrong. The build was wrong. The legs were wrong. And she was woefully nervous, this being her first speaking role since leaving college. I felt sick with the disappointment. Not with her inexperience, but with her looks. I'm not saying she wasn't lovely. She was very lovely. But she wasn't you. In the advert... In the advert she was you. For two seconds. Shaking her sleek dark hair. She was you.

Kelly could tell I was disappointed. I tried to hide it, but she knew. She took me to one side during our coffee break and apologised, and I assured her the fault lay entirely with me, and I told her a few things about my past. Only a few.

She said I was forgetting about the wonders of make-up. With the right make-up she said she could look like Margaret Thatcher. I said, "Good god, no thanks, let's just make sure you end up looking like you did in that advert."

'And did she?'

Exactly. It's quite remarkable what the make-up department achieved. She starts off as an Estuary-speaking blonde and is slowly transformed into a posh pallid beauty with sleek dark hair. Kelly was fabulous as Judy.

Poole: (*obsessed*) I said a short skirt and ribbed tights. This... this isn't what I meant.

Judy: (*distressed*) What's wrong with the skirt?

Poole: It's... far too long. And the tights are wrong. I said ribbed, not... (*Snatches the packet and tosses it aside*)

Judy: I never wear ribbed tights.

Poole: From now on you do. Preferably black.

Judy: You can't make me do anything.

Poole: You said you loved me.

Judy: I do. But you, you just want me to look like her. You don't want me at all. (*Stares*)

Poole: (*looks guiltily away*) That's not true.

Judy: (*rounding on him*) It is and you damned well know it.

Poole: (*after a long pause, without looking at her*) Go. Just... leave, will you?

Judy: (*quietly but intensely*) Maybe it's best if we don't see one another again.

The phone didn't stop ringing for her after that episode was shown. In her recent BAFTA speech she acknowledged that I was the person responsible for her first major break. "Thanks, Jim!"

'Did you not want to go out with her?'

I told you, she wasn't right. She was lovely – phenomenally lovely, in fact – but then so are a million other women.

'Plus you only ever wanted me.'

Precisely. Accept no imitation, that's what I say.

'You must admit, you've led a very lonely life.'

Far from it. I don't need anyone when I've you to keep me company. Anyone else would be an intrusion. I've lost count of the lunches and parties I've missed because I needed to be with you. I even turned down the chance to meet Tony Blair: Rudd Snubs PM: "My sock drawer needed sorting out." Which though true, wasn't the actual reason I declined the invite to Number 10. I was busy filming.

'What I don't get is why you liked me so ardently. I wasn't that nice to you, if you really think about it.'

I didn't simply like you, I loved you. Loved you with my

entire being. Still do.

'But wasn't I just the sister you – you and Martin – never had? After all, I'd been hanging about doing sisterly things since early nonage.'

You became far more than a sister to me when puberty put ideas into my head. I know you were not a sister to Martin. He liked looking at you in a very non-brotherly way. Particularly when you got those legs of yours.

'Ah, my famous legs.'

The photo I found of us wrestling in the garden: do you remember that being taken?

'Very clearly. What happened was we'd gone outside to check on your nephew, who'd climbed into next door's garden to play with the kids who lived there. For some reason we started chasing each other around the garden and ended up wrestling. Your brother saw us mucking about and rushed out with his camera.'

Correction. My brother saw you were wearing shorts and wanted to preserve the moment.

'I was so naïve. How old would your brother have been?'

Almost twenty-two. And miserable. It's like this. He's trapped in some joyless insurance job in Lowestoft. He's not sure if he loves the woman he's married to anymore, and he's had it up to here with parental responsibilities. Meanwhile, his younger brother, who has no responsibilities, is relatively free to do what he pleases, he's even thinking of applying to drama school, and to top it all his pretty-but-stick-thin-and-sexless childhood friend Alison has turned into a cracking bird with squidgy tits, child-bearing hips and famous legs.

'You have a lovely way of putting things. You could be a poet.'

You're forgetting I was at one time: *Gorleston*, by James Rudd.

A broadshouldered urban ghost,
Gaunt, herringboned and salt-cloaked,
Arrogantly slouched about the sea-swerving shore,
It stares out with dull, fixed eyes
At the unerring rhythm of the tide.

All eight verses of it published in the *Mercury* in 1979.

'My turn to ask for permission to yawn –'

I liked my '*merrybugling, wind-rapt gulls that croon and wheel smugly unavailable to the sea*'. I liked the '*dark, foul terror of the touch-and-go town*'.

'Very Dylan Thomas.'

He was the master. I loved to read his work aloud. It was the equivalent of filling your mouth with your favourite chocolates. I used to recite his poems to you and Martin. Not that he appreciated my renditions, the Philistine. He only used to hang about in order to ogle you in his peripheral sight.

'My secret admirer.'

He was obsessed.

'Like you.'

No, not like me. I liked all of you.

'Did you? You hardly ever took photos of me.'

I had no need to. I saw you in the flesh every day.

'I have to admit, Martin did photograph me relentlessly. That day we all went to Fritton Country Park. When I slid down the slide, he was waiting for me at the bottom.'

Snap.

'Swinging on the swing.'

Snap. Snap.

'Diving for the frisbee.'

Snap-snap-snap.

'In the rowing boat on the lake, while you and I pulled the oars.'

Snap-snap. His lens was tumid. Begrudgingly he took the odd one of Lizzie with the Boy, but the majority of the other forty-seven exposures taken that day were mostly of the view up your skirt, or of your face. His wife never got to see them. He claimed the back of the camera hadn't been closed properly and the films had been ruined. If she'd looked in the shoebox on the top shelf in the garage she'd have found the two packets, hidden as if they were porn. As in a way they were.

'You don't think –?'

I wouldn't rule it out. Men can turn absolutely anything into porn. I used to get turned on by the cover photo of a pattern for crocheted swimwear. A lovely nineteen-sixties blonde, she was, sunning herself in monochrome on a beach. And if you let your imagination look closely, you could make out her nipples in the holes. I used to study that for hours. And then there were the bra pages of the mail order catalogues...

'How did you know about my photos?'

I went through a phase of poking around in hard-to-get places. It was good training for my Inspector Poole character. He's forever poking around in hard-to-get places.

'Under people's beds, for example?'

Most memorably in season 3, episode 4: *An Inspector Crawls*. Anyway, you can't talk. You're worse than me, reading secret diaries.

'Guilty, as charged.'

I searched my brother's house from top to bottom. Even ventured into the loft. Eventually I turned my attention upon the garage and found what I was looking for in less than ten minutes. There were a few token ones of me, some ducks, the lake, Lizzie and the Boy, but I'd say ninety per cent of the photos were of you. There were deliciously lecherous too, like preliminary shots for a porn mag striptease.

'So do you think he...?'

Leg shots, most of them. It's funny, but it wasn't until I saw your legs in the photos that I realised how lovely they were in real life. After that I began to notice them.

'Muscles, sinews and bones, that's all legs are.'

And shapeliness.

'Shapeliness is in the eye of the beholder. Big tits, small tits, no tits: different men enjoy different things. Not all women are turned on by receding hair and a paunch. Your brother's halfway to fifty. What does he look like these days?'

I shouldn't think you'd like him. Not like you used to. Because you did like him at one time.

Do you know, that in all those years we lived in Gorleston, and all the places we went, we never went to Benacre Ness by ourselves?

Benacre Ness, you remember. Just a short drive down the coast from Lowestoft. No, we never went there as Jim'n'Ally.

' _ '

Although you went, didn't you.

' _ '

With Martin.

' _ '

And not just the once.

' _ '

How many times was it?

' _ '

Two? Three?

' _ '

I'll tell you, shall I? I've done the necessary research.

' _ '

I'll tell you, shall I? Mm? Alison?

' _ '

Shall I? Because I do know.

' _ '

I've known about your visits for some time.

ELEVEN

It is during the trip to Fritton that my suspicions are first aroused. Not the incessant snap of the shutter so much as the posing I glimpse sidelong, the legs you splay for Martin's mechanical eye, the practised doleful look, the sultry stare through wind-tousled fringe, the tongue playing wetly at the corner of your mouth. They are momentary signals, and you think I don't see them, but I see them perfectly. You are not as surreptitious as you think.

The developed photos confirm my suspicions. It's clear why they have to be concealed. They document a pact, a secret pact between artist and model. You and him. It sickens me to see the love of my life reduced to aping glamour girl clichés; and yet at the same time I am probably as delighted as my brother with the results. Some of them give me a real buzz of desire. Interesting, though, how your eyes never give up any of your secrets to the camera. They remain as impenetrable as the mechanical iris that captures them.

It's easy enough, isn't it, to meet Martin out of work in Lowestoft. Three times that summer you go to tea at your Nan's, midweek, catching the Lowestoft bus late afternoon. In all the years I've known you, you've gone to tea there no more than once a month, and always on a Sunday. And yet suddenly you've developed a conscience and a taste for her home-made scones. She's getting old, you say. She's over sixty. She may not have many more years to go. (Now that I have reached middle age, sixty is beginning to sound remarkably young.) You invite me, but ever since the bolster incident, I've not dared to show my face. I suspect nothing because I love and trust you.

Where do you wait for him? There is a bench outside a newsagent's a few streets away from his office. You arrange for him to collect you as he drives past, sometime between five past and ten past five, depending on the traffic, and tonight the main road is bumper to bumper, constipated. Bored men call out to you: requests to see your mammaries or offers of a lift. By half past, convinced he's had second thoughts and won't show, you start to walk away, but something makes you return to the bench, and moments later his car draws alongside. Once he has you in the passenger seat, he taxis you swiftly south out of Lowestoft. You communicate not with words but sidelong smirks and raised eyebrows. Your right thigh nuzzles up to the gear-stick like a cat craving attention, and after he has changed up to fourth for the main road, he introduces his hand to your bare knee. His fingers trace the outline of your kneecap, the tightening hamstrings. He smoothes at last the flesh he has craved for months. Coveted. And he is not disappointed. It shows he is not disappointed. You reach over to feel, and the car instantly strays towards the white line.

Where he is taking you remains a secret until he leaves the main road and you read the sign. Benacre. You are going to Benacre Ness. You have been to this out-of-the-way place once before, aged eleven, James' guest on a Suffolk day out courtesy of his parents. You don't recall Martin being there. Presumably he was off doing his own thing, as usual, although subsequently, independent of his family, he was to become a regular visitor to this stretch of the coast, first on bicycle, later by moped and car, drawn to the windswept desolation with a poet's passion. Usually he brought Carl with him. They would smoke joints and compose songs and plan their first four album covers. There was little else here to occupy a pair of fledging adolescents. Martin also brought Lizzie here before they were married in order to have sex. Wilson has been here too, by bicycle. He took photographs; arty, low-angle views of the shingle with foreground sorrel. It will bring back memories when you see these pictures two years later.

You wind down your window and gratefully toke the hot aroma of newly-mown grass, nettles, chickens. Here is the church and the orderly churchyard in which you and I competed to find the oldest grave. Here is the huddle of houses Mum purred over; beyond them the long straight road where Dad pretended to have brake failure and you and I cried out *no, no, I don't want to die* so convincingly he relented and dropped his speed to twenty.

The road ends at a farm. Martin parks close against the hedgerow in case tractors need to pass. You are obliged to clamber through the driver's door. He grins lasciviously when your hem snags on the gear stick, then relents and offers his forearm. A short hike now, single file past the farm and along a track towards the sea. Assorted chirrups and trills. One unseen bird speaks like a mattress spring.

The beach is deserted. You scrunch, scrunch, side-by-side, searching for a suitable fastness. Martin takes your hand and grips it tightly as if he fears you will abscond. The not-talking annoys you and you offer him a selection of pertinent facts acquired in Geography and History and extracurricular reading. Glaciers. Tribes. Uh-huh. Mm. His interest is feigned. The only Saxon he cares to know about is the rock band, not some first millennium predecessor.

He begins to walk more quickly. Close by the freshwater broad is a perfect greenery-fringed scrape in the shingle. You fall into it together and lie down and immediately he is greedily kissing your throat and chin. His day's growth of stubble abrades like a gym mat. Enough. You pinch your lips hard together. The kissing stops and he turns his attention elsewhere. Without asking he removes your underwear and sets about stroking you with two spittly fingers. He invites you to reciprocate, unaware that you are making this up as you go along. You fumble at the button and zip of his trousers. What you release shocks you. It is every bit as rigid as it looks. You were expecting something more user-friendly, whippier, no larger than a tampon.

And now? Leave it to Martin. He's married; he has sex all the time. He kneels between your legs and sheaths his thing with smeary grey so that it not longer resembles a body part. Good. You notice his hands are shaking. Perhaps it would help him to relax if he were to touch your breasts. Men enjoy breasts. On rare occasions you have even caught James admiring yours. You lift your t-shirt and advance them through the alphabet by squashing them together. Martin groans appreciatively and suckles. You notice scurf around his crown. He ought to change his shampoo. Clouds pass swiftly overhead, southwest to northeast. You look for shapes in them. A longboat. A Scotty dog. A coelacanth, is that? They were believed extinct until one was netted. A flower.

The modicum of arousal you were feeling vanishes as he pushes in. In spite of his care there is immense pain. *Girls and Sex* warned there might be for those who hadn't spent puberty astride ponies or inserting things they oughtn't. For the rest, you decide, there should be an anaesthetic. You grind your cheeks and heels into the cold shingle, hoping to demote the pain by creating more elsewhere. You growl and you sink your teeth into his shoulder.

Martin gasps, tenses, slumps. It appears to be over. The hurt has vanished and all you are left with is a nagging discomfort independent of your pulse. A cloud shaped like a different sort of flower speeds past. You fix your eyes on it and follow it.

After a pause, he whispers into your ear: 'You could've bloomin' warned me.'

'I didn't think it would've made much difference.'

'Understatement of the year. Yes, well, next time won't hurt.'
He raises himself up, draws around your mouth with a finger that
has your biscuity smell on it. 'Next time'll be nicer for you. For
one thing, it won't hurt. It sounded as though it hurt.'

You hadn't planned for such a thing as a next time, but
curiosity demands a next time. As many next times as it takes
until your curiosity is satisfied.

'Did you... enjoy it?' you inquire, relieved that he is
disengaging.

'I'll enjoy it more next time,' he says.

'So you hated it.'

'I didn't say that.' He kisses your button nipples.

'What was wrong? Did I do something really wrong?'

'It was your first time,' he says, brushing the tip of his tongue
over your navel knot. 'I had to go easy.'

'Easy?'

He mimes a thrusting motion. 'Usually there's a lot more of
that.' You detect disappointment in his voice.

'I wasn't sure what to do. Sorry.'

He retreats to past your ankles in order to attend to the sheath.
'You were fine. You'll soon pick it up. Maybe you could get in
some practise with my brother.'

'Hardly. We're just mates.' You resent this mention of me,
here, after what you've been doing.

'I always thought you two – you know – while you were
babysitting for us.'

'Well now you know we weren't. We were simply watching
the telly and getting a bit pissed. Show me. I want to see.'

'What?'

'What came out.'

Martin dangles the candy-striped sac of captured fluid.
'Millions and millions of baby me's,' he says, before casually
tossing it into some vegetation.

'That's disgusting.'

'It'll degrade.'

'No, I mean that stuff. It's like snot.'

'Most girls don't have a problem with it. You'll get used to it.' Martin sniggers. 'Lizzie was exactly the same as you when we first started going out. You'll soon pick it up.'

'I do not want to hear her name,' you tell him as you hunker to pee. 'Hey. Don't watch.'

'But you've got a lovely looking –' He hesitates, unsure which noun you'd prefer him to use. He laughs. 'Say: Mike Hunt.'

You do and scrunch your nose. 'She's not a bloke. She's *Meg* Hunt.'

Martin leans to observe more closely. 'Lizzie –'

'I told you to shut up about her, you pervert.' You rotate crab-awkward to hide yourself. When you look back, you see Martin is hosing the shingle. 'Yuck!'

'Only natural.'

'Like some old dog.' When you mop yourself with your hanky, you discover the pee is streaked pink and red. 'Oh fuck.' You look to Martin who merely shrugs. 'I'm still bleeding!'

'Only natural,' he replies, adding with undisguised sarcasm: 'I thought Alison Dury was supposed to know everything there was to know about everything.'

When you are back at the car he attempts to feel your leg. You swat his hand away. 'But I love your thighs.'

'I don't want to be mauled. I hurt.'

'Ah, you'll feel better tomorrow. You'll be ready for action.'

'Just take me home.'

'You'll get a taste for it now. You see.'

That night you consult *Sex for Girls*. There is no chapter on infidelity, and only one sentence on the pain that might be expected the first time. Surely there could have been more written about the excruciating pain you suffered. There was plenty about disease and pregnancy. Nothing on how to do sex properly, how to enjoy it; the implication being you are not supposed to. You hurl the book into the waste paper basket.

Anne is incredulous when you tell her about Martin.

'You idiot! That's so irresponsible. He's married with a kid. *And* his brother's your oldest friend. What's James going to say if he finds out?'

You blot your eyes on one of her mum's best cushions. 'He won't find out.'

'You don't know that. Like Caroline Parker never thought anyone would find out about her and that student teacher.'

'All I want you to tell me is how to come. I want to be able to get something out of bonking, otherwise – what's the point?'

'There's no magic method. It just happens. If you're really excited you won't have any trouble coming.'

'But how do you get really excited?'

'Well the important thing is not to screw your best friend's brother.'

The next time with Martin is a week later. Same itinerary. Same place. Even the weather is the same: mild, breezy, scudding clouds. This time, however, the sex is nicer. You follow the advice Anne gave you and put your imagination to work. Sex, she explained, starts up here, not down here. You imagine he is a local fisherman returning home after a day at sea and chancing upon you sunbathing. An intensely shy fisherman who has never been with a girl before.

A few days later you bump into my sister-in-law and nephew in Gorleston high street. You are emerging from the butcher's carrying a bag of assorted innards for Oliver. Lizzie is clearly preoccupied with something. There is a faraway look in her eyes. The whites are bloodshot and pinkish.

'How's things?' you inquire, pinching the tip of my nephew's nose to make him laugh.

Lizzie huffs out her cheeks. 'Oh, you know.'

You don't, and you wonder if her misery is a consequence of

her husband's joy with you. Could she have found out? The photos?

'How's Martin?'

He has told you intimate things about Lizzie. Things you wish you hadn't heard. You think of them now. Her multifarious blemishes: moles and stretch marks. Her knock knees. Her fantasies involving Warren Beatty. The grunting pig noise she makes during sex. What she likes Martin to do to her in bed. What she doesn't.

Lizzie's eyes grow big with tears. Hastily she swipes them with her sleeve before anyone notices.

'Is something wrong?'

Lizzie smiles at you for your concern. 'No, sweetie, I'm fine. I'm just... That time of the month, you know?' A lie because the box of tampons appeared in the bathroom just over two weeks ago.

'Chop, chop, chop,' the Boy suddenly yells out with relish. He has been observing the butchery through the window. 'Look Mummy, look Aunt Ally.'

Lizzie is not interested but you look, in time to see the ginger-haired assistant satisfyingly cleave a section of carcass on the chopping block.

'Chop, chop, chop.'

At Benacre Ness, as Martin gropes and burrows and possesses with even greater relish and satisfaction than before, thoughts of the virgin fisherman dissolve and you find yourself remembering Lizzie's grey despair. You imagine her standing over you, watching, her face a complex of condemnation and heartfelt regret. This is the moment you decide not to see him again. As soon as he has loudly and vigorously come, you push him off, even though the sneeze you have learnt to achieve with your fingers had been about to happen with his penis. You have to stop all this. For Lizzie's sake. Besides, he is getting too familiar with you. He assumes you are on his side now, and criticises his wife's dullness, his brother's arrogance. ('I know he's your mate, and all that, but you have to agree he's so full of himself, isn't he.') He wants you to have sex with him more often. ('We don't have to come all this way. I'll send her out to her sister's and we can play in a proper bed.') He wants you to do more than just lie beneath him. ('I'm going to dress you up in stockings and a nurse's uniform and you can do a strip tease for me.') More alarmingly, he wants you to go on the pill. ('I hate wearing these flaming things.')

It is definitely time to call it a day.

You don't tell him until he has driven you back to Gorleston, just in case he becomes cross and leaves you stranded in the wilds of Suffolk. You get out of the car and address him through the passenger window.

'You what?' His expression hovers between laughter and irritation.

'That was the last time.'

'You're joking. Why?'

'It's wrong, Martin. You're treating your wife like shit.'

He is genuinely surprised. 'What do you mean?'

'When you go indoors, take a good long look at her.'

'No ta!'

'Martin!' Your finest scolding voice shocks the smile from his face. 'She's really unhappy.'

'Whose fault is that?'

'Just yours.'

'Takes two to tango, Ally.'

'We're finished, okay? Not that we were ever an item.'

His eyes narrow. 'Have you told anyone about us? Does Jim know?'

'There was never an us. It was just – sex. And I didn't enjoy it.'

This is interpreted as a slur upon his virility, his ability to satisfy. 'You spiteful little slag. I hope you're not going to try and blackmail me, because if you do, it's not just me who's going to suffer. There's her, and the Boy.' He waves his arm in the direction of the house, which is nearby. 'Anyway, if you say anything, I'll just tell everyone how crap you are.'

'Crap?'

'The pits. You're eye candy; nothing else. Just eye candy. Lizzie says all you are is a tart with a posh voice.' He makes the car growl before accelerating off.

You stay away from my brother's house. I have to baby-sit on my own. I know something is wrong, but figure you'll tell me when you are ready, which you never are.

Eventually, half way through October, you are returning with Oliver from a brisk walk to the beach when Martin's car draws up alongside. You could ignore him but decide it is more of a *coup* if you behave in a suitably grown-up manner.

He hastily winds down the passenger window. 'Hello.'

'Hello.'

'I'm sorry.' He looks pallid and shabby. 'Please come round again. We all miss you. The Boy always asks where you are.'

You allow Oliver to pee against one of the tyres. 'We should never have – done what we did.'

'Let's forget it happened. Mates again?' He raises his hand tentatively towards the window.

Were you ever mates? 'Those things you said.'

'I was angry. I was being dumped.'

'It had to end.'

'I know, I know.' He waggles the hand and you shake it, warning: 'You are never ever to try and make a pass at me.'

'I swear, I swear.'

'Or take any more stupid photos.'

'I promise I won't.'

'Or allude to what happened between us.' Seeing his blank look, you elucidate: 'Drop hints. Make remarks.'

'Gotcha. Won't happen, Ally. I promise.'

TWELVE

He kept his word. It wasn't long before you were babysitting with me again, while Martin and Lizzie went to *The Links*, or further afield to a night club in Yarmouth. It was just like old times, except I carried around the memory of those photographs. I chaperoned you obsessively those first few visits.

'Meanwhile I was still reeling from Martin's comment. That I'd been crap at sex. No one wants to hear that. Even though he'd recanted, I knew he'd meant it.'

What did you do about it?

'Practised.'

What, sex?

'Self love.'

Ah.

'Don't sneer. It's perfectly normal for girls to do that. It even warrants a mention in *Girls and Sex,* although there's no advice on improving your technique.'

Mm.

'You're embarrassed.'

No.

'It's perfectly natural. You did it. You did it all the time. I expect you still do. Do you?'

Hm.

'Of course you do. And I suspect you think about me every time. What do you have me do in your fantasies? Do you dress me up, or put me in diamond-pattern stockings?'

I don't.

'What do you think of when you're ravishing a girl a quarter of a century younger than yourself?'

Southwold.

'You think of Southwold.'

Our so-called pleasant mistake.

'A few days before Christmas 1980.'

THIRTEEN

'I've not bought you anything yet,' I confess.

'Ditto.'

Christmas Day is four days away, on Wednesday. We are sitting on a bench in a shelter on the upper esplanade. Oliver is pacing restlessly at the end of his leash. It is a bright cold day. A thin crust of snow has fallen. School finished the day before.

'"To begin at the beginning..."' I say for the hundredth time that morning. I am still buzzing from success of the school play. Yesterday's *Mercury* had remarked that my performance was near-perfection.

You say: '"It is spring..."' Also for the hundredth time. Our in-joke. The repetition is what we find funny. No one else would be amused by this apart from us. You pinch the collars of your expensive bronze coat to keep the heat in. I study you. Your face is framed by bronze and dark brown, so that the paleness of it becomes ghostly-beautiful. Even the grey of your eyes is ash pale, while the sunlight has shrunk your pupils to pin-pricks. I feel close to you. And I really am close to you. These are the halcyon days, and I have not given much thought to my brother's crush on you for many months. Maybe there was no crush. Maybe I'd been suffering from paranoia. Paranoid delusions, yes, brought on by jealousy and hormones. I'd read in the problem pages about the effects hormones can have on the sanest of minds during the teen years. Some kids even saw things, heard things that weren't there.

I stare out to sea. '"To begin..."' I change to a camp voice this time. '"Ooh I say, ducky, at the beginning."'

And you preacher-boom in caricature Welsh: '"It is sper-rrring..."' rolling the r's with relish.

'Sper-rrring,' I mimic. 'Hey, that's what a Welsh telephone sounds like: Rrring... Rrring!'

Tiring of this game suddenly, we admit we are bored shitless.

'Why don't we go shopping in Norwich?' I suggest.

'We went there last week.'

'But we still don't have pressies for one another. How about Yarmouth?'

'We won't find anything in Yarmouth if we had no luck in Norwich,' you say.

Oliver starts to pee against the end bricks. A pale cloud of steam rises from the barley twist and the dark pool it makes.

'You boys are so-o-o disgusting,' you say. 'Girls pee so much more politely. We hunker.'

I've never seen a girl pee, so I can't compare and comment. Instead, using my *Narrator One* voice, I intone solemnly: 'Idle Rudd and his Norfolk broad, Nogood Dury, abandoned their wall-wetting pooch and journeyed sunward, along the switch-backing, sea-swerving lanes to Lowestoft.' We're able to see the hazy promontory of Lowestoft, the most easterly point in Britain, from where we're sitting.

As soon as you've translated what I've said, you poshly declare it a most splendid proposal. Springing up suddenly, you reach onto the shelter roof and bring down an avalanche of snow onto me. I throw my arms around you and lift you high up, locking my hands under your bum.

'Leggo or I'll fart.'

Undeterred I squeeze you more tightly and spin you. Oliver circles us, yapping, desperate not to be excluded from the game.

'I'll piss myself.'

'Go on, then.'

'I will. In your face. *Pssss*.'

'Fart and piss all you like,' I tell you. Turning you so that you're facing the sea, I totter backwards towards the edge. One false step and we'll be tumbling uncontrollably down and down the slope and possibly leaving no bone unbroken by the time we reached the tarmac at the bottom. You scream and swear at me, frightened but exhilarated too.

'What did you just call me?' I say.

'Nothing.'

I teeter and totter some more. 'Tell me,' I demand.

'James, no!' You scream shrilly. '*Okay, okay*.' People are staring at us. 'I said – I called you a Clucking Hunt. Sort of.'

'Where'd you learn disgusting language like that?' The game's over, I've decided. I plonk you down and stare disappointedly at the horizon.

'Are you really upset? James, look at me. Look at me. Please.'

When I can bear to, I discover how genuinely horrified you are that you've hurt me.

'I swear I'll never say Clucking Hunt, or anything remotely like it, ever again. Cross my heart. Hope to die. Hug?'

I make a performance out of forgiving you, and enjoy the drawn out hug that follows. As we're pulling apart, you kiss me on the cheek. 'What was that for?'

'It was a thankyou. For being my best friend. You are, aren't you?'

'Daft question. We're Jim'n'Ally, aren't we? Friends for life. No matter what.'

Satisfied, you walk away from the shelter. I hurry in your footsteps to catch up with you.

*

We have the upstairs of the red Eastern Counties double-decker to ourselves. There's no heating. The floor is a palimpsest of soles. We sit at the very front, and wipe holes in the condensation in order to see out. We light cigarettes, trusting that no one who knows us or our families will get on and catch us. I recommend we look for Scott's top secret listening station; the top secret listening station every *Links* regular has heard about.

'We could bribe him,' I suggest. 'Free drinks for ever, otherwise we pass its map coordinates to the Kremlin.'

'Scott doesn't seem the bribable type. He'd more likely assassinate us if we posed a threat to national security.'

I like this idea. 'One dark night,' I whisper, 'we'll hear footsteps behind us, then – *fttt...ffft*.'

More puzzled than troubled: 'He's going to kill us using toxic farts?'

I lean close. 'It's the sound of our throats being slit. Insanely sharp butcher's knife.'

You push me away. 'Charming.'

A trio of unruly lads is waiting for the bus at Corton. Archetypically unsupervised hoi polloi, they are incapable of being in a place without having a detrimental affect on it. They use a passing cat for target practise. When our bus approaches they throw snowballs at this instead. Before I can lean back they see me at the window and excitedly point and gesture. Predictably, the first thing they do on entering the bus is to clump-clump upstairs and sit immediately behind us and across the aisle. The icy hand of fear grips my stomach.

'Where you going then, eh?'

They are wildly dissimilar in appearance, but wear the same basic uniform of denim jacket and jeans. The lapels of their jackets are decorated with metal badges of their convictions: an intriguing combination of a vees-up , the anarchists' capital A, a Union Jack and a Nazi Swastika. The oldest is our age and heavily encrusted with acne; while the youngest, with a fluorescent worm of snot observing us from the entrance of its burrow, is no more than thirteen. The third is possibly fifteen although, as much of his face is concealed by an extravagant peroxided quiff, he could be any age. On their own, they would have ignored us, but as a multi-organism they have the combined strike power to tackle anyone.

'Giss a fag,' demands Spotty.

'Wass yer name, love?' says Snotty. (This to you, relatively politely.)

'Wattya doing wiv him, eh?' Quiff chimes in.

Spotty leans his face too close. 'Giss a fag.'

To retort would be a mistake. To retort using RP would be a bigger mistake. 'Haven't got any left,' I mumble, yokel-local.

'Where you from, love?' (Snotty. Again, this to you.)

'Gorleston,' you announce, jolly-hockey-sticks bold. 'Where are you guys from? Round here?'

It's patently obvious they live in a midden, bath in cow slurry, probably dine on cow slurry and are mentally impaired from centuries of intermarriage, but your interest in them (they are too pig-ignorant to know you are faking it) throws them temporarily. 'Corton,' the oldest meekly responds, before launching a fresh verbal assault on me: 'Do you give her one? Can you manage to keep it up?'

You notice me shifting uncomfortably. 'He gives me one all right,' you tell them. 'He's a magnificent lover. Hung like Harry the Horse.'

They cackle. They like that. They like you. You're different. You're not afraid of them. They hate me.

'Oo d'you support?' Snotty asks.

'The same team as you,' I say quickly.

'Come on. 'Oo d'you support?' Snotty says, more insistently this time, while Spotty is prodding me on the shoulder.

'I – don't follow football.'

They cannot comprehend a person who does not align himself with a team of ball-kicking males.

'Are you a poof, or what?' asks Quiff.

'I enjoy a spot of Wimbledon.'

"''Kin poofter.'

(I wonder if ten years later he will open his tabloid (assuming he can read) and see the campaign to out me, and recognise me as the possible homosexual he once took pleasure in persecuting. 'You could tell ee was a poof even then. He didn't like football.')

I want to crawl under the seat and curl up. My entire body is chilled with the anticipation of violence. Getting my head stoved in four days before Christmas. If I survive the attack, will I be allowed home from hospital to unwrap my presents?

You round on them, genuinely annoyed. 'Just what do you think you're trying to achieve?'

The question is too complicated for them to understand. And you deliver it like a teacher. Spotty tells you to shut up. We are now disliked equally. We will be spending Christmas in hospital together.

Snotty thinks it's amusing to tweak your hair, while Quiff rams the hood of my coat over my head. Spotty produces a disposable lighter and waves it in front of our faces. The other two find our panic utterly hilarious and so the lighter-threat is repeated, only this time the flame is close enough to singe my fringe.

You seize Spotty's wrist and shake it and shake it, digging your nails in until he drops the lighter, which deflects from your leg onto the floor, where you crush it under your heel. It is nothing short of a declaration of war. Swearing at you, Spotty grabs a handful of your hair and roughly jerks your head back. You shriek satisfyingly loudly, inspiring him to repeat the jerking three more times. As cowardly as I am, I have no choice but to intervene somehow. There is no room for diplomacy.

I have just taken hold of his hand when there is a furious cry from behind of, 'Oy, you little sods, you get off my bus now,' from the irate driver, who has abandoned the journey after watching proceedings via his periscope and fish-eye mirror, and is now bearing down on all three parts of the organism at once. He flings Quiff, who I notice has elementary breasts and is therefore a variety of girl, down the steep stairs after Snotty and is about to manhandle Spotty when the sneering yokel feebly surrenders and slinks away, threatening to search for us in Lowestoft and 'kick our 'kin heads in'. I don't doubt that he will.

'Don't pay any attention to those idiots,' the driver says, hurrying to resume his place at the wheel.

Easier said than done. We are both thoroughly shaken. As the bus pulls away, an enfilade of snowballs hit the upper stage windows and make us recoil.

'Are you all right?' I ask.

'I'm sorry.'

'What for?'

'For shooting my mouth off. They might have left us alone if I hadn't got all cocky with them. Look, I'm actually shaking.'

'They had no intention of leaving us alone,' I say. 'They were pig-ignorant yobs. No-hopers. They need flogging.'

'You sound like a newspaper reporter. *Couple in Yob Bus Siege Drama.*'

'*Busty Beauty Demands Retribution.*'

'Busty? In whose dream? And no words of four syllables, please.'

'*Leggy Lovely In Thug Horror,* then. *They Must Be Flogged.*'

'That's more like it, although I don't like the sound of all this flogging. Makes you worse than the felons, because they were opportunists. They weren't picking on us in particular. We just happened to cross their path. Tabloid-style retribution is premeditated, and far nastier. It's sound bites from the manifesto of the Knee-Jerk Party. It scares me how many millions of people are paid up members... Stop glowering at me.

End of lecture.'

'Shut up and bugger off to Oxford,' I say. Oxford is very much on my mind at the moment; you will be applying in the next few weeks. I'd prefer it if you applied to a university in London, so that we can share a flat and preserve the continuity of our shared lives. The thought of not seeing you for days, perhaps weeks, causes my chest to tighten. I suppose it is a kind of bereavement.

*

We are reluctant to leave the bus at the bus station, and are contemplating returning to Gorleston when we spot the Southwold double-decker waiting to pull out. We have a symbiotic brainwave.

'Let's go there.' You haul me towards it and buy tickets with the fiver your mother gave us for lunch. This time we take no chances and sit downstairs, surrounding ourselves with peaceable-looking middle-aged and elderly couples.

Low golden sunlight turns everything in the bus to brass as we rattle south through Kessingland. We agree not to let the encounter ruin our day out and combine like lovers, arms linked, heads resting together, to regard wintry Suffolk through the dirty glass.

You say: 'Do you remember when your parents took us on a picnic to Kessingland? Nineteen –'

'Seventy-four. You were so terrified of being bitten by an adder, you refused to leave the car and sit in the gorse with us.'

'So you stayed with me. That was sweet. You didn't even laugh at me.'

'Maybe I was scared too.'

You squeeze my gloved hand. 'I'm not looking forward to next year. There's going to be a lot of changes, aren't there. A-levels.'

'Oxford.'

'It's not far from London.'

'It's this far.' I hold my forefingers apart. 'At four inches per mile. And at one inch per mile...'

'I prefer the four-inch scale.'

'This is sixty miles per inch. We'd only be an inch apart.'

'I don't want to be any inches apart.'

We press our cheeks together. Yours feels warm, so mine must feel cool to you. Affection makes my head woozy, like the onset of drunkenness. I want to tell you something I've been wanting to tell you for a very long time.

You lean away from me, brushing your lips against my face. Deliberately. Like a kiss. We have never kissed. You are smiling, your teeth tipped with brass. Your suddenly marigold eyes read my features, as if you are memorising them. Or merely interpreting them. It is impossible to tell.

'To begin at the beginning...' I whisper.

*

The light is already starting to fail by the time we arrive at Southwold. We walk hand in hand along the main street, enjoying the windows that have become overgrown with tinsel and coloured fairy-lights, and rimed with both spray-on and genuine snow. There is an old-fashioned feel to the celebrations here. The Santa figurine in one long-established shoe-shop is definitely from a different social background to the pink-cheeked plastic incarnations you might see in Yarmouth. He is genteel-looking. He is not moulded in Hong Kong. I can easily imagine him wearing tweeds and monocle the rest of the year, and stalking Rudolph with a shotgun.

You suggest we split up to do our shopping and then meet back at the diminutive market in half an hour. Next to the town pump with its motto Defend Thy Ryghts.

It hurts to see your bronze coat disappear into the crowd. I want to follow. To keep you in my line of sight. But tailing you would not find you that elusive present. I dive into a gift shop.

Girls like smellies, but do you prefer lavender or

sandalwood? Do you have any need for lavender sachets for your drawers, or incense sticks? You've not used them up to now, so I assume you can continue without them. Besides, they are so strongly scented, you would guess what I'd bought you from several paces.

How about enabling you to play god with the elements with a model of Southwold lighthouse in a glitter-storm?

A Southwold letter opener for when we have to correspond?

Handkerchiefs embroidered with a copperplate-style A?

A mug with your name on it? I search the rack... Adele. Amanda. Anne. No you, just a space where you should be.

I am drawn to a display of stylised wooden models. Gulls. Fishing boats in three sizes. And serried next to these, brightly painted beach huts that look more like sentry boxes that have been got at by hippies. I like the beach huts. If I like them, chances are so will you. I chose a white one with a bright blue roof and door. While I'm queuing to pay I notice some posh-looking chocolate coins, eye-catchingly wrapped in gold, silver and green foil and presented in a green netting bag. You will like these as well.

I need something else, though. Something truly unusual to show I've taken the trouble to use my imagination. Spotting you heading my way along the opposite pavement, and with ten minutes to spare before we meet again, I dive into the nearest shop.

It is an antiques shop. One of those antiques shops where the stock is so plentiful it resembles a pirate's hoard, accumulated rather than arranged so that, in order to examine any single item, it will be necessary to reposition at least ten others as if battling Mr Spock at three-dimensional chess. Thus discouraged, I satisfy my curiosity with a swift glance and head for the door.

'May I help you?' A middle-aged woman with a kindly face peers at me from behind a glass case containing a variety of pocket-watches and ladies' old-looking wrist-watches.

'I was just – browsing.' My RP is not as natural as hers. Hers is the real thing.

'Christmas present?'

Perhaps she tells the future in addition to reading minds. 'That's right.'

'What kind of budget do you have?'

I glance at some of the price tags. The decimal points are in the wrong place. 'Small.'

'Try me, you might be surprised.'

I feel in my pocket. 'Three pounds.'

I expect the woman to laugh and point me to the door. Instead she directs my attention towards a tall glass cabinet illuminated from the side by a low wattage spot. Several glass shelves are arrayed with small items. Thimbles, rings, necklaces.

'Who's the present for? Your mother?'

'A friend. A girl who's a friend.'

'There are some lovely Edwardian brooches for under three pounds,' she says. 'Anyone can wear brooches. They never go out of fashion.'

I've never seen any female contemporary sporting one of these. I find it hard to imagine Quiff swapping her anarchy badge for one of these. But they are compellingly dainty and lovely, and I feel you ought to have one. Several are like small shields, constructed from metal weave-work with coloured glass embedded in the centre. Some are naturalistic flowers and fruits. I like these.

'That one. Is that old?'

'The red one?' She reaches into the display. 'It's genuine Edwardian. It's a nasturtium. That's flower code for patriotism.'

'Oh. No thanks.'

'How about this bluebell? In flower code that means constancy.' She hands it to me.

'Perfect. But there's no price.'

'It's not especially valuable. Call it a pound. Here, I'll wrap it for you, my dear. I'm sure your young lady will love it.'

My young lady is already at the market place. You have bought a bag of peanuts from the greengrocer's and are voraciously splitting the shells. 'Any success?'

'That, Madam,' I say poshly, 'would be telling. One will have to wait and see. Now, may one please request a fortifying nut or two?'

We warm ourselves with tea and a toasted bun in a small café, draping ourselves over a hot radiator, deciding what to do next. It seems too soon to be heading home. The last bus isn't for ages yet. We decide to explore the town away from the shops.

'You know, it's strange, but I haven't seen any yobs,' I say. 'No yobs, no graffiti.'

'I haven't seen anyone under twenty. Do you think kids are shipped out once they hit a certain age so as not to upset the status quo? I reckon we're the youngest people here. They'll have the police out.'

The back streets are silent. Front room lamps and fairy lights have been switched on in many houses. We observe families immobile in front of TV sport, or else silently reading, unable to see us for their own reflections. It's rather like a strange kind of zoo; Homo sapiens preserved for ever as it was at Christmas 1980. I try to imagine returning to this zoo twenty years hence, middle-aged, a survivor of World War Three and its aftermath, keen to remind myself how we used to live before rationing, identity cards and military rule.

We drift aimlessly through these wintry streets, ending up at Gun Hill, with its six cannon pointing at the leaden North Sea. Sole Bay, where, you delight in informing me, the English and Dutch battled in 1672. From here we descend to the beach.

'Decidedly crepuscular, dear chap,' you say.

'Decidedly chilly too.'

'In which case...' You wrap yourself around me. 'Better?'

'Much. Ta.'

We advance like this along the scrunching sand, slowing to the slow rhythm of the shingle-worrying sea, past serried rows of brightly painted beach huts now two shades of grey in the twilight. As far as we can tell, we are by ourselves on the beach.

I hear myself say, 'I love you,' without meaning to.

You halt, and plant yourself in front of me, your face ill-defined like an aquatint in close-up, oddly skull-like now that the eyes lack glister. 'What did you say?' Not angry, not scolding, not bemused. Then what, exactly?

'I said, I love you. I love you.'

You catch your breath. Four times the sea swipes at the beach before you respond. 'I love you too, James. I really do. With all my heart. I love you, *I love you*.'

This kiss that follows I have dreamed of for centuries, this salt-seasoned taste of you, this banquet of nimble tongue and saliva. We consume and slowly combine until there is only Jim'n'Ally then JimnAlly. All else, every person and thing that is not-us, is nugatory and ceases to exist. We are the extent of the universe, our souls a double star at the inconceivably far-off centre of it.

Love. I, you, thee, we. Your, mine, thine, our. I love you. You love me. We love we.

Gently you lean away. Not to bring this to an end but to suggest a continuation. 'Why don't we find a place in those dunes over there,' you whisper. 'For a cuddle.'

'A cuddle?'

'A lying-down cuddle.'

'Lying-down?'

'*James*, I'm not spelling it out. Do you want to? With me?'

Of course I want to. However, I point out that the weather is hardly suitable for a lying-down cuddle in the sand.

'Then maybe – maybe we should catch the bus home.'

Terrible idea. I can predict what will happen. 'By the time we've waited at the bus stop – in the freezing cold – caught the bus to Lowestoft and waited for a bus to Gorleston – in the freezing cold, and with the Midden Gang breathing down our necks – we'll have had more than enough time to talk ourselves out of doing anything.'

'Where do you suggest we go, then?'

My hand closes in my pocket around an idea. I've never been so certain about anything in my life. Dragging you after me like a pillaged maiden, I stride seven-league strides towards the line of beach huts. We shake each door in turn, hoping that one owner has neglected to padlock and before long discover a hut partially deconstructed for repairs. The door, window frame, balcony planks and balustrade have been stacked across the opening. We help one another climb over them and embrace in the pitch dark of the hut.

We agree that in order to begin the lying-down cuddle, we must first be lying down. I strike matches to explore intermittently the darkness and discover dustsheets. Two, three dustsheets, and decorator's overalls. They are not too dirty and smell pleasantly of paint and putty. After folding these to form a makeshift bed and sloughing our coats, we lie on the bed, arranging the coats on top of us.

You kiss me fancily. 'I love you, James.'

'I love you, Alison.' There must be better words. These particular ones are useless, overused and inadequate, a mere summary of the great and complex feeling I have and wish to convey. I love you, but I also love a sunny day and Shakespeare, while my dad loves his job and the RE teacher loves Jesus. There ought to be a moratorium on the word. *I love* for amatory declaration; *I like* in every other circumstance. The police could deploy snitches and hidden microphones.

'I love you, James. I love you and I need you inside me.'

I need desperately to be inside you too, but hesitate. I whisper my concern.

'My period's due in the next couple of days,' you whisper back. Is this a good thing or an impediment? You squeeze my hand assuringly and explain. 'It means don't worry. Don't worry about anything. Let's just love each other.'

I regret that I am unable to see your body. My inch by inch study of you will have to wait until next time. We help one another push our trousers and our underwear down to our ankles. Your thighs are radiator hot. Your knees, conversely – I've missed the cold kiss of your knees first thing in the morning. You move me so that I'm on top and ask if I can remember Action Man and Barbie. From dread or joy I begin to chuckle uncontrollably. You interpret this as crying and palpate my eyes and cheeks for tears. We kiss a new sort of prolonged kiss. You reach down. 'Oh, beautiful,' you tell me. 'We're going to make a perfect fit.'

'Are you really sure about this?'

'I'm going to die if we don't.' Carefully you hold me against your notch and position me to your liking.

'I'm not going to be much cop.'

'Just love me, James.' You push hard unexpectedly, determinedly. Ninety-eight point four feels hotter than I imagined. Hot enough to melt steel. Instinctively – for how else would you know how to do this; certainly not a priori from books or videotape – you start to move, each push followed by a drawing back with a wriggle thrown in now and again to break the rhythm. We've made an engine of ourselves, a soft machine that would chug more efficiently were I to match you, not just be put on my mettle. But time has run out. I moan loudly. For a brief moment I'm terrified it is my bladder that I'm emptying into you. You clutch me reassuringly. 'Oh, James, *James.*'

It is over swiftly, sweetly, every nerve from scalp to toe singing with joy.

'Did I hurt you?' I inquire.

'Don't be a berk.'

'I thought that the first time –'

'a) It didn't hurt and b) it was lovely and c) I'm not letting you out until you've come again and again, my lovely boy James.'

*

Afterwards, while we lie cocooned under our coats, you cry. With sadness? Regret? You won't tell me, but I know the sobs are welling from deep inside. I hold you tightly against me. You cry us to sleep.

*

I strike a match. It is three in the morning. The cold has penetrated us to our bones. Striking a second match, I see snow has blown through the open doorway. We make love again, hungrily, hastily, connubially, then get dressed.

'I am going to be hanged, drawn and quartered,' you say.

'Tell them it was all my fault. I don't care.' My joy was armour plating.

'I wish it worked like that,' you reply bitterly.

We hurry through the deserted and silent streets to find the nearest telephone box. You call your parents first. Having been on sentry duty by the phone for the last couple of hours, they express at full volume their relief that you are still alive. You tell them where we are and hold the phone away as your father exclaims incredulously, '*Southwold*?'

'Could you collect us?'

'*Southwold*?'

'There was this party, you see, and –'

I hear him barking directions about finding somewhere safe to wait while he drives to collect us.

While you amuse yourself drawing love hearts in the condensation I call my parents. They have been asleep in bed.

'I'll be home in about an hour,' I say, calmly. 'Found a party.' The lie is only necessary so that our stories chime.

Dad yawns. 'Okay.'

'Thought I'd better tell you.'

'Righty-ho. Are you drunk?'

'No.'

'Wacky-baccyed or otherwise?'

'No.'

'Are you in any immediate physical danger?'

'Not at present, but there is a fire-breathing Mr Dury heading this way.'

'In which case, I advise you to write a Will pronto.'

'Unfortunately, no pen or paper,' I say. 'In the event of my untimely demise, Alison is to get everything I own.'

You grab the handset. 'Everything except the underpants and the dirty mags.'

Dad is still replying when I return the phone to its cradle. 'Now he thinks I've got porn. Git.'

'Berk.'

'Hey. We're having our first domestic,' I point out.

'We'd better kiss and make up, then.' You girdle me inside my coat with your arms and offer your hot mouth.

*

Your dad's anger has had a chance to abate during his twenty-minute drive. I notice he is still wearing his pyjama top under his coat. 'You had us so worried. You should've have phoned earlier. I'm very surprised at you, James.'

Can he tell we have been making love? I feel he can. He can probably smell the smell of you on my hands, a rich, biscuity odour I have no intention of ever washing off. I sit on my own in the back, my hands gloved. I am afraid of speaking in case I let slip something incriminating. You describe the mythical party we have attended. I am impressed by your improvisatory prowess. Poised on the edge of sleep, I begin to doubt we were ever in that beach hut at all.

I have to remove my glove to remind myself that we were.

*

When I call on you in the afternoon, I find you reading beside the log fire. Your eyes are bleary through lack of sleep, and your right cheek is red from the flames. The left one colours as you stand and move around me.

I wait for you to hug me so that I can hug you powerfully back, but you make it clear there is to be no hugging, no physical intimacy at all. You put on your coat. Flakes of dried paint have adhered to it from the dustsheets. We leash a jubilant Oliver and head for the seafront. Usual route.

'About last night...' you begin, briskly brusque, as though you want to get this out of the way with the minimum of fuss.

About last night, dot dot dot. Like three bullets fired straight into the heart.

You won't even take my hand. 'You're okay? You're not –?'

'Pregnant? Oh James, I wouldn't be able to tell this quickly. The thing is, I do love you, and I intend to always love you, which is why I think it's for the best if we nip it in the bud now, before we get too involved.'

'I don't understand.'

'You love me, don't you? Well, say in a month, or two months, or six months' time we're thoroughly fed up with each other? It might happen. We might end up tearing each other's hair out.'

'Hardly!'

'As friends we're great friends, but we may not be so compatible as lovers. In nine months, if all goes according to plan, we'll be living apart for the first time since we've known one another. That's going to hurt enough as it is. Being lovers would make it hurt ten times more.'

I cannot see where I am walking. I bury my face in a handkerchief.

'Oh, James. Don't do this to me.'

You allow me to cry into your neck, where it is warm and

soap-fragrant. Your hair smells of wood smoke. Roused, I try to kiss you. You turn away, but place a compromise kiss on my cheek as soon as I pull back. 'We never should have gone that far.'

For a moment I think she's referring to the journey, not the joining. 'If you say so.'

'It was a mistake. A very pleasant one. A lovely one. But a mistake all the same.'

'A mistake,' I echo bitterly. Not for one second do I think of what we did as a mistake. I put my hand to my nose and remember.

*

Christmas Eve, as I assemble my presents together and settle down to wrap them, I discover with horror that some of the chocolate coins have been crushed during our lovemaking; but worse, far worse, the brooch is missing. It is not in my pocket, nor has it found its way into the lining. It could be anywhere. The likeliest place for it to be now is the floor of the beach hut, probably concealed under a layer of blown snow, but it is too late to go back there. You will have to do without.

In fact, it turns out Mum has a suitable replacement in her sewing box. It was her mother's, and is a meticulously observed recreation of a pansy flower. 'Pansies for thoughts,' she tells me, quoting the Bard. She has no compunction that the brooch is to be yours: as far as she's concerned, you're part of the family, as much her daughter-in-law as Lizzie.

I'm not sure what you are.

FOURTEEN

'I loved the brooch. I would have loved the other one, too.'

This is one of my favourite memories of us. We ate the coins in the beach shelter. They cheered us up.

'Can you remember the presents I gave you?'

A giant Toblerone. A pair of socks. And that diary for the year 1981.

'And did you use it? No.'

I was hardly in the mood for filling in diaries. But I still have it. I have it in a box of Alison-related memorabilia. 'For my dearest friend James, with much, much love XXX'. Breaks my heart every time I read it.

'What else do you have in this Museum of Me?'

One hair band. One pair of navy blue nuclear-blast-proof tights still in the packet. Your sixth-form coursework, your cramming notes. Your purse containing forty-seven pence (almost the price of a pint of bitter) and a lucky half pence, four first class stamps, a strip of passport photos of you and Anne, you and me, you Anne and me, and me and Anne (she's prettier than I thought at the time, though not as attractive as you) and a tiny snap of Oliver scissored from a larger photo in order to fit the back compartment. Assorted pencils and Biros, some with chew marks. Several compilation C60s with your favourite pop now irretrievable (I tried to play one once; heard a wildly distorted fragment of *Japan* from paranormal afar before the oxidised recording permanently mushed my player).

Paperbacks you annotated. A pebble you chose from a billion billion beach pebbles because it was 'special'. Wimbledon treasures. A CND badge. Beer mats filched from *The Links* over a long period. A photo from *Look In* magazine of an actor you had a serious crush on, Oliver Tobias, dressed to play *Arthur, King of the Britons*. A Rubik Cube one-sixth solved (the red face only). A self-portrait from school, intaglio in kitchen foil. Ten sets of birthday cards. Your homemade birthday and Christmas cards to me. Postcards from Dorset. A tampon.

'Please specify unused.'

Of course unused. Also in the Museum of You are the letters you sent me. We started corresponding after leaving Gorleston. In spite of the way things had turned out that last summer, I was determined to hold on to you.

FIFTEEN

I've kept the letters in an A4 padded envelope. While the photo of us in my brother's garden went walkabout for umpteen years, I've always known exactly where the letters have been: for much of the eighties in my parent's loft until they moved into a smaller house and rationalised their possessions. When they did, I reclaimed four sizeable cardboard boxes of memorabilia: my books, my schoolbooks and toys, and the collected juvenilia. I discovered the letters buried deep inside one of the boxes, although I couldn't remember putting them there. I have kept them here in the Museum, and the Museum in my study, ever since.

It surprises a lot of people that an actor has a study, as if he has nothing to study. I shelve my scripts here, and plays, and various books. There is no view from the window, which suits me fine. The side wall of the neighbour's garage doesn't distract when I'm learning lines.

I never married. I have no interest in sharing my private life with anyone. Some people are irritated by this: my parents, who would like grandchildren; Poole's spinster fans, who presume I'm the perfect mate; and the tabloids, of course. Several years ago the red tops decided I was interchangeable with my debonair and womanising screen character. One of the 'Ten Things You Didn't Know About James Rudd' was that I had five girlfriends dotted around the country and frequented orgies. The stories eventually ran low on oxygen and burned themselves out. They were rekindled a couple of years later, but this time I was gay. In their effort to out me, the papers fabricated revelations. I attended the *de rigueur* orgies – gay, of course – and cruised the dunes near Bournemouth (their photographic so-called proof was in fact a production still). As for boyfriends, disappointingly, they merely gave me three. The only crumb of near-truth in all those stories was that I collected erotic paintings. Obviously someone had been aiming the crosshairs of a telephoto at my windows and misinterpreting what they could see.

I never married because I am too selfish. I like what spare time I have to be mine. I go on holiday by myself, once a year, always to the same place. (At the height of the campaign to out me, the telephoto lenses came too. From a distance the paparazzi resembled a raggle-taggle band of mercenaries. But I was so boring they lost interest and dubbed me Inspector Yawn.) As I am still in touch with many of my old friends from *The Links* days, when my filming schedule allows me to, I meet up with them for a pint in their particular necks of the wood. (Which is perhaps how the rumours of my multiple lovers began.) They assure me I have not been changed by my success as an *ack*-tor. They are right. Acting is a job I do because I enjoy it. I enjoy the wage. I enjoy the company of my fellow actors. What I take no pleasure in is the fame. Feigning indifference to fame can get tiring.

I never married because I have never met the right woman. The right woman would have had to have been indistinguishable from you. Who knows. Perhaps you have a doppelganger and our paths have yet to cross.

There is a faint mustiness inside the envelope, which is a surprise. Perhaps I have been expecting the air inside to be the same air from my parent's house when I sealed your letters in. I tip the contents onto the desk. There is a baker's dozen of them, each one still in its envelope. I fan them like a card sharp's losing hand.

By September 1981 I could no longer be counted as your closest friend. That was Wilson's privilege. Our cursory farewell at that party masked my real feelings for you. I was an expert at feigning indifference even then.

It was my indifference, strangely enough, that spurred you to write to me. You began the letter on the coach, even before you arrived at Oxford. Giant looping letters that filled a side of A4 independent of the ruled lines.

"I left that stupid party not long after you when Wilson started molesting Julie, who let him. People thought I was crying because of them. I wasn't. I was crying because of you. Us."

Good. Glad to know I wasn't the only one driven to tears.

"What we'd had and lost."

Correction: thrown away.

I confess that when I originally read of your misery, it was with considerable glee. Had you not ended with "I wish I could go back in time – don't you? – and see what might have happened had we stayed lovers", I would have thrown the page into the bin and not been moved to write back. In spite of everything, we were friends, with a history. Hence my replying so promptly.

I forget what I said. I recall it was brief, business, lacking the warmth of the letters that followed.

"We've never needed to write to one another before," you pointed out in your reply. Clearly now we did, because this letter runs to four pages of condensed handwriting. Two decades on I'm impressed by the neatness, the straightness of it, the absence of any crossings-out. I wonder now if it is a second draft. "Do you miss me as much as I miss you?" Yes. Yes. I do, yes. "Tell me that you do. I feel so alone here."

You were not alone for long. You quickly made friends. Same as I did. Yours were called Miranda and Crispin and had double-barrelled surnames, while my most immediate friends were my flatmates, the angry Scotsman (who was opinionated and addicted to imitating pistol shots with his finger joints, but who was ultimately generous with his comestibles) and the two young women (jealous and emotional when together, but hilariously funny apart). When I wrote to you I described my life outside of drama school as a social whirl. Really it was just Maxwell, Bella and Julie, and me, sitting in a run-down pub night after night. We were a behavioural psychologist's experiment. We were a comedian's opening line: 'There was an Englishman, a Scotsman and two lesbians...' We never vacuumed or dusted, we washed-up once a week, we allowed food to moulder in the fridge. While we never cleaned the bath or the bathroom sink, we did spruce up the toilet bowl from time to time by pouring bleach into it. We never thought to clean the windows, which were so grimy you had to open them to see what the weather was like. The only oases of hygiene were our beds, the sheets of which we laundered once a fortnight. I sprinkled talcum powder on them as if it was magical cleansing dust. It was, too.

You didn't fare at Oxford as well as your teachers and family had hoped. You found the work-load burdensome and the town-and-gown snobberies of some of the staff and fellow students intolerable. You had a run-in with your tutor over his dismissive remarks about peace protesters. You marched with a banner on an anti-Thatcher demonstration and were reprimanded for doing so by your college authorities. Miranda's parents blamed you for their daughter's descent into the madness that was CND membership. You announced that you had cropped your hair, and some time before Christmas you put your legs into retirement. Henceforth it was to be trousers only. No skirts or dresses, and no tights.

The letters from late November and December are full of polemic. I couldn't understand a word of it. What was so wrong with these dead white males on your syllabus? Was there a league table of who was or wasn't acceptable, with the dead white male at the very bottom and facing relegation? What did 'hegemony' and 'hegemonic' mean? (I was, and still am, too lazy to consult a dictionary, though I doubt if I'd be any the wiser even armed with the definition and correct pronunciation. Inspector Poole is frequently called upon to use polysyllables I never look up.) Your chief enemies were Mrs Thatcher and the American government. You mocked the Protect and Survive campaign. You wrote bitterly of the evil of privatisation. Even pop culture didn't escape your attention: neo-romantics were pilloried as lackeys of capitalism. And *Under Milk Wood*, our beloved *Under Milk Wood*, was no more than a textbook example of dead white male-ism.

In short, you'd become someone else.

SIXTEEN

I am dreading meeting the new you. I am afraid that you'll direct your ire at me. However, when I see you in *The Links*, chummy with your ex, clearly enjoying his company, my dread turns to anger. He is a white male (though not yet dead, a suitably cadaverous specimen). It is a mystery why you are giving him the time of day.

You do not see me enter. I hide in the crush at the bar, delaying my order so that I can watch you. Your hair is bobbed, not as cropped as you've led me to believe, and it very much suits you. Ironically, the jeans you wear to conceal your legs simply emphasise the length and shapeliness of them. They make your bottom delectable.

'Ah, the traveller returns.' Scott works his way along the bar. He is wearing his TA camouflage. 'Off on a night manoeuvre.' He glances at his special watch. 'In the woods at Lound Waterworks,' he adds, not remotely interested in what I've been up to these past thirteen weeks. He glances towards you. 'Said hello yet?'

'Not yet.'

'You've not seen her since September?' He whistles in disbelief. 'We caught up the other night.'

Since when did this army of one need to catch up with you?

You glance across to see me looking and beckon enthusiastically. I am glad of the excuse to get away from Scott.

'One may kiss one's hand,' you say, mock-queenly. Your

manner is noticeably more confident. I kiss your hand like a gentlemen, but draw the line at hugging you.

'To be or not to be, that is the question,' Wilson says. 'Hi.' He is drunk. 'Done any Pinter yet? *The Caretaker*, that's a post-war masterpiece.'

To satisfy his need to be taken for an intellectual, I tell him I've acted a scene from *The Birthday Party*. He nods, saying nothing. He is clearly not familiar with this play, though by tomorrow he will doubtless be an expert on it.

'So how's life treating you?' you say. Before I can think of a reply, you turn to Wilson and say, 'Show James your photos.'

'"They do not move."' Wilson freezes. A password is required. I indulge him and say it – Godot – and he is free to reach into his charity-shop tweed jacket. 'My latest work.'

I'm not sure what I'm looking at, or indeed if they are the right way up. They are half-painting, half-sculpture. ('Assemblages,' he explains. 'That one's about twelve feet high. I like working big.') He has eschewed realism in the pursuit of Art, with a capital F, and the results are correspondingly art-school gimmicky, anonymously bland. Pretentious. ('They're based on Schlop – er – Schop, Schopenhauer.') Good for getting through tutorials and earning degrees, and for impressing Civvy Street, yet ultimately hollow and useless. Interestingly, nothing from this period will be included in his Reading exhibition.

Wilson goes to the bar for more beer for himself and a vodka and orange for you.

'Hello,' you say. 'Again.'

'Hello.'

You pass your eyes over my face. 'You're all stubbly.' I tell you my shaver is still packed. 'Better unpack it, then, hadn't you.' Mock haughtily. Or perhaps not. You don't sound like you anymore. You sound like the old you playing pretend.

I'm stuck for something to say. 'How're your parents?'

'Glad to have me home. Looking older.'

'Oliver?'

'He's my lovely boy. He was beside himself.' You smile at the memory of being reunited with your beloved pooch. Aren't you going to ask me about me? Clearly not: 'Gorleston's pretty much the same. So is everyone.'

Apart from you, I think. Why do you keep glancing over to the bar? Are you back with your ex? 'Who the hell is Schop – Schop-thingy?' I say.

'German philosopher.'

'Never heard of him.'

I've stumbled into a trap. 'So you're assuming Schopenhauer's a guy.' You grin, but unpleasantly, at my mistake. 'You haven't mentioned my hair.' You shake your head.

'It's very smart.'

'Smart? Is that all?' You kick my shoe.

What would you prefer me to say? Distinctive? Chic? It is these things, but it is also sexy, and for some reason my big mouth chooses to say sexy.

Bad choice.

If only real life can be edited like an episode of *Inspector Poole*, scenes re-shot as many times as you need, muffed lines re-recorded and, if necessary, re-recorded *ad infinitum* in post-production. I would definitely re-record this last reply. I would say distinctive, which is what you'd have preferred to hear. Sexy is stoking the furnace of anger you carry inside you. Sexy is body fascism. Sexy is a no-no.

That grin again. 'What's your opinion on the subject?'

'I don't have an opinion,' I mumble.

'I know,' you say. 'You go out of your way to avoid having an opinion.'

On a stage I can do confrontation till I'm blue in the face, I enjoy the dynamics of it; but in real life I shy away from it, finding it unsettling. I sip my drink.

'I mean,' you continue, 'you go into immense detail about all these parties you go to, all these wild nights down the pub... But where's the serious stuff?'

I've completely forgotten about my lies.

'I mean, what do you talk about down the pub?'

'Not a lot.'

'You must do. Everyone talks. Especially in pubs.'

I'm not enjoying this reunion. I'm glad when Wilson returns. '"My papers are in Sidcup",' he says, quoting again. '*The Birthday Party.*'

'*The Caretaker*,' you and I correct together.

'That's what I meant. *The Caretaker*.'

I hand back his photos. 'No life-painting any more?'

He glances at you momentarily. 'Nah. All that artist and model stuff is considered a bit on the old fashioned side.'

I think I understand. 'You mean, it's not Modern Art enough?'

Shaking your head, you cut in before he can respond. Words. Wordswordswords. A concatenation of polysyllables I'd need your shorter OED and a pile of textbooks to wrest meaning from. As you are well aware. Do I detect a sneer, like Wilson's supercilious sneer? Except his is self defence, to cover his inadequacies. Yours is plain aggression. Nasty.

'What the sodding hell does all that mean?' I demand. 'We're in a pub in Gorleston, not some university debating society.' I regret this. For twenty minutes you outline your political beliefs. The annoying thing is my pint runs out after ten minutes, and you leave no suitable break in your lecture in which I can visit the bar. I envy Wilson. He can get up and wander off. I hear him saying to Simon: '... having a go at Jim.' And you are having a go. You are blaming me for all the ills in the world, the injustices, the propensity of the human animal for conquest and destruction. Me. Jim. Formerly of the Jim'n'Ally partnership. Except Jim'n'Ally no longer exists, and it seems as though you're quite capable of banging on for another twenty minutes. I take the bold and uncharacteristic step of telling you to 'shut the fuck up'. It comes out louder than I'd intended, as if it had been meant for Oliver, but it's too late now.

You do shut up. Instantly. So do half the bar who've overheard. Even the jukebox and the video game shut the fuck up. It is like a scene from a Western when two gunslingers are squaring up for a duel. Wilson and the others watch, waiting to see how this is going to develop. We stare each other out. The expression you wear is a fifty-fifty mixture of hurt and horror. I stand. 'Well, seeya.' I nod at the others. '*Th-th-th* – that's all folks.' I'm good. Just one term and I've got Porky Pig to a T.

As soon as I am outside, I drop my act and run, howling, towards the sea front.

I keep away from *The Links* for the next few nights. I hermit myself in my room and read, or try to because all the while I'm waiting for your face to show at the window, disconsolate, contrite, or for the phone to hear your voice. You don't contact me. The old you would have. When I do venture back to the pub, I learn that you have gone to Lowestoft to stay with your Nan. I am never to see you again.

In spite of his know-it-all-ness, his earnestness, his self-importance, Wilson shows me great kindness. He buys me a drink, offers me a fifty per cent share in his crisps, and attempts to give me his undivided attention; although the presence of an attractive female in the form of Joanna, Julie's friend and a newcomer to *The Links*, sorely tests him. His eyes are darting from me to her as if he has a courtside seat at Wimbledon. It is his lechery that results in a momentary loss of concentration and a slip of the tongue.

'We weren't at all compatible,' he reflects. 'Not like you two were.'

'Were,' I emphasise.

'She's getting involved in things that are important to her,' he says. 'She's bound to change. Out with the old, and all that. I've changed since I went away. What I believe in, more than who I am.'

'Do you reckon you were in love with her?' I ask, my tongue lubricated by beer.

He shakes his head. 'I thought I was at the time, but... Nah. And she definitely didn't love me. She said so. Or Mart –'

He notes his slip too late. 'Martin?' My head has gone dizzy. I feel the weight of the photos in my hand.

'Shit.'

'What's Martin got to do with this?'

'Sorry.'

'Did she have a crush on him?'

'It was nothing serious. They didn't... It didn't last long.'

'*Did* they have a fling?'

'Mm, well.'

'For god's sake, did they?'

'Please don't say I let it out.'

'Did they?'

'Sorry.' He tells me what he knows, which is the bare bones of the plot.

'Alison was actually fucking my brother? Who else knows?'

Wilson is looking over my shoulder. I turn to see everyone, including Simon, Julie, and Nuclear Scott, everyone, staring back at me, dumbstruck by what my big mouth has just broadcast. If they hadn't known before, they certainly know now.

'Oops,' says Julie.

'I had the feeling –' I can hardly speak. ' – in Southwold – she wasn't – I wasn't –'

'Pipped at the post, mate,' says Wilson. 'She could hardly have told you, could she.'

I shake my head. 'I'm never getting involved with any woman ever again.'

'Flagon of medicinal bitter for the gentleman,' says Scott.

*

A letter, the baker's dozenth, arrives at my parents' the following day. A Lowestoft postmark.

Dear James, I was very sorry we parted on such bad terms. You may not believe this, but I walked up to your house a thousand times (well, twice) to apologise for going on at you. I was totally out of order. I'm sorry. I bottled out of telling you to your face. I've even run away, as you may have discovered.

I knew our worlds would drift apart when we left Gorleston. It was inevitable. I suppose if we're honest we'd admit they'd already started drifting a long time ago. I had hoped we could remain good friends. Maybe we still can. You might think I want you to change. I don't. I love you exactly the way you are. My priorities have changed, but that doesn't mean I should dump my bestest friends just because their priorities are different.

I'm sorry, James, for snapping at you. If you'd like to talk to me, please phone me. I'll be here for another few days.

With all my love,

Alison xx

Love? Love me exactly the way I am? All your love? What species of love? Friends' love, or the lovers' love we confessed to in Southwold?

I phone your Nan's number. She answers and goes to fetch you. I hear you approaching along the echoing hallway we have walked along together.

'Hello, James?' You are out of breath.

I swallow. 'I found out about you and Martin,' I say quickly, and put the receiver down.

You phone back immediately. 'James, that was ages ago. And I'm not proud of –'

'Go fuck yourself.'

This time I unplug the phone. My knuckles look as if I'm on a funfair ride.

'Popping out, Jim?' my mother inquires.

'Going to see Martin,' I say, between clenched teeth.

I'm not sure what I intend to do when I see him. Hit the bastard? Swap anecdotes? All I know is, I have to see him.

He is crawling around on his living room carpet supervising the Boy, who is laying out a railway track in the shape of an infinity sign. 'Help yourself to a can.' He nods towards the tower of seasonal booze next to the tree.

'I can't stay long,' I say. My voice comes out all thin and tuneless. I find I am imagining him with you. On you and in you. Here, right here on the floor. Like the moustachioed actor and the leg-warmers girl while a camera roamed for the clearest view.

He looks disappointed. I reconsider.

'Okay, then. I'll have a Guinness.' I perch on the edge of the sofa.

'I've not really had a chance to talk to you since you got back,' Martin says, satisfyingly snapping two sections of track together. 'How's the acting? Like it?'

'Love it,' I say. 'Can't imagine doing anything else.'

'Remind me to get your autograph before you're too famous for Gorleston. I'll get you to sign all your photos. I can flog them and pay off the mortgage when you're in Hollywood. I'll sell my story to the papers.'

(And so he does, a decade later, in the article *My Brother is not Gay*.)

'Alison was in *The Links* the other night.' I say, emphasising your name to catch his attention. I'm treating this as if it is an improvisation exercise: two brothers, one has been sleeping with the other's friend.

He barely looks up. 'That must've been nice for you.'

'It was. I've really missed her.'

'Nice girl.'

'You used to see a lot of her at one time,' I say.

'Mm?'

This is like fishing without bait or hook. 'Didn't you... She once said something about...' I check to see if my sister-in-law is out of range. 'Alison said something about...' Martin looks up, suspicions aroused. 'Sh-she mentioned,' I stammer, thinking how this would be a piece of cake if I was armed with a script.

'Daddy, you're not helping,' my nephew scolds. 'Uncle Jim, *you're* not helping.'

While Martin fiddles about, getting the battery-operated train to work, I begin to wonder if dragging up events from one-and-a-half years before is such a good idea after all. He and Lizzie appear to be going through one of their fragile happy periods. They've had a good run-up to Christmas. I have no right to jeopardise their happiness and the stability of my nephew's life.

'What were you going to say about Alison?' He glances at the clock.

It's no good. I can't go through with it. 'Oh, only that she used to enjoy coming round here babysitting.'

Martin nods slowly, and for a brief moment contemplation passes across his face like a scudding cloud. He looks up. 'Shouldn't think we'll be seeing her round here again.'

'Why not?'

'She's in a different world now, isn't she.' He stands up. 'I don't mean to be rude, but I've got to nip out for a while,' he says. 'I won't be above an hour. Help yourself to beer. It's there to be drunk.'

*

I don't stay after he drives off. Lizzie is keen to clean the house and I'm in the way. I don't go home in case the phone has been plugged back in and you've left me a message. I take myself off to our shelter on the upper esplanade. Chain-smoking my way through half a packet of hand-rolling tobacco, I write you a letter. What was meant to be an angry note swiftly grows and grows like a disease and eventually contaminates an entire exercise book. You know much of it already, or will be able to guess it. It is the History of Us. Putting it into words, assembling my feelings towards you on the page, gives me an opportunity to deconstruct our relationship for the first time. I realise I have been like the faithful hound, accepting your mastery (mistressy) without question. Southwold had not been a very pleasant mistake, it had been an intensely beautiful experience, and we might have had many other beautiful experiences had you not been so cautious. Conversely, letting my brother lie between your legs had been a genuine mistake.

My motive for writing the History of Us is revenge. I even admit this on page one. I want to hurt you as you have hurt me.

You will never get to read it.

SEVENTEEN

After seeing Wilson's exhibition in Reading a decade later, I track down the artist and arrange to visit him one morning. He is living in a rented cottage near Winchester. He is teaching painting in the art college. He is still weasel-like, emphasised by an artist's goatee. The congenital smirk has left a permanent crease, enabling him to wear the expression permanently and without effort. The fringe has been pruned, and he wears spectacles with trendy frames (for reading). The fingers I clasp and shake are no longer ochre-stained.

When I follow him into the gloomy, low-ceilinged cottage, I discover he is not alone. There is a lanky, flaxen-haired female sitting at his kitchen table. Her age I guess at around twenty. She is wearing black-and-pink stripy ankle socks and a long t-shirt, and judging from the state of her hair she is not long out of the shower. She is munching toast and half-heartedly pointing a camera towards the countryside through the window.

'Louise,' she says, beaming at me. 'I've seen you on telly.'

'Presenting the famous Jim Rudd,' announces Wilson. 'My old mate from Gorleston. Louise came to – ahm – live with me after my wife left me.'

'Wife number two,' Louise adds. 'And she left you because of me.' She looks at me. 'He's probably got my replacement already lined up.'

Still the fickle philogynist, I think.

I refuse the offer of whisky. Louise volunteers to make coffee while Wilson takes me outside to the building in the garden he uses as his studio.

At first I think it is a shed until closer inspection reveals it to be a substantial brick workshop extending across the width of both his and the neighbouring garden.

'It dates from turn of the century,' Wilson explains in his bogus RP. 'Originally it was a forge. The chap I rent the place from used to run a joinery business from here.' Pronounced *hair*. He has never been able to completely iron-out those Norfolk vowels, unless I am mistaken about him and in fact he is trying to hang on to them. He draws my attention to the clear panels in the corrugated roof. 'The light's beautiful. It's perfect for painting in. I work in here all the time.'

There are plenty of heaters dotted around to keep the place warm, two or three art deco sofas and armchairs for models to arrange themselves upon, and a double mattress laid on the floor. The walls are covered with drawings and studies for paintings, with inspirational material culled from porn magazines; and there are a few film posters too, including that one for *Tess* he had stolen. Tables are piled high with sketchbooks, boxes of materials and empty whisky bottles. A 1960s kitchen cabinet serves as a bookcase for art books and magazines, exhibition catalogues and various porn publications and more empty bottles. There is a small mountain of multi-coloured knitwear which leads me to wonder if he moonlights as a children's TV presenter. The place is a mess. I couldn't work in such conditions. But then, I'm not an artist.

There is painted porn in progress on the easel. A woman seen from behind and slightly above, incandescent against a dark background, face-down on a bed with her knees planted widely apart and her backside tilted in an unequivocal invitation to mate with her. Louise, I guess, judging from the hair. Almost life-size. Painted with a loose realism. I can hardly bring myself to look, because every time my eyes sweep across the large canvas, they are magnetically drawn towards the centre of the composition.

'It's very in-your-face. But amazing,' I say, meaning it.

'Getting there,' he says. 'It's for my next show in Scotland. Not what Americans would call politically correct. I do get slagged off in the journals. Someone hurled eggs around at my last show. I didn't mind. It was free publicity, wasn't it. Of course, I can't let anyone from the college see this particular picture.'

'Student?'

'Second year.'

'Are you two –?'

Louise comes in as he's nodding. I find myself blushing as she hands us our coffees. His, I can smell, has been laced with whisky. Seeing we are contemplating her portrait, she flicks her eyebrows at me and puts her arms around him. 'Want anything in town, you disgusting old man?'

'Milk and an *Independent*,' Wilson says, magicking a fiver from his pocket. He kisses her and grapples with her buttocks through the t-shirt. I look away as the hem starts to ride up. I'm certainly no prude – buttocks and boobs are a staple of my show – but I do believe in decorum.

Louise breaks away from the mauling. 'Is Inspect – I mean, is Jim staying for lunch? If he is, I'll buy some food.'

Wilson looks at me. 'Jim?'

I consult my watch. 'I've got an appointment with my agent this afternoon. Another time, definitely.'

Louise says, 'Then I'll be able to boast that I cooked for Inspector Poole. So what do you think of this?' She nods at the canvas.

'It's –' It's what? Celebratory? Virtuosic? Porny?

'Precisely,' she finishes for me, seeing I am at a loss for words. 'Brilliant, but very, very provocative. Just like the mad bugger who's painting it.'

When she's gone we get down to the reason for my visit.

'You said to name the price.' He grins at me. 'What would you say to twenty grand a picture? Sixty grand total.'

I've expected something like this. Having originally told Wilson on the phone that I would be prepared to pay any price, however eccentric, I have come to an arrangement with my bank manager, who also happens to be a big fan of my TV work. I swung it so that he could perform as a pedestrian in a recent episode.

'No problem,' I say.

'In that case, forty grand a painting. All major credit cards accepted. Cheques. Postal orders. Cash even.'

'*Forty*?' This sends my eyebrows scuttling towards my low-tide hairline. 'I'm not Hollywood.'

Wilson grins. 'Sorry. They mean a lot to me.'

'Not as much as they mean to me.' I can see the paintings I want leaning against a partitioning wall. To be so close to them and at the same time to be denied them is almost too much to bear. If I can't have them, then I will have to steal them. I will commit murder for them. Without asking if he minds, I march over to them and space them out for a viewing. Seeing them again, seeing you again, life-size, alive almost, is overwhelming. I have to catch my breath. 'You were so lovely.'

Wilson stands beside me. 'Not bad.'

'*Not bad*?'

'The paintings. Not bad for a beginner, although I confess I did tidy them up before showing them. *She* was lovely. Difficult at times, to put it mildly, but lovely.'

I dab my eyes with a handkerchief. 'I loved her so much.'

Wilson places a hand on my shoulder. 'I know you did. That's why I want you to take them. For nothing.'

'What?'

'They're yours. I had no intention of asking for money for them. I never wanted to get rid of them until you phoned. It seemed indecent to get rid of them. Take them. I'll know where they are, if ever I want to look at them again. You're the rightful owner, old chap.'

I forgive him for his un-Gorleston endearment and hug him passionately. His clothes smell of turps and his breath is heavy with whisky. It is this embrace that Louise glimpses through the open doorway as she passes through the garden and decides to photograph for use in her college work. (A few years later she will sell the photo, which she develops but never uses, to the tabloids; not just to make money by producing apparent outing evidence, but to seek revenge on Wilson for dumping her and replacing her instantly with another girl. Denying any involvement with me, Wilson goes on to admit a predilection for bedding students and promptly loses his job. And yet in the long term the scandal does him more good than harm. His *Louise Reading, Louise Asleep* and *Bonjour Louise!* are bought by a major gallery. The postcards of them sell very well, I'm told. Particularly the last.)

'There's something else,' he says. 'I dug it out when I knew you were coming.' He goes over to the kitchen cabinet and takes something from the drawer. A book bound in wallpaper. His diary for 1981. He opens it. 'I thought we could divide this between us.'

At first I think it is the head of a paintbrush he's archived, but it is a lock of your hair, girdled with thread and secured to the page with a strip of sticky tape brown-brittle with age.

'I used to –' He removes the trophy. 'Used to kiss this. Daft, really. Made me feel as though...'

I can't find the words. Any words.

He divides the sable into two equal halves and places one on my palm. How could something so small and insubstantial weigh so much?

'Wife number one caught me kissing it. Never trusted me after that. Demanded I get rid of the paintings. When I refused...'

I gently brush my lips.

'Made sure wife number two never caught me going back to 1981.'

I can taste you.

'Of course Louise wouldn't bat an eyelid. She likes the fact there have been lots of girls before I chose her.'

I can reconstruct you, every square millimetre of you, all one hundred trillion cells of you from that fragment.

'Oh Jim, perhaps I shouldn't have – Here, come and sit down and – and we'll have some more coffee as soon as Louise – Poor old Jim. Poor old Jim.'

EIGHTEEN

And so I came to own the pictures of you, my dear Alison. One of my cameramen and I collected them from Hampshire in a hired van. I hung them where I could look at them all the time. It is the closest I can get to having you around. Inspector Poole learns his lines in your company. When I use the telephone, I do so with you listening. And when I lay in bed, you glance up from your reading to coyly smile at me. Your hair I keep sheaved with a loop of cotton in the top draw of my desk, easily accessible. I hold it for luck when I am memorising a new *Poole*. One of my fancies is to hold out the sheaf and see you grow from it, like a genii emerging from a lamp, hair, face, chest and arms, middle, famous legs, feet. And I become eighteen to be with you.

For you are forever eighteen. Had I not hung up on you that morning after Christmas, had I not unplugged the phone (so that when you called back you would have been able to chat to my mother instead of getting fobbed off with the ringing tone), had you not despairingly insisted on cycling back to Gorleston in order to speak to me, you would not have been slipstreamed under the wheels of Scott's delivery van and sliced in two at the waist.

Just ten seconds would have made all the difference. My mother would have provided you with them. She always had time for you, Alison.

*

One minute Martin is at home playing with his son, the next he is parked in a lay-by on a Suffolk dual carriageway hammering his fists against the steering wheel. He is the principal witness. He sees what is happening from the lay-by on the opposite side of the road, where he has pulled over to – I forget what—to change the cassette? Inadvertently he has ended up with a front row ticket.

He describes the sequence of events to the police.

You appear in the distance. It's clear you are in a hurry because you are standing on your pedals for speed. As you get closer, he can see that you are crying, once or twice mopping your face on your coat sleeve. The van approaches. Too fast? Definitely too fast. When a gust of wind catches it the driver loses control, and as he swerves, he erases you, immediately slamming on the brakes and slewing the van into the hedgerow. He remains in the driver's seat until the police and ambulance arrive. This is all Martin is able to remember. He never does satisfactorily explain where he has been going, or why he has pulled over to change the cassette when there is only the one cassette. Odd that he knows both the girl and the driver of the van, but Gorleston is a smallish town, and in a smallish town coincidences like this are hardly unusual. About that gust of wind, sir. Are you absolutely certain about this? We've checked with the weather experts who say the air has been Beaufort 1 for days. And did you not think to go and check on the cyclist? Oh, you were able to see she could not have survived. Thank you for your help, sir. That will be all for the moment.

He never does speak to me about the accident. I have to read his words in the paper.

*

A corpse. A broken mannequin. And cold; cold at the core. Your father is the only one of us with the courage to identify your body. He was changed for ever.

A funeral. I recall little of that afternoon. The sky was the colour of lead, resting as heavy as lead on my skull. It had snowed lightly, but the snow was grey like fallout. All colour had drained out of the world. I forget who was there. Everyone. No one. Anne. At some point Anne said a few words. God. Heaven. Eternity. I should've stopped her, but the words were for the benefit of friends and kin, not for you. You were absent.

It felt inappropriate to watch as your box was dispatched to the grey flames. I looked away. And then I was in a car surrounded by people but on my own, looking out of the window. Then I was in a crowded room on my own with a glass of whisky being pushed into my hand and someone (my mother? your mother? Anne? you? Yes, you. You smiled) folding my unthinking fingers around it, then I was on the seafront on my own. Then you were there too, big-smile, me-engirdling arms, and I was fine.

*

There was never any doubt in my mind that your death was my fault, not Scott's. I'd caused the tears that had blinded you. Scott lost his licence for driving without due care and attention, and after he was pictured on the front page of the *Mercury* he quit his job and the TA and as far as I know has never stepped outside of his parents' house since. Appropriate punishment, perhaps. But didn't I need to be punished too? I wanted to die; and *slowly*, so that I was aware of every pull on the torturer's ratchet. Ignoring your good advice, I took myself out of college and went to earth so that you couldn't find me. I fell into decrepitude on the streets of London for three or four months, where I starved and dehydrated and was periodically beaten up, laughed at and gleefully pissed on by the great British public, until one of my lecturers recognised me behind the wild hair and beard and reek of piss and decay. He took me home with him, dusted me down, repaired me (my teeth had particularly suffered), and eventually returned me to drama school. And you.

I thrived. There was a passion in my acting that had not been there before. My grief was a power source I quickly learned to harness. (I still get letters about my Hamlet, and my run at the Edinburgh Festival of Beckett's monologue *Krapp's Last Tape*.) I revelled in not being me. I was only truly happy when I was learning lines. When I was offered the role of Inspector Poole, initially for a six-part series, I was so overjoyed with my new alter ego I ceased being me altogether, and continued to be Inspector Poole when the cameras stopped rolling. It was like hiding in a locked room. And I stayed in that room for three seasons. Eighteen episodes and a Christmas Special, to be precise. James Rudd only emerged again after a day trip to Reading, where he chanced upon that exhibition.

To be honest, on the surface there was not a great deal of difference between Inspector Poole and James Rudd. My relatives could not tell it was he rather than I who visited them. The main difference between us was perspicacity. I had none, while the good Inspector, thanks to a succession of excellent scriptwriters, solved all his cases during the first visit to the scene of the crime. James Rudd wouldn't pass muster as a switchboard operator down the nick.

For the past few years I have been holidaying in Southwold. It is my favourite place. I stay in one of three B&Bs; which particular one depending on how booked-up they are: in my line of work holidays are not easy to plan for.

When I could afford to, I bought one of those highly expensive and sought-after beach huts. Not our beach hut, which I discovered was called Maiden Voyage, but one close to it called Repose. Five years ago Maiden Voyage went on the market and I immediately sold Repose and bought it. I'll never sell it. I'll sell my house first. I'll advertise burgers manufactured from minced gerbils first. I have had the roof repaired, and the floor replaced. I spent a very enjoyable weekend lovingly repainting it cerulean and white, having discovered these had been the colours of Maiden Voyage back in the early eighties. I keep a selection of fold-up chairs inside, and a camp bed, and brew tea on a primus. Occasionally my ageing parents will spend some time here with me. I never invite anyone else. This is where I come to relax. The only exception was when I was being outed. A bored reporter, who was hanging around waiting for some swim-suited six-packed stud to drop in on me, got himself bitten on the shin by a hot and bothered poodle. The sight of him hobbling about was funny at first (I laughed my loudest stage laugh), but as I am not prone to Schadenfreude, I soon felt guilty enough to invite him to join me for a mug of tea and the use of my modest first aid kit. Dubbing me *Inspector Yawn* was his way of repaying me. After his article appeared I was left alone to contemplate the sea and to read my diary.

Amazingly I don't get recognised too often. Once, twice per holiday seems to be the norm. I have Inspector Poole's moustache and sideburns to thank for that. Without them, I'm Joe Public. When I am spotted, it's no hardship. My fans are sedate late-middle-aged, and they usually demand little more from me than an autograph and a quick pose for a snapshot. I presume I am the talking point in a thousand flip albums from Totnes to Tokyo.

*

They still feel immensely private, these diaries of yours. Anne told me where in your room you'd hidden them and I dug them out and stole them. I had the idea of sending them to the crematorium with you, but in the end could not bear to see your handiwork turned into smoke. I've read them as far as December 19th 1980. I am too afraid to read further for what you may have written about our Southwold adventure, for there is a good deal of acid in your pen. Julie you describe as 'a flicker-book chick for boys to animate'; Martin as 'a big knob attached to a bigger knob'.

I was interested to learn what you have to say about my brother. Your mistake is to underestimate the effect flirting is having on him. You are highly intelligent, and yet you know nothing about men. Your first trip to Benacre Ness is described with forensic detachment over twenty-one pages: ten extra pages needed to be glued into the diary to accommodate your telling of events. There is no mention of your finding him physically attractive, just plenty of trepidation, and much disappointment.

While you refer to me on almost every page of your diaries, it is a relief that not once do you say anything derogatory about me, beyond the to-be-expected good-natured chiding of two people living in each other's pockets.

If I live to extreme old age, I will read on.

Until then I will have to assume that you loved me as I loved you.

And to remember you.

WILSON

KAFKA TOWERS REHAB CLINIC
(Actually, LAKE HOUSE CLINIC)
FLUFFY BUNNY LAND
(Actually, MIDDLESEX)

1994 (although it could be 1884 for all I know. Or 2004.)

Dear Jim,

Re: The Unicorn. For the record, I no longer believe I espied the fabled beast clip-clopping through the centre of Winchester.

But yes, at the time I did, which is why I panicked and was heard to exclaim: 'Unicorn! A unicorn's going to suck our brains!'

It gave off a malevolent vibe, you see, assessing passers-by for the most satisfying feed; its horn drooping to one side of its sugar pink muzzle – or whatever a horse's face is called. Next thing I knew, it had singled me out and was careering towards me, whinnying, sparks flying from its dinner-plate hooves. Change of underpants required! No matter where I hid – Woolies, WH Smith, the bank – it found me, bore down on me. To cut the story short, five mad minutes later I was being chased around and around King Alfred's statue, getting increasingly knackered until a pair of kind policemen grabbed me and stowed me safely in the back of their motorised carriage. You should've seen the exasperated look on that creature's face as we zoomed off. Tee hee.

I've been describing the unicorn to Suzie, my counsellor. We agree it's a symbol. As a painter, I'm forever translating concepts *et cetera* into their visual equivalents. It's one of the things in a painter's armoury. All my addled brain had done was find an appropriate way of representing my messed-up state of mind. Flaccid; that's pretty obvious. But unicorn? According to Brewers Dictionary a *bona fide* unicorn should have the legs of a buck, a lion's tail and a horse's body. The body should be white and the head red. Mine was pale pink all over and the long mane was bright yellow.

After much discussion with Suzie, and a flick through the current Argos catalogue, I discovered my unicorn was a mutant species of My Little Pony. It's my goddaughter's birthday soon, and I'd been searching for a present.

Could've been worse, I suppose. I wouldn't have wanted to mess with a vengeful Air Hostess Barbie.

Anyway mate, thanks again for the substantial cash gift. I promise, vow, never to reveal the identity of my benefactor, and promise, vow, I'll use my time here wisely to reflect on my miserable existence and change for the better. And I do want to change. I do. I just need to be shown how. I should've come here years ago.

Lake House is delightful, as peaceful as a nun's bed. Lots of picture windows on the ground floor, each with a several-acre view; sprung flooring, a rain forest's worth of leafy indoor plants, tinkling water features. The staff smile as if they're moonlighting from Disneyland. And Suzie's cool.

While my fellow inmates are pleasant enough, some are more pleasant than others. Angela, for instance. Yonks ago she sang backing vocals on the B side of *Love Me Like No Other – Love Me Then Leave Me* – by The Cogs, a minor post-punk, pre-Neo Romantic band. It was on *The Links* jukebox. You'll know it when you hear it. Angela hit the bottle after The Cogs split in'83. A decade or so of hard tippling has certainly taken its toll, but she's a trouper, determined to turn her life around. We get on extremely well.

Then there's Nigel. He's bearable when he's in a good mood, but unfortunately his moods tend to swing. One minute he's all 'tum-ti-tum', then some tiny thing triggers a period of self loathing. He's been holidaying here on and off for years. Another minor pop personality, Nigel used to wield a chainsaw during performances by the experimental German rock band *Drang* back in the mid eighties. Thus is explained the missing earlobe and the scarred shins. During his last stay here he oversaw the pollarding of the lakeside willows, so his stage career and his professional sawing certificate served a practical function outside of the music biz.

Nigel threw one of his famous wobblers a couple of nights back. There we all were, about six of us, enjoying the latest *Poole* (I'd insisted), when all of a sudden Nigel starts to complain that 'in real life Poole wouldn't knob an old girl like her' (a reference to the lovely Mrs Williams character). Angela tells him to stop being so vile and shut up, which Nigel takes great exception to. Maria (daddy's little girl; alcohol and cocaine) tells them to stop arguing because she's missing the plot. Simone (former Miss Isle of Wight runner up; alcohol and cannabis) snatches the remote from me and cranks the volume so that the speakers make you sound like Mr Punch. At which point Suzie marches in and demands to know blah-blah-blah. Nigel gets spooked, kicks over the coffee table and his chair, and forms interesting new combinations of the only two swear words he knows. Suzie switches off *Poole* (sorry) and calls a meeting. Nigel recommends we have sexual intercourse with the meeting and launches into what appears to be a Linford Christie tribute, lapping the room like it's an Olympic stadium, kicking any furniture that gets in his way out of his way.

The girls were either angry (Angela, Simone) or upset (Maria), while Suzie, a professional to the core, merely observed him as if she'd placed a bet. I missed it, but apparently he kept up this athletic display for several minutes; not bad when you consider he's been on twenty a day since he was fourteen. He was still going strong when he changed his course. While attempting to clear an overturned table his unfashionable flares caught on one of the legs and misdirected him onto a treacherous patch of milkshake (raspberry). He slammed face first into the back of the TV, knocking it over and killing it dead. (Angela, Simone, not happy; many tears flowed.) He's currently slumped in a comfy chair, too embarrassed to talk to anyone, plasters on his nose, reading Suzie's in-house publication *Steps to a Better Life*. His face is very David Cronenberg. In fact, with the bruising, he's scary enough to star in his own chainsaw slasher gore fest. Fancy producing it? I envisage lots of violence and a herd of malevolent unicorns running amok. Just the sort of thing the yoof of today crave.

Like I said, I missed his unfortunate accident because at the time I was happily ensconced in Maria's room. Guests are discouraged from inviting fellow guests into their private rooms (known as 'Me Domains'; as opposed to the dining hall and TV room which are 'Us Domains'. Lavatories, I suppose, are 'Wee Domains'), but Suzie and her colleagues were being distracted by Nigel's antics and failed to see us slip out of the communal lounge. We enjoyed a cuddle and a snog and I was permitted to feel her boobs through her clothing. Maria's quite trim but has been blessed with an ample bosom which she further emphasises by wearing clingy v-neck jumpers. I've been eying her ample bosom and her face since she strolled past me during registration several days ago.

Did we? I hear you beg.

Alas, no. Remember the unicorn-pony and it's erectile malfunction?

Maybe when I've got this crap out of my system, I'll be able to do the business again. I really hope so, because after breathing, doing the business is my favourite pastime. Hopefully I'll be doing the business with Maria. We're getting on extremely well, enjoying long walks around the lake or watching *Neighbours*. (We like to catch both the lunchtime showing and the evening repeat whenever possible in order to see how much of the script we can remember, supposing this provides a kind of Jane Fonda workout for our remaining brain cells.) While we're officially 'together', we've been discreet enough for no one to have cottoned on. I'd love you to meet her when – if – you visit. She admires your work, even though your character reminds her of her daddy, who charms the underwear off at least twenty temps a year while his wife slowly and painfully grows rigid in a wheelchair.

*

~~LAKE HOUSE CLINIC~~
KAFKA TOWERS

Still 1994, I think.

Good friend,

It was truly lovely to see you, albeit fleetingly last week. I'm sorry the place gave you the willies. It does its best to look like a hotel, but now and again the façade slips and a vomiting guest destroys the illusion. Still, ten minutes with my earthly hero is better than no minutes.

How anyone – gay, straight or abstaining – cannot fancy Maria, or be hypnotised by her shrink-wrapped goodies, I do not know. She liked you a lot, relieved that you look nothing like Poole without your make-up. I ought to be jealous. Instead I'm proud. 'That man is my friend.' 'I am the friend of that man.' To think, at one time you thought I was – what was it now –? a flick-fringed forgery. Ha ha!

Suzie is chuffed with the *TV Times* you autographed. She's

having the page framed and hung in her office. The woman's got a PhD, but you had her squirming in her sling-backs like a Brosette. (You won't know what one of those is; a follower of the now defunct (?) pop group Bros.) She's finding it difficult not to tell anyone how we came by our new television set. It was a mightily generous gesture of yours, and you'll be pleased to know it has been attached out of harm's way, high on the wall by metal brackets forged on an anvil in Nibelheim. First programme we watched was an afternoon showing of *Vertigo*. I love *Vertigo* – that amazing red restaurant, into which Hitch places his actress, dressed in complimentary green. I'd love to do a painting based on the movie as soon as I get my painting head back. I still feel as though I don't know which end of the tube the paint comes out of. Good thing I don't work on a dairy farm, eh?

By the way, it wasn't a good move to tell Suzie that Maria and I have formed an attachment. While Suzie's hardly going to split us up, she sincerely believes (page 3 of her *Steps*) that relationships formed at the clinic complicate the healing process and are in themselves doomed. She's seen it before: guests falling in love and falling apart as soon as they pass through the gates. And of course, the first thing they do when this occurs is find solace in their preferred drug. Result: more self-destruction and, if they're lucky enough to survive, another sojourn in a place like this.

It's a risk, but Maria and I have decided to continue dating. She's eleven years younger, but we have much in common – our admiration for Poole, for example, and our love of early eighties pop. Very mature of us, I know, but we're foregoing any consummating until we get out of here. Easier than it sounds, because one of the several little tablets we're plied with each day makes consummation impossible. Think: partially inflated bicycle inner tube; letter box.

*

~~LAKE HOUSE CLINIC~~
KAFKA TOWERS

1994

Dear Helena,

Thank you so very much for the latest jumper and matching hat. They are the talk of the clinic. Both are a trifle roomy, but my good friend Maria, who knows about these things, reckons it could set a trend. Pink and green is such a winning combination, too.

It would be wonderful if you could visit during your half term. I've calculated that you and I haven't met for eight years; which is mad, seeing as how we live less than a hundred miles apart. But that's adult life and responsibilities for you. Maria's keen to meet people from my past. I'm sure you'd get on. She's a Cancer. Taureans are supposed to bond with the crablike ones, aren't they?

Kafka, by the way was a writer (died 1924). He penned weirdy stories, such as *Metamorphosis* (a guy wakes up transformed into a giant insect) and *The Trial* (a guy gets entrenched in endless bureaucracy). Remember Terry Gilliam's *Brazil*? That's a very Kafkaesque movie. I suppose *Nineteen Eighty-Four* is Kafkaesque-ish.

Now I come to think about it, Lake House Clinic isn't remotely Kafkaesque. I was just showing off.

*

LAKE HOUSE CLINIC

Dear Helena,

Sorry sorry sorry sorry sorry sorry. I should've warned you. These days my fuse blows at the slightest increase in emotional current. (It has taken me half an hour to think up that analogy – and seven sheets of Lake House stationery.) I suppose I didn't want to frighten you into not coming. Please forgive the outburst – I understand fully why you decided not to hang around. And please continue to write to me. I've always loved receiving your letters. Your curvy cursive is a comforting cuddle for the eye.

Maria reports that she is impressed with her sleeveless pullover. Yellow was a good choice; it contrasts nicely with her dark brown hair. It is roomy enough to double up as a kind of skimpy dress. Eventually I know I will find it hugely sexy.

*

GORLESTON seafront

1994 [BUT UNSENT]

Dear Jim,

I'm writing this on my knee in one of the shelters on the lower esplanade. Weather not bad – blue sky, scudding clouds and warm enough for rolled shirt sleeves. As the schools have gone back, there are no holidaymakers. A few locals mooching about. Was spotted by a guy I was at school with. He looked pretty much the same, only greyer and more creased. He used to work at Bird's Eye in Yarmouth until that closed down. Since then he's been on benefit. He assumed I was a fellow dole-drawer. When I said I was recovering from alcoholic dependency, he demanded to hear 'my story'. So I told him 'my story', leaving out really embarrassing stuff such as my indefinite suspension from teaching until I'm detoxed and have learnt self control. He wanted to know if swigging from a half bottle of gin concealed in a paper bag meant my recovery wasn't going well.

So why had I been on the gin? Why is my handwriting so appalling?

Where to begin?

Maria and I decided to visit my relatives for a few days, trusting the sea air to blow some Hampshire cobwebs away. I decided to show her one of the old haunts we avoided on our previous stays: *The Links*. While we'd made no pledge to stay away from pubs, this was the first time we'd been in a hostelry since quitting Kafka's Castle. We crept into the saloon like burglars. It was a weekday lunchtime and deserted. Believe it or not, the barmaid was Julie. A mother now, she works there part-time. She's very bored with her life. As soon as her sprogs are old enough for big school, she intends to go back to the beauty salon in Yarmouth she owns. Time and child-rearing have taken their toll, although she's still shapely, and attractive, with that Miss World smile of hers. I've been asked to tell you that she's your number one fan. Number two, actually; I am number one. (I promised to acquire autographed photos for her. Please could you oblige? One of you as you, not Poole.) She was intrigued by Maria. Correction, by Maria's wardrobe. I don't know these things, but it turned out that Maria's clingy v-necks retail at well over a hundred quid each, while her slacks and designer sandals cost as much as Julie would earn in several weeks behind the bar. I felt very uncomfortable for Julie and attempted to lighten the mood by making a joke about Maria having stolen her daddy's credit card and hitting the sales. Not a joke, I discovered. High on coke and completely bonkers as a result, she'd acquired four and a half thousand pounds' worth of goodies in a three-hour guerrilla assault on Oxford Street and environs. Unable to carry so many bags, she'd had them delivered by a succession of taxis to a friend's flat south of the river. Included among her purchases were two dozen of her favourite jumpers in almost as many colours and over twenty belts. When Daddy found out, Daddy was most displeased. He returned ninety per cent of the goods and had his daughter arrested for possession. It was only by agreeing to check into Kafka's Castle that she avoided prosecution and imprisonment.

We sat at a window table, as far from the optics and the ciggies as we could get, watching the traffic pass on Marine Parade, enjoying our pot of tea and our scampi and chips. This was the happiest and most relaxed I'd felt for years. In fact, I was so happy I started crying and laughing at the same time, which set Maria off, which led to Julie administering extra serviettes for hankies.

We stayed in the pub until chucking out time at half-two. I fancied a stroll along the beach, but Maria was tired and so we decided to head back to my parents'. Not far from *The Links* I halted outside a neglected-looking house. The paintwork badly needed seeing to, and there were weeds in the gutters. The front garden hadn't been touched for a long time. You get the idea?

'Who lives here?' Maria asked innocently.

'Just a bloke we all used to know,' I said. More accurately, used to poke fun at. I suddenly felt guilty for all the times I'd taken the piss without his realising, and for my being in the great outdoors, happy as an East Berliner the night the wall came down.

His mum answered, unlocked and unbolted the peeled red door and opened it as far as the chain permitted. A funny smell leaked out – gone-off milk and landfill; the house I assumed, not her. She hadn't a clue who I was, but from the way she was peering at me she'd clearly decided I might be the sort of person who intended to pull a gun on her. I asked if Scott was in. I said I used to know him.

'Of course he's in,' she said. 'He only goes out when it's dark.'

Long pause.

'Could I see him? To say hi.'

Another long pause. 'And you used to know him?' she said.
'Long long time ago.'
'Were you in the TA?'
(Do I look like a soldier? I look more like the person who's been incarcerated for years, tortured, starved and dragged into a yard to face a TA firing squad.) 'Just a fellow quaffer at *The Links*,' I said, jollily, nodding unnecessarily in the direction of the nearby pub. 'I left the area to go to college. Thought I'd say hi, as I was passing. I am aware he's been – unwell.'

This euphemism satisfied her that I wouldn't be shocked if her son either refused to see me, or behaved oddly if he did. She opened the door wider and called his name. A few moments later, much creaking and a door opening and Scott appeared at the top of the stairs.

I say it was Scott. It could've been anyone between the age of thirty and fifty. He was unrecognisable; skinnier than me, even emaciated, and bald. He was probably what you'd be left with if you cracked the shell off a tortoise. He wouldn't come down, just lingered at the top of the stairs as if he had a communicable disease. Or as if we had. To be honest, he didn't have much of a clue who I was, which is understandable, seeing as how he wasn't part of our 'gang'. So I said I'd been a boyfriend of Alison's. Alison Dury?

Oops.

For a moment he looked as though he was going to collapse and take a tumble. The strength seemed to drain out of his legs and he hugged the newel as if his safety depended on it. Then he started wailing for his mum, who immediately grabbed a jar of tablets from one of the downstairs rooms.

'You ought to be ashamed of yourselves,' she yelled at us. 'Coming round here and having a go at him. He's only recently plucked up the courage to leave the house.'

I tried to assure her that I'd never 'have a go' at anyone, but she wouldn't listen and slammed the door. I heard her thump upstairs to administer the calming medicine. We could hear Scott's pained ululation from the end of the garden path as we fled.

All in all, then, a mistake.

Mistake number one, because I made mistake number two the following morning.

That night I hardly slept, in spite of some excellent help from Maria (at one-thirty, two forty-five and five past six). Kept thinking about Alison; the bonks; the nights down the pub, along the seafront or at the cinema; and all the occasions she'd posed for me, from her first timid freeze-frame smile to the final porno display.

Straight after breakfast, and without phoning, I dragged Maria round to Mrs Dury's.

Now, I'm no stranger to the woman – I usually hand deliver a card when I'm paying the old dears a pre-Christmas visit and always make a point of chatting with her on the doorstep – but I've never made a social call before. It really threw her at first. For a moment I was scared she was going to start wailing like Scott, but once the initial baffled look had passed, she relaxed and invited us inside. We were plied with coffee, cake, biscuits; all the stuff that's not recommended on our diet sheets, in fact. We scoffed like piranhas.

She was fascinated by Maria. So was the terrier, Oliver (the Third, suitably taupe and unruly), whose idea of a greeting was to shove his muzzle into Maria's crotch, not once but persistently, in the hall, the kitchen, and most embarrassingly when she was on the sitting room sofa. He was obsessed and visibly delirious. He left saliva. Good thing Maria was wearing trousers and not the little skirt. Eventually Mrs Dury tired of shouting instructions and excluded the beast.

(Mrs D sends her regards, by the way. The latest series of *Poole* is the best yet, apparently. Shame you never call round when you visit Gorleston. You'd be most welcome.)

Every December when I've spoken to her she's asked if I'd paint a picture of Alison to hang above the mantelpiece. She asked again now. Quite frankly, I can't think of anything more upsetting. While I can cope with retouching old work painted from life, the thought of enlarging the mantelpiece photo into an oil portrait makes me want to reach for the bottle. The photo's heartbreaking enough. It was the one they used in the *Mercury* and on Anglia news, taken in the upper sixth, some nine months before she died. She's at her inscrutable best. The photographer must've asked her to grin, but instead she gave him a wry Mona Lisa-style smile and a slightly raised eyebrow. I'd not realised it before, but it's truly unsettling. The grey eyes don't simply follow you round the room, they peer inside you in order to see whatever secrets you've got squirreled away. It's as if she knew I still had erotic thoughts about her, or that I was itching to let Oliver out of the kitchen just for the pervy thrill of seeing him provoked by Maria's odours.

Weird I know, but in my darkest moments – and over the years I've had my fair share – I've summoned Alison from 'the other side' to be with me (I've decided you must do this too). She takes hold of my hand and, like some ghostly social worker, proceeds to talk me out of yet one more for the road, or from snorting just one extra line. She's good; always says the right thing. In real life, of course, Alison wouldn't have intervened, even if I were to have mixed a toxic cocktail of meths, aftershave and cough mixture. She'd have let me take a few swigs and then observed, scientifically, the nature and degree of my suffering... before dialling for an ambulance, that is. Is this ungenerous of me? I make her sound as though she wasn't capable of love. She was, surely. She loved you, didn't she? Possibly me, for a short while. Not Martin.

Getting back to the portrait, I told Mrs D the truth, that I'm finding it impossible to paint, barely able to write my signature, let alone wield a brush in the name of Fine Art. It's as if I've forgotten everything. But while Maria was in the loo, and Mrs D fixing more coffee, I grabbed the photo for a closer look and found myself evaluating the flesh tones, working out how I'd mix them, and just how much violet was in those grey eyes, those unbelievably cold eyes. I could see the finished picture, enormous, and I really do mean enormous, like those billboard portraits of Communist dictators and Middle Eastern autocrats you see on parades. Half a building big. Mrs D came in and caught me scrutinising the photo like a watchmaker. She offered to loan me a spare for when I was ready to work again. She showed me how large the picture needed to be (about three feet by two, hardly billboard, but obviously more practical). I said, wouldn't it be better to have a nice landscape? I'd plenty of unpeopled scenes for her to choose from. For free. But she was adamant. She wanted her daughter, three by two, in oils. I said okay. She said would I be able to make the background a darker blue to go with the sofa and curtains. Oh, and would I be able to change the school colours (chocolate jumper and sky blue blouse) to something jollier? I advised her to consult other photos and choose some new attire. Then Mrs D went a bit cagey and started chewing her bottom lip.

Guess what? She couldn't bring herself to chuck away any of Alison's old clothes. They're in the loft. I was gobsmacked. What a plonker. The first rule of bereavement is to dump the clothes. It's madness not to. But of course, it's too late now.

Maria went back to my parents' to catch up on her sleep. I stayed at Mrs Dury's. Armed with a torch I ascended the rickety aluminium ladder into the loft. Boxes, boxes, boxes. I looked inside some of them: crime paperbacks; runs of *Woman's Own* and *Radio Times* from the seventies; election leaflets and blue badges from 1979. I also found Alison's lower school exercise books. She was a meticulous student. Turn to any page and you'd find A+ or A- along with some gushing commentary in red biro. 'Well researched, Alison. A+.' 'Excellent work. A+.'

'Well argued.' 'Outstanding.' English Literature and History were her strongest subjects, her Achilles' heel being Mathematics, at which she rarely achieved anything above C+.

I found the suitcases beside the chimney, under a grey blanket. When I lifted the blanket aside I discovered it had once been bright red, now impregnated with thirteen years' worth of dust. Wedging the torch between the roof trusses, I snapped open the upper catches and raised the lid a few inches, releasing the inert, anaerobic fustiness of stored cloth. I threw the lid wide then tried to understand what I was looking at. A vortex of some kind. Tights. Alison's trademark 10,000 Denier ribbed tights, bottle green, navy and black, writhing like snakes. There were even some attached to their cardboard packets. Eighty pence? They would set you back three quid now. There were smaller snakes too, wriggling among the larger ones, busily consuming their own tails: scrunchies and hair bands.

Below these, a few flimsy-looking white bras and a collection of knickers, their elastic long-perished, at least a month of days' worth, mostly off-white, although there were also striped and patterned and red ones; dark blue for PE. Carefully, so as not to disturb the ecosystem too much, I searched for a pair I could recognise. But I'd seen so many knickers in the intervening years and I gave up, delved instead to the very bottom of the case. Denim. Denim skirts. Now these I could remember. Short enough to rule out bending as an option. Perfect for gropes and quickies. Once, she'd accepted my challenge to wear one of these on a shopping trip to Norwich without undies. Neither of us had reckoned on so many people ogling her legs on stairs, necessitating the purchase of emergency knickers from a stall on the market.

Keeping out one of the skirts and choosing a pair of bottle green tights and matching undies and a scrunchie for no other reason than I wanted to covet them, I closed the case and swapped it for the one underneath. At first I thought I wasn't meant to investigate this, imagining ghostly fingers frustrating my effort to open the catches, but they were simply cheaper quality and reluctant to move. Far fustier than the undies case, this was crammed full with blouses, jumpers, shorts, jeans and shoes. I could remember every item stored here. Each one was a story. These shoes: purchased the summer I'd dated her, these had rubbed her feet and left a mark. The uppers still looked new, her toes hadn't had time to leave an imprint. Turning them over, I could see the heels had been bevelled from walking. Closer inspection with the torch revealed grains of sand and dirt trapped in the ridges. I imagined her striding along the esplanade, past the yacht pond and the bingo parlour and the open-air pool and the amusements, into the chip shop and hurrying up the stairs to my studio, where I pretended to have been immersed in my painting when really I'd been on sentry duty at the windows, scanning the holidaymakers, desperate for the first glimpse of her.

In addition to the sixth-form blouses, there were three or four out-of-school ones. These looked dated, with outsized collars and overstated seams, all the rage when they'd been made. I decided the lilac one would work best with the background blue and the pallid flesh and retained this as a reference.

Up to this point I'd managed to avoid an outpouring simply by swallowing back each bolus of misery as it appeared. However, as I was closing the lid, I noticed several tiny squares of white cloth squeezed into a pocket at the back, each a larger square folded twice like the signatures of an unbound book. I opened one out. It was monogrammed with a copperplate A. Instantly I pictured her using this, to dab tears, perspiration or snot; or tamped into her gusset to swab whatever was draining out of her. Living fluids. Living girl. Now she was not just dead but obliterated. Incinerated into the ether a third of my life ago.

Jim, it was just too much for me.

Mrs D appeared at the hatch and talked me into coming

down. She hugged me like a mother and cried herself, admitting not an hour went by when she didn't think about Alison: what she might be doing now, what she'd look like, if she'd be a fan of *Next Generation*, what she'd have thought of the Gulf War. Every hour, every day.

She asked how often I remembered Alison. I told her the truth: usually when I was drowning and needed a lifeline. Otherwise, hardly ever. I had my mementoes – letters, a few not very good snaps, a curl of hair – but by no means were they holy relics, clasped and kissed during some sort of ritual.

Mrs Dury asked if I'd take Oliver for a walk. She thought it would be a practical way of clearing my head of sad thoughts. I dragged him along the beach to Hopton, then back along the narrow lane by the golf course, a round trip of two-and-a-half, three miles. Alison came too, barefoot along the warm sand, dangling her sling backs on a finger, sprinting ahead on Warren Lane so that Oliver strutted on his back legs like a circus dog in his desperation to reach her. At one point we paused to kiss and she told me I'd never settled down because unconsciously I measured all my partners against her.

I went home. The old dears were out. Maria was asleep on the sofa. She'd used cushions as a duvet. I woke her by kissing her toes. As soon as she opened her eyes, she noticed I'd been upset.

'Please tell me you didn't go back to Scott's.'

I explained about the suitcases. 'Fancy her mother having kept all those clothes. Maybe I ought to offer to take them away for her.'

'And do what with them?'

'Charity shops. Or just dump them.'

Maria laughed at this. 'Are you telling me you'd be able to get rid of them now?'

I suddenly wanted to make love. We had a smooch on the sofa but Maria said she'd be able to relax properly upstairs on the bed. So I chased her upstairs, pretending to be Oliver, thrusting my nose up her bottom and snapping at her bum cheeks. She liked that.

Maria launched herself onto the bed and waited for me. I hesitated. A couple of hours ago she was the most beautiful woman in the world; eminently desirable; perfect. Yet now –

I stared at her. She frowned. 'What's wrong?'

'Let's play a game,' I said.

'The sniffy dog game?' She squirmed and squealed at the thought of my muzzle.

'Dressing up,' I said. We often played this back home. Maria pretended to be an au pair, or room service, while her favourite for me was naughty teacher or Customs strip search. I rattled the carrier bag containing Alison's things. No reaction, so I took out the skirt.

'I am not putting on a dead girl's clothes,' she said bluntly.

'I'll never ask again.'

'Definitely not. It's sick. Besides, I'm about two sizes bigger. I'll split the stitches. Wait until we're back in Winchester; I've got skirts exactly like it.'

'Not exactly,' I said, placing the garment on top of her.

'It stinks. I suppose you fucked her when she was wearing this.' She examined it, as if looking for tell-tale stains. The zip was stiff, but opened. 'Stinks of mildew.'

And chip fat and sun-rotted curtains.

I worked on her.

Maria sat up. 'So what else is in the bag?'

I showed her. She laughed at the bra. 'Poached eggs,' she said. 'And we wouldn't be able to do anything if I was wearing these.' She smoothed out the tights and the knickers. 'I assume these were washed when they were packed away.'

'Maybe we don't have to do anything,' I said. 'Maybe putting them on would be enough.'

'Enough for what?'

'For me to see.'

'If I look like your old sweetheart?' She waved the knickers like a flag. 'I don't need to put these on to answer that.' I'd already started pulling down her trousers and undies. 'I must be off my head,' she said, sloughing the jumper.

'Utterly bonkers,' I said. I pressed the bra into her hands.

'Better if you leave the room,' she said. 'For the full effect.'

She was right. I waited on the landing, sniffing the hanky as if I could get high from it. A few minutes later: 'Okay. You can come in.'

I hardly dared open the door, just gripped the handle, terrified.

'If you don't come in by the time I've counted to three, I'm taking all this off.' She started to count. I threw the door open. In a broad Norfolk accent she said, 'Hev you come to see you old girlfriend, then?'

'She was posh,' I said. 'And don't tuck your hair behind your ears.'

Maria held out her arms and slowly turned. She was a good deal shorter in the leg than Alison, and hourglass-shaped, which Alison was not. The lilac blouse gaped at the cleavage. 'Close the door,' she demanded, using RP this time. She came towards me and enveloped me.

Mildew and cold chip fat. To kiss kissable sable.

'You're nothing like her –' I began.

'Good.' She groped me. 'Wanna do anything with this?'

' – But when I shut my eyes –' I groped her bum and reached under the skirt.

She tensed immediately. 'Open your eyes,' she insisted. 'You're with me, not her.'

Was I? 'Alison –'

She pushed me away. I grabbed her and examined her eagerly. Uncanny, but her boobs had withered. Her hips too. She was taller.

'You're freaking me out,' she said. 'Open your eyes. Look at me.'

'Alison,' I croaked, desperate for her to love me. 'Ally.' And it really was her. I could feel it was her. Smell it was her.

Next thing, Alison was kicking me in the shin and slapping me around the arms and head. 'Thought so. Your pupils. You've been taking something.'

'Just a tiny, weeny sniff,' I said. My emergency ration, hidden in foil and Clingfilm in my shoe. I'd tied Oliver to a fencepost while I'd snorted. He was still there.

Alison melted like the Wicked Witch into a heap of cloth. Maria glowered. 'Stay away from me. Jesus, I reek.'

'I'm sorry, Ali – Maria.' I fell onto the bed. I closed my eyes and heard a door slam, and then far off another door slam, then footsteps on the pavement outside, then footsteps disappearing into the distance.

[ONLY FRAGMENT OF LETTER THAT WAS EVENTUALLY SENT]

And so here I am, my friend, a little pissed (sorry) and feeling about as isolated and guano-plastered as Rockall. No job, no income, unless I rent my place, and I'm loathe to do that because it's my home. The old dears have made it clear they'd prefer me to bugger off back to Hampshire, which I will as soon as I find out if Maria's going to forgive me (highly unlikely; if you are a betting man, you'd have more luck with Laughing Boy, 700-1 in the Glue Factory Cup), but in the meantime I'm going to be crashing down above my cousin's café. Fortunately the flat isn't being rented out at the moment.

(Later.) Excuse the scrawl. I'm somewhat wasted, to use the scientific description. Sat in *The Links* all evening talking to Julie (have I mentioned she works there?). I lost track of how much I was knocking back. Beer mainly, although I ended up on the hard stuff. I think I started to flirt with her (a married woman with family! Shame on me). And Julie is very flirt-withable. She always was, wasn't she. With Weltschmerz added to the mix, she's game for anything out of the ordinary.

This place is haunted, I'm sure it is. I keep hearing noises – assorted creaks and clicks and scrapes – and just now, when I was sitting on the loo, I swear I sensed someone outside the door, trying the handle. From now on I'm always going to leave the door open, and, when I'm just pissing, I'll stand to the side so that I can see if anyone or thing tries to creep up on me. I'd like to do something about those bloody skylights above the loo and kitchen – I'm sure someone has been looking down at me. Trouble was, every time I looked up: nothing there.

Heebie-jeebies notwithstanding, I'm hoping to stay here for a week or so. I'm planning on getting some work started. My cousin's loaned me cash for materials. I suspect I spent a small portion of it this evening – I daren't tally the change – but I've phoned my old friend Helena and she's promised to mail me some dosh.

*

GORLESTON

1994

Dear Jim,

Thank you SO much for the box of goodies. I agree, it's safer to send me the materials rather than trust me to buy them. I've already started work on a couple of large oils. Julie's able to pose for an hour a day. Not nude, cheeky; fully clothed. I'm also doing a LARGE portrait, six by four feet. I've checked to make sure I can get it down the stairs as I don't want the fuss of taking it off the stretcher.

An additional 'thankyou' for sorting out my residence for

me. Never a good thing to have the electricity people threatening to cut one off. Are you absolutely certain Maria hasn't left any forwarding address? Shame if she hasn't, because I did want to offer some kind of apology to her. And let her know how lost I feel without her.

*

GORLESTON

1994 [UNSENT]

Dear Jim,

Couldn't send you a Xmas card without enclosing a letter.

Progress on the paintings is painfully slow. At first I missed not having Julie around, but she was all wrong anyway – not skinny enough. Not only that, she fidgeted, and never talked about anything interesting, like books or jazz, so in a way it was a good thing that she freaked and fled when she did. Shame I daren't show my face in *The Links* ever again, but the *Cliff Hotel* is a decent alternative. They have comfy sofas and armchairs like a gentleman's club. And if I'd never gone in there, I'd never have met Lisa.

Every evening, between eight and ten, a group of young people would come in for drinks. They'd been away at college or university and were catching up. Three guys and three girls. Ian (loudmouth, know-it-all) was an art historian (I refuse to take seriously anyone who condemns Victorian painting as 'shite' without explaining himself and while using a Norfolk accent). Very opinionated about what's good and what's not, but okay with my correcting him on Futurism when we found ourselves elbow to elbow at the bar. The following evening I was consulted for my opinion on the state of current British painting and my amusing irreverent reply earned me an invite into their clique.

I was glad of this, not only because I thrive on the company of young people (educated ones – I admit it, I'm a snob), but also because I'd taken a fancy to one of the girls: Lisa. The other two girls were mouthy and vain and both fair-haired. Lisa, brown bobbed, pretty with hazel eyes and a fixed, enigmatic smirk, was more to my taste. She was a trainee librarian, content to listen rather than contribute, yet chatty enough when engaged in one-to-one conversation. She had a boyfriend back in Aberystwyth, but for once I wasn't after sex. Using my x-ray vision, I had seen through her baggy jumper and jeans. She was trim and flat-chested and long in the leg. Perfect. Perfect to be my model.

Asking outright would be no good – 'Would you pose for me,' sounded too much like a really wet chat-up – so I invited Ian to my 'studio' and asked Lisa if she'd like to come too.

They turned up the following afternoon. I'd stayed sober on purpose. Ian was awestruck by the six-by-four. 'It's like a Chuck Close,' he said, 'though more painterly.' (Obviously he'd only seen his Closes reproduced in art publications, because Chuck Close is a very painterly photorealist.) He was so impressed, he grabbed a chair and contemplated my handiwork from the far side of the room with a can of bitter in his hand, intermittently offering up praise of my brush strokes, my colour, my composition. He said he wanted to write about me for his next college essay.

It was Lisa who bothered to ask the identity of my subject. I related the abridged History of Alison, leaving out that we'd been intimate. Her smirk disappeared for the first time since I'd known her. 'Is this supposed to be her, too?' she said, scrutinising the unfinished front view of Julie.

'Supposed to be,' I said with meaning. I explained that my model hadn't been a good physical match, neglecting to mention the part about her calling me a weirdo and running out on me. 'I'm still looking for someone more suitable,' adding, 'I don't suppose you can recommend anyone?' I suggested those other two girls, knowing full well that Lisa disapproved of them.

'They'd be no good,' she said. 'They wouldn't sit still. Wrong colour hair, too.'

'Shame,' I lamented. 'I'll just have to leave it unfinished.' Heavy sigh. Ah, the unhappy lot of the professional painter.

'Lisa will sit for you,' Ian said, without taking his eyes off the six-by-four. 'She used to sit for me when I was on the foundation course.'

'Oh god,' Lisa said. 'You won't want me.'

'Why not?'

She shrugged. 'Would I have to dress up like this?'

I nodded. 'I'd be happy to paint you, but if you don't feel like wearing the props...' Dot dot dot.

'Do it,' Ian urged, the booze already have worked its three point five per cent magic on his brain. 'You know what? Next term I'm going to start doing the life drawing module. I've really been inspired by this guy.'

'Okay, I'll pose,' Lisa said. 'Tomorrow.' We shook hands.

'Let's all go get some chips,' Ian said. 'The smell's making my mouth water.'

Lisa arrived at ten the next day. I'd been working on Alison's eyes since half eight and was brought out of a trance by her stamping up the stairs. There was something different about her. She'd washed her hair and blow-dried it so that it was several times the usual volume. And when she stood at the window, I saw she was wearing a shit-load of eye make-up. I told her she looked gorgeous (she did, too), but it would all have to come off.

As soon as she'd cleaned up and wet-combed her hair so that it was flat to her skull, she disappeared into the loo to change. I heard her bolt the door, obviously worried I might try to check out her bod.

You'll probably laugh – or maybe you won't – but I was

actually shaking with nerves when I heard the door opening. I pretended to be watching something out of the window.

'What do you reckon?' she said.

I looked round. And gasped loudly, as if I was about to suffer from a heart attack. The clothes fitted her perfectly. *Perfectly*. 'Legs,' I croaked, pointing as if at an apparition. 'A librarian with legs. Whatever next.'

'These jumble clothes pong,' she said. 'Mind if I have a ciggie? Smoking might desensitise my nose.' She took a packet from her bag. 'Want one?'

In spite of my ongoing abuse of alcohol and occasional (non-dependent) experimentation with opium derivates, I'd quit smoking years ago, hating the foul taste it left in my mouth and the ashtray reek I could never get out of my clothes. But seeing Lisa puff in her exaggerated way like a nineteen-forties Hollywood starlet made me eager to join in. So I took the proffered ciggie and whipped out my Zippo. Yes, I still have my Zippo (you were an inveterate match striker, I seem to recall). I've carried it around since the early eighties for no other reason than it occasionally comes in handy, like the diminutive blade you sometimes have on a key fob. The chemicals hit my brain soon after the first few drags. I reeled and thought I was going to throw up.

'Where do you want me?' Lisa said.

I gestured towards the chair Julie had fidgeted upon. 'Let's finish our cigarettes first, though.' As there was no ashtray, I opened one of the windows. We knelt, leaning over the sill. '*Déjà* flaming *vu*,' I said. It came out more bitterly than I'd intended.

'You and that girl?' Was she reluctant to speak her name for fear of triggering an emotional outburst?

'One summer, yonks ago,' I began. Then I did the maths. 'You'd have been about five. Crikey.' I changed the subject. 'Do you ever watch *Inspector Poole*?'

'Sometimes.' She scrunched her nose, Jim. You're not her thing. Sorry. Her mother, on the other hand, was an avid fan. Her mother had watched every episode.

I said, 'Alison used to go out with him. They were best mates.'

Lisa was suitably impressed, the smirk broadening into a lop-sided grin. 'How come you're so obsessed with her?'

'Obsessed? That's a strong word.'

'Aren't you?' She leaned out and stubbed her cigarette on the bricks. Sparks danced on the breeze. I found myself remembering the unicorn's hooves.

'These are commissions,' I said. 'Obsession would be if I'd painted these off my own bat.'

Lisa stood and straightened the skirt. 'Got any music to listen to?' I nodded in the direction of my cassette player and the stack of tapes beside it. She went to investigate. 'Who's Evan Parker?'

'Improvising saxophonist. Uses extended techniques.' Blank look. 'Funny noises,' I explained.

'Funny noises. Doesn't sound as though I'd like it.'

'Probably not.'

'Kate Bush!' She held it up as if it was something laughable.

'They're good songs,' I said. 'Revolutionary at the time.'

'Yeah?'

'Not many people had written pop songs about having periods, or guys 'hitting the Vaseline',' I said.

'Hitting the Vaseline?' She'd discarded the tape and chosen another before I could explain. 'Madonna's acceptable.' She dropped it into the player.

After checking no one was below, I flicked the dog end into the road and closed the window. When I stood I discovered I had new-born foal's legs. My head was woozy with nicotine. 'Not so loud,' I said. 'You'll have Sharon up here.'

Lisa reduced the volume and went over to the chair. Using

the painting as a guide, she put herself in the identical pose. As soon as I'd recovered, I carried the painting over to the easel and set to work.

'Do you ever do nudes?' she asked, inevitably.

'All the time,' I said. 'I run – used to run life classes at the college.'

'I wouldn't know where to look.'

'You get used to it,' I assured. 'After all, just because a person's nude, doesn't mean they're sexy.' She didn't follow. 'There's nothing more natural than nudity. It's not erotic at all. Clothes make a person erotic. What's sexier, you stark naked or you in a flattering bikini?'

Seeing the picture of the two Lisas I'd put in her head, she slowly nodded.

'Sexy is imagining what you can't see,' I continued. 'I mean, this picture's going to end up miles sexier than if you'd been kit-off because the viewer is required to imagine the body under the clothes.'

'Since when have bottle green tights been sexy?' She laughed, plucking at them.

'It's what's in them that's sexy.' I said. 'Weird question, but have you ever seen any porn on video?'

Her cheeks coloured. 'Why?'

'Yes or no?'

'You're not going to make me to watch porn, are you?' she asked wearily.

'No, I'm not. The point I'm trying to make is that for me, the sexiest part of the show is at the start, when the actors are fully clothed, pretending to get to know one another. As soon as the clothes start flying off all sense of mystery evaporates. Naked people are boring, unless you're a Lucien Freud painting them.'

She seemed greatly relieved I thought so. 'Yes, I have seen a naughty film.'

'Hated it?'

She scrunched her nose. 'Just found it daft,' she said.

I painted without talking, scraping off as much of Julie as I needed to before redrawing the pose. As soon as the Madonna tape finished we had another fag break, this time with coffee. While the water was heating up Lisa sidled over to the easel and asked me if she was modelling okay. I assured her she was doing a sterling job. When she queried the proportions of her legs, I explained about foreshortening and perspective.

'Plus you're a leg man,' she added. 'It's pretty obvious.' She drew my attention to the heap of preparatory drawings I'd made of Julie.

We went and sat at the open window again. 'Must be weird being back.'

'No weirder than being in that rehab clinic,' I said, having forgotten I'd neglected to tell her about my holiday there. Her eyes grew large and she lost interest in her cigarette while I explained I'd become addicted to booze.

'Then how come you tipped some whisky into your coffee just now?' (Sorry, Jim.)

'Because I can handle a seasonal tipple,' I said. 'I'm cured.'

'Rehab clinic.' She shook her head disbelievingly. 'My mum would kill me if she knew I was up here with a reformed alcoholic.'

'So where does she think you are?'

'Out with Ian.' As if worried her mother might stroll past, she moved away from the window and sat with her back to the wall and her legs stretched out. 'So how much longer will you be staying in Gorleston?'

'Until these two piccies are finished.'

'I reckon you'll still be here when I'm back for Easter.'

I was horrified. 'What makes you say that?'

'Just a hunch. To me, you haven't really moved on.'

'Been re-shelving the Psychology section, have we?' I kicked the sole of Alison's shoe. Lisa kicked me back.

'Admit it. You feel at home in Gorleston. Your family's here. You were happy when you were here. Do you honestly believe you'd have ended up in rehab if you'd not gone away to college and had got a job here instead?'

'Depressing thought,' I said. 'I wouldn't have been a painter, would I. I might even have ended up like one of those guys down there.' A pair of men lugging rods and equipment for a high tide's fishing off the pier.

Lisa peeped over the sill. 'Snob. Judging people when you don't even know them.'

'I suppose the guy on the left could be a major novelist,' I reconsidered.

'Possibly,' Lisa said. 'But why would his being a 'major novelist' make him a better person?'

'I didn't say 'better'.' I was regretting opening my mouth. 'I meant 'more interesting'.'

'So you're saying he's not interesting because he goes fishing. Ted Hughes enjoyed fishing. So did Ernest Hemingway. What if their day job hadn't been writing?'

I didn't know how to wriggle out of this one. 'Go and sit down,' I said.

She laughed – 'Snob' – and ruffled my hair as she passed. I managed to get in a quick retaliatory slap on her bum.

Lisa left late afternoon, and returned the following morning with a carrier bag of supplies: biscuits, a half bottle of scotch to fortify our coffee and a selection of music cassettes (American guitar twangers and *Carols from Kings*). 'Plus I felt you needed a few decs.' She shook the carrier onto the worktop.

'Condoms?'

'Balloons, you twit. And we had these going spare.' A string of coloured lights. 'Thought you could hang them up, seeing as how you'll be spending Christmas here.'

Today, after instructing me to look away or risk injury, she donned her costume in front of the hot-air blower instead of in the unheated loo. I looked, of course. Briefly. Out of curiosity rather than lasciviousness. Saw a good deal of thigh and a narrow moley back.

She caught me. 'Don't even think about it,' she warned. I asked her what she meant. 'Trying anything on. I'm spoken for and you're way too old.'

Again, Lisa stayed with me all day. We had lunch downstairs; egg and sausage and chips. She dared to remain in costume. No one noticed, although Sharon kept giving us funny looks from the counter, obviously trying to place where she'd seen that getup before. Gobshite Ian paid a brief visit in the afternoon. Apparently I'm a genius. He took some snaps of me painting and Lisa posing and several of the giant portrait, which I'd worked on after the pub. Unable to resist offering his opinion on the Lisa picture, he drew my attention to a troublingly blank area on the bottom right.

'It's been bothering me, too,' I said.

'Needs something in it.' He stroked his chin as I supposed he supposed genius artists did as an aid to contemplation. 'Pile of books? Or maybe her shoes?' I asked why she wouldn't be wearing her shoes. What would be the meaning? In a composition with only one element – a girl on a chair – to place the shoes beside her would have great significance. Ian, who as an art historian ought to know better, asked if it mattered whether or not it needed to mean anything. Disgusted, I sent him packing.

Lisa was curious to know more about the girl she was impersonating.

'Ally was very brainy,' I said, remembering the school books. 'Political.' I recalled you and her arguing full volume in the pub on your return from London. 'Fiercely independent at times, but she had a tender side.' And a powerful erotic impulse I sometimes found unsettling. I mean, what sort of person would want to have sex immediately after having sex? 'She was very fanciable, but after going out with her for a while, I realised I preferred my girlies a tad warmer. Ally had a touch of the Hitchcock blonde about her.'

'So you didn't love her.'

'Jim – Inspector Poole Jim – he loved her. And she loved him. But she loved Oliver most of all.' As I was explaining he had been her pet pooch, inspiration struck. 'That's who I could put in this blank area: Oliver. It's so obvious.' Very roughly I outlined a rudimentary dog lying with his head resting on his paws. 'You're not allergic, are you?'

Before my nightly quaff at the *Cliff Hotel* that evening I called on Mrs Dury. Pleased I'd started the commission (I didn't mention the second, full-length picture), she thought it would be a great idea to include Alison's beloved dog. She had umpteen snaps of them together, but I hate working from photos if there's an alternative, and said I'd prefer to borrow Oliver the Third, promising this time not to return him two hours later than agreed (fortunately he'd still been tied up where I'd left him). First thing the following day, I collected the pooch and took him to the studio.

Lisa was Christmas shopping in Yarmouth and wouldn't be arriving until after lunch, which gave me a morning to settle and draw the animal. At first he was frightened and intractable, circling the flat and yapping at the exit, but eventually, pacified by doggy chocs, he settled into a position I could use and I sketched furiously, rewarding him for his patience with a jumbo sausage and gravy and a brisk walk to the end of the pier, where we shared a packet of chips. When I got back, Lisa was changing. I introduced pet to mistress. First thing Oliver did was shove his muzzle under her skirt. But Lisa was far better than Maria at dealing with unacceptable doggy behaviour and soon had him snoozing beside the chair.

Lubricated with coffee, we sang along with the carols.

'Day three and you haven't tried anything on with me. I'm impressed.' Lisa grinned.

'Sounds as though you're expecting me to misbehave,' I said.

'Like Oliver?' She shrugged. 'Maybe. You like me.'

'I do. But you've got someone, and I – well I *might* still have someone.' I was hopeful that Maria would contact me before long.

'You haven't even flirted, though. Me sitting here dressed as your teen sweetheart.'

I said, 'What would you do if I came over and tried to kiss you?'

Was the coffee affecting our judgement? Succumbing to our lusts, we conjoined on the sofa bed, fully dressed, with the tights scrunched down by her ankles. I called her 'gorgeous' and 'sweetie'; she implored me to 'give it to her'; which I believe I did. Then she gasped, I roared and Oliver barked. Off came the tights and, after the briefest of pauses, we were away again.

Several gasps, roars and barks later, while I was busy snogging with Lisa's hamster, my cousin Sharon banged on the door and informed us the customers could hear everything so could we please either do what we were doing quietly, or preferably not do it at all.

It was now too dark to paint, so after draping the Christmas lights around the fireplace and plugging them in, we turned the sofa bed back into a sofa and cuddled under a blanket, swigging from the whisky bottle and competing to remember beyond the first verse of the most popular carols.

We dozed, then slept. When we awoke it was after seven. Lisa suggested we get some wake-up air by returning Oliver. 'Then back here for a shower. Then you can treat me to a slap-up meal at the *Cliff Hotel*. Preferably something without chips.' She was still wearing the blouse and skirt, and decided there was little to be gained from changing until she'd washed. She pulled on the tights, her own shoes and her coat, and we went outside.

Not greatly cold, considering it was late December, though bracing enough to revive us. Few bods were about, just the odd dog walker and people fishing off the beach. Hurricane lamps pinpricked the blackness at diminishing intervals along the beach, thanks to the whisky restlessly looping-the-loop like fireflies. Lisa and I held hands as we strode along the lower esplanade. Now and again we'd pause for a kiss, and each time we did, Oliver would take the opportunity to pee. I realised I was already falling in love with Lisa. I told her.

'But what about Maria?' she said.

'I love her too, immensely, but differently.'

'Maybe you just fancy me,' Lisa said. 'Me and my hamster. You spent a lot of time down there.'

'Maybe. And I'd been doing so well, keeping my hands to myself.'

She leaned against the railing. 'You have my permission not to keep them to yourself for a quick naughty grope. No one's about.'

I was suddenly eighteen again, mauling Alison on the bus or in *The Links* when no one was looking. In the orange light Lisa became Alison. I cupped my hands over Alison's boobs, smoothed Alison's waist and hips and bum, slipped my hand under the hem of Alison's skirt. She threw her head back, inviting me to kiss her throat while I worried her clitoris with my finger.

Suddenly, behind me, the ululation of a Lake House internee, very loud and very close. We fell apart. Oliver yapped and barked frenziedly, almost garrotting himself in his effort to escape.

'But you're dead! I killed you!'

Out for his evening constitutional, Scott had inadvertently strolled into one of his nightmares.

For a sick man, he was surprisingly nimble; he was on us

before we'd had time to appreciate what was happening. Flinging me aside, he lunged at Lisa, grabbing her by her lapels and mercilessly shaking her as if this might transform her resemblance to Alison. Freed, Oliver bolted, as I would've done had Lisa not been ensnared. I hugged Scott around his knees and overbalanced him, Lisa too, although she managed to spring up again. I yelled at her to run. Instead she stayed to haul me to my feet, repeatedly stamping on Scott's bullet head when he doggedly clung to my coat.

'I killed her,' Scott kept saying. 'She's not here.'

Lisa reached into my pocket for the whisky bottle and slammed it hard against his skull. In Western bar brawls and *Laurel and Hardy*, bottles always shatter into a million pieces, but this one remained intact. It made a dull clump sound. The pain was instant and considerable. Scott instinctively went foetal, clasping his skull and wailing to himself.

'Alison, come on,' I urged, having noticed a hurricane lamp floating towards us.

'We can't leave him,' she said.

But she refused to budge. 'Alison, for god's sake.'

She shook herself free and hunkered beside him. Scott was crying. I suspected a trick, but he really was hurt. 'You know him?' she said.

'Unfortunately.'

She peeled Scott's fingers aside to investigate the wound. 'Skin's not broken,' she said, but there's a massive bump. He ought to go to Casualty.'

A burly-looking man in donkey-jacket and wellies ascended the steps from the beach. His lamp was as bright as a photoflash. 'What the heck's going on here,' he said in a broad local accent. 'Fighting over you, are they, girl?'

I explained how he'd attacked us, and that I knew him. 'He's on medication,' I added, as if this might satisfy his curiosity.

He lifted Scott to his feet. 'Alright son?'

'Alison,' Scott murmured to himself.

She shot me a look. 'What's going on?'

'Alison –' More pained this time. He started sobbing. 'I killed you.'

'How?' she said.

'Flattened you. My van.' He doubled up as if he was going to be sick. 'Lights,' he said.

'What lights?' Alison said.

'Lights. All down the sodding road.'

'What sort of lights?' Alison persisted. 'Headlights?'

Not headlights. I'd realised Scott was using butcher-speak. I saw what he'd seen. A nasty taste bubbled in the back of my throat. Two swigs washed it down. Three. Then the bottle was empty.

'We'd better get him home,' I said. The man offered to help, but Scott wanted to be free of us. Still nursing his head wound, he staggered up one of the steep tarmac paths that criss-cross the grass incline and disappeared over the ridge.

'Rum old business,' the man said. Having made sure that Alison was okay, he left us to return to his fishing.

I reached for her hand. 'Let's go get ourselves a drink.'

'I don't think so.'

'Let's go home, then.

'What's my name?'

'Your name? Don't you know?' I laughed.

'You don't appear to.'

I couldn't see what she was getting at. When she told me, I still couldn't. When she walked away, I still couldn't.

'One of those and one of those,' I said to the woman in the off licence.

'What am I going to have?' Alison asked, punching me on the arm.

'And a bottle of that for the young lady,' I said, and we went back to the studio to resume work on the paintings.

*

GORLESTON

JAN 95

Dear Jim,

Excuse the typing. It's a damn sight more rEAdable [sic] than
my godawful usual scrawl.

Plese [sic], please could you send me a wee drop of not-filthy
lucre for the diminishing funds. You're a gent. You are. And

BrillAnt eipisode [sic] of *Poo[le]* last night. Wept buckets at
your brilliant defuctive [sic] powers[.] I didn't half fancy that
woman you humped. We have the same taste in women
obviously.

You're a gent Jim. Jim the gent.

*

GORLESTON

FEB 95

Dear Ian,

Thank you for your letter and your request for biographical
information to help you with your essay research.

I have to confess that I am experiencing great difficulty
trying to place you. You seem to know me, but when exactly did
we meet?

*

GORLESTON

FEB 1995

Dear Ian,

Most perplexing! But then, I've been a little unwell these past few weeks.

I look quite the famous artist in your photographs, don't I. The pictures no longer exist. I overworked them and was obliged to destroy them. The attractive girl modelling for me is my girlfriend Alison Dury. She lives away but often visits me here in my studio.

Ten things you didn't know about me:

1) I am best friends with James Rudd aka Inspector Poole.

2) The postcard of my painting *Bonjour Louise* is the best selling art postcard at whichever gallery the picture's hung at (I've forgotten. You'll have to find out).

3) I know the woman who sang backing vocals on *Love Me Then Leave Me*, the B side of *Love Me Like No Other* by The Cogs, a minor post-punk, pre-Neo Romantic band. You'd have been about five, so before your time.

4) I know the guy who used to wave a chainsaw about during stage shows by the German rock band Sturm [should be Drang Ed.] back in the mid eighties. You'd have been into Wham.

5) I have a sizeable collection of hand-knitted jumpers, scarves, ties and hats. A friend hand-crafts them especially for me. She is a knittaholic.

6) My favourite pop music is early Kate Bush and German period Bowie.

7) But I prefer modern jazz. Like Evan Parker.

8) My parents won't talk to me.

9) Quite a lot of the time my cousin won't talk to me either. She doesn't charge me rent but I am expected to pay the

utilities, which is sometimes a struggle.

10) I'd really love to teach again, but am not allowed to.

*

~~LAKE HOUSE CLINIC~~
FOR COMPLETE PLONKERS

1995

Dear Jim,

Excuse the deplorable writing. Holding a pen is far from easy.

We lost touch again, didn't we, but you found me Under the Volcano and saved me again.

My counsellor reckons I don't deserve a friend like you. I agree with her. I'm a shit. A worthless shit.

Bye.

PS When you visit, please can you bring some swimming goggles? I've started as part of my keep fit campaign. Ta.

*

LAKE HOUSE CLINIC

Jim, Jim,

You are my rock. I don't know how I'd manage without you. How the hell do you do it? I mean, she was gone for good, wasn't she.

At first, I couldn't believe it was her. I thought you'd paid one of your actress friends to dress up as her. I saw her heavily distorted by the goggles as I crawled towards the edge of the pool.

Overjoyed. Utterly.

Mere words are unable to express et cetera.

Maria. Impeccably groomed and wearing a too-tight v-neck and slacks. Her first words to me were: 'You're doing it all wrong, you know. It's all about regulating when you breathe.'

I climbed out. She saw I was putting on weight at long last. I stood dripping in front of her. She said, 'Have you learnt your lesson now?'

'Definitely,' I said, shivering. I reached for my towel, but she grabbed it and held it behind her. 'If you ever deceive me again, over anything. *Anything*.' Long stare.

'I'm a hundred per cent clean,' I assured. 'This is the new me. It's taken me four months to get here.'

'Because of you – I got into a right state. I went on a month-long bender. Almost died when I set fire to Michelle's kitchen. Look –' She rolled up her sleeve. The skin around her elbow was yellow and green. 'Had to jump out the window into a tree, and she's four floors up. Dislocated it and fractured it here and here and here. I was so pissed I didn't know. There are so many pins, I could pass for the Bionic Woman.'

Just because I failed to cry, didn't mean that I wasn't ashamed. I simply apologised and begged her forgiveness.

Then she handed me my towel and said yes.

ALISON

[1979]

I think he fancies me a little. Men like to look at breasts so I pushed my chest out a few times to raise his eyebrows. Sat next to him on the sofa and leaned artfully so that he could peer down my top. My thigh was an inch away from his hand. He moved his hand in order to 'accidentally' brush my skin. A little later he experimentally 'accidentally' brushed me again. I think he is what is known as a leg man.

[1979]

Lizzie was upstairs getting the Boy dressed, James had nipped to the loo and I was downstairs with Martin, who was slumped on the sofa pretending to watch the snooker. I wasn't wearing my tights, and I knew that if I were to bend down, he would get an eyeful of my blue ones, so I went over to the sideboard for an apple and 'whoops' dropped it. Spent ages trying to retrieve it, stooping this way and that. When eventually I straightened up and looked round, Martin had contracted an eye disorder, the symptoms of which were swelling and transfixion, while Lizzie, who was standing in the doorway behind him, having witnessed the tail end of my show, so to speak, was suffering from the same complaint, only a far more virulent strain.

[1979]

The Parents, bless their cotton socks, were down the Conservative Club all last night, and have spent the day celebrating the Great Victory down at the *Cliff Hotel*, the

Conservative Club and a palatial residence by the golf course. They rolled home a few moments ago very drunk and silly. I am ashamed. Oh yes, I am ashamed. Why can't I have normal parents, like James'? Mine used to be normal. They've turned into tub-thumping Tories. It's the equivalent of birds de-evolving back into the lizards they came from. No wonder the more liberal-minded Rudds don't have anything to do with them anymore. Our mums used to be so close at one time. I can't remember the last time they stood and chatted.

I would describe myself as a socialist. But more accurately, I would describe myself as a Punk. Not the common-or-garden gob-on-you tartan tart whose *raison d'être* is to induce vomiting. I'm a political Punk. An Anarchist. I'm against The Establishment, Authority, Tradition, the Conventional, the Boring, the Bland, the Ordinary. You get in my way, you better watch out!

[1979]

Anne has seen a real live human penis in the erect state. The lanky guy she met last week in the *Ocean Room* was there again last night. He went into one of the shelters with her and displayed himself while she directed the bicycle light. She was not greatly impressed by what she saw. She said it was just like a big fat finger with a raw-meat-coloured swollen end. That girl has such a nerve. I wouldn't dare to ask to see one. She wouldn't touch it or show him her furry hole so he had a strop and stomped off.

According to *Girls and Sex*, a lot of men enjoy porn. Even our dads, I wonder? Anne reckons that men of advanced years are more likely to rely on porn as their wives are no longer interested in sex. Anne has lately discovered this to be true. Her dad, her polite, cheerful, boring, ancient dad, who reads Hammond Innes and the *Telegraph* possesses a dirty video. I was shocked when she told me. Her dad is such an unassuming man, surely too grown-up to bother with sex. Anne reckons he must have had dirty cine films as well because no one was allowed to touch the projector and film boxes without supervision. I don't think I'll ever be able to look him in his bloodshot eyes again. Or be alone in the same room with him.

When I'm middle-aged I'm going to make a point of being interested in sex, just to be different. I'm going to be so *hot*, my husband will need porn to cool himself down!

Conducted a thorough search of my parents' bedroom while they were out. No porn, although I did find the colour supplement in Dad's bedside cabinet. It was suspiciously open at a full-page portrait of Mrs Thatcher. Does he peruse this to inspire erotic dreams about our Prime Minister?

[1979]

Anne's parents went out this afternoon, so we took the opportunity to watch that video. I suppose it's because I'm not a man that it failed to make me feel sexy. The opposite, in fact. Anne reckons it would definitely turn James on. I don't agree with her. James is above lust. In the interests of Science I have suggested we sit James in front of the porn and see if a bulge appears.

[1979]

'Say cheese.'

'Cheese,' I said, ventriloquially.

'Properly.'

Snap.

'I thought you said you were taking my portrait. You're too far away.'

Snap.

Martin moved closer to the sun-lounger. 'Say cheese, then.'

'Pervert,' I said.

Snap.

[1979]

...and headed back to the others, leaving Robert to sulk. To my horror I found Anne and James not only snogging, but scratching each other's itch. I intervened. If I can't have James, no one can, unless I deem her suitable; and Anne is most certainly not suitable, being a close friend. I pulled the dirty bitch off and claimed him for myself.

I could warrant my own Aesop fable.

[1979]

The play wot we rote when we waz bored rigid tonight:

Fishing for Compliments

He: Hello there, miss. Out a bit late, aren't you?

She: That's a lovely long rod you've got.

He: Good for catching fish, love. It's manufactured for that very porpoise.

She: What's your name?

He: Ray. Yours?

She: Annette.

He: You'll make a fine catch, Annette.

She: Do you have much tackle? Mind if I hold it?

He: Ere! You be careful with my prize rod.

She: There's nothing I don't know about tackle and flies.

He: Blimey, love, that was an impressive cast. Far out!

She: Deep enough for you?

He: Can't wait to tell me mates. Ere, you only wearing flip-flops, come and warm your eels by my Tilley lamp.

She: The end's twitching already.

He: Looks like a big one. They do say if a rod twitches like that...

She: There's no time for cod philosophy. Hold me round the middle while I reel the beast in.

He: (much grunting) Blimey. We're getting dragged towards the surf. Ere! What's happening to your legs?

She: Oh Ray, promise you won't mention my tail to a single sole.

He: Shame. You'd make a big splash down the pub if you were to a-pier. Are you married? Is there a buoy in your life?

She: I'm happy drifting. I've never wanted to be tide down until now. Yourself?

He: Currently shingle.

She: Why don't you kick your wellies off and come to My Plaice? It's a bit of a dive, but I'm sure you'll love to see my sandy bottom.

He: I'd prefer to sea chest.

The End.

We were having fits of laughter in the glass shelter, nearly pissing ourselves, as we devised our sketch. An elderly couple scowled at us, assuming no doubt we'd been taking drugs. We had the idea of writing several short two-handers and performing them down by the yacht pond. Only trouble is, I'm not as extrovert as James. I'm okay if there's a crowd, but I'd get terribly self-conscious if there were just two of us.

Other ideas for sketches: Mad professor invents robotic woman to keep himself company, but she takes over and he has to invent robot man to put her in her place... Boy asking big sister about the facts of life. Turns out he knows more than she does... Two goldfish discuss life etc... Two porn actors talk really intellectually while bonking... Talking weighing machine (James stole this idea from NF Simpson)... Artist and model. The model gradually takes over the painting and the artist becomes the model...

[1979]

After years of going there with our parents, James and I have ventured into *The Links* by ourselves. It felt weird to be ordering our own drinks – proper alcoholic ones at that. We were afraid the barmaid might chuck us out, but as she's seen us so many times before, I suppose it seemed natural for her to serve us. She even asked how my mum was. We stayed in the saloon bar, which is where the people of our age hang out. A few interesting-looking regulars, such as the ginger-haired army-type whose dad's the butcher in the High Street. Nuclear Scott is convinced the US is poised to eliminate the Soviets in a war that could be over in a few minutes. We've done all that in school, and I think he's probably right to be alarmed, but I disagree with his belief that stockpiling weapons is going to save us. Also in *The Links* was a tall, very pretty blonde called Julie, who had better not make a play for James otherwise I'll pluck her bright blue eyes out and throw them to Oliver. We sat sipping our beers with Julie, who's actually quite nice. At fifteen, she's a fellow under-ager. Nuclear Scott has an off-putting habit of staring at people. Not people: me. He leaned on the bar just gawping at my legs. He must have been enjoying himself because when he ordered a fresh beer, the landlord said, 'Two pints in one evening, Scott? That's the first time in three years.' Next time, if there is a next time, I'll make a point of sitting out of his line of sight. I refuse to be some kind of free porn.

[1979]
'Cheese!'
  'Cheese.'
  Snap.
So what if he could see my white ones? It was only a bit of fun. He's married, for goodness sake. Besides, aren't I a kind of pseudo-sister? Brothers and sisters flirt, I'm sure they do. Flirt and fight. I'm James' sister, near-enough, aren't I?
  Lizzie stopped speaking to me by the end of our day out. I offered to carry the Boy and she just walked off. The sour-faced bitch ought to thank me for cheering up her husband.

[1979]

James was rehearsing so I didn't take Oliver down to the beach as usual, just along Marine Parade as far as *The Links* and back. Martin was out walking. He caught up with me and we walked together. He was in an odd mood. Said I looked nice when I looked the same as I usually do. Laughed too much at my not-particularly-funny funny remarks. Kept make a clicking noise at Oliver to bond with him (Oliver ignored him totally, he's very particular). Wanted to know if James was rehearsing tomorrow as well.

[1979]

M is definitely pursuing me. He claimed he just happened to be out walking when he ran into me. Asked an awful lot of questions about my taste in boys, and about me and him, how I felt about him. I began to enjoy the attention. It was like having my hair brushed by someone. The fact he is a married man made it all the more exciting.

[1979]

[...]

He promised I'd enjoy the next time more. I can't see how. I consulted Anne on the subject. She's an old hand these days: once a week at least. She wanted to know if I'd succumbed at long last to the temptation of James. When I told her who, she called me an irresponsible idiot and ordered me not to see him again.

[1979]

No pain this time. No pleasure either, once the initial warm-up had ended. To pass the time I timed him by his thrusts. Assuming that one thrust equals one second, today's FABULOUS fuck lasted four-and-a-half minutes. When you add that to the warm-up of about three-and-a-half minutes plus the ten minutes recovery time, that's a total of eighteen OH SO WONDERFUL minutes. If you were to add to this the walk to and from the car, plus the car journey each way and a whole week of waiting, just for a three-second squirt of goo, you have to wonder if this lust thing is perhaps Nature's cruellest joke. Would it be the same if I was someone else? Why does he not drive Lizzie to Benacre anymore? Is it because he is bored with her? When will I become boring? Does he have his next conquest already lined up? Julie? Anne? Oliver?

[1979]

It is OVER, thank cod, thank COD. No way was I going to let him screw me in the marital bed dressed as some stupid bloody *Carry On* nurse. What's the matter with me as I am? Lizzie wears stockings and suspenders and high heels. Lizzie wears crotchless knickers. Well if Lizzie is so wonderfully sexy why is he so interested in fucking me? Apparently I'm crap at sex, whatever he means by that. Inexperienced, I suppose. Not enough rock and roll.

[1980]

James overacted his way through *Salad Days* in order to impress Julie, who was in the front row doing her best not to appear as bored shitless as she obviously was. The more she tried not to look bored, the hammier James grew, so that by the end he was romping about like a panto dame. The worst performance of an otherwise illustrious career, although the audience thought he was a hoot, which I suppose is what matters. The next production is to be *Oklahoma!* I was asked if I would like to participate, and I've put my name down as one of the townsfolk. Yee-ha!

[1980]

Just call me Your Majesty from now on. I am the new Head

Girl! Huzzah! Three cheers for me!

The downside is, I'll have to sit on the stage during assemblies, next to that supreme nerd Jeremy Gowan. He is sexually repressed. And boring. We had to ascend the stage this morning to receive the official handshake, and already loads of people have been coming up asking if I'm going out with him.

[1980]

Nice seafront cuddle with James in the dark spoilt by his yakking about my applying to Norwich instead of Oxford. If I apply to Norwich, so will he etc.

Twit.

[September 1980]

'This morning's reading is taken from *The Gospel According to Mark*...' I'm not remotely religious. What a hypocrite I was, therefore, to stand in front of the school and spout scripture. I felt like substituting wrong words to create a stir, but I don't have the guts. I was so nervous having all those eyes trained on me, my left leg started twitching like one of Galvini's frog leg experiments. I tried to disguise it by putting my weight on it, but that seemed to make it worse. Plus, I got hissed at by the Head to speak up.

I could resign, but it won't look good on my report. I stand a better chance of getting into Oxford if I see out my reign as Head Girl.

Prefect duty at lunchtime. I was assigned Smokers' Corner, and reluctantly went to check it out. Half the bloody school was there puffing the weed, including people I socialise with down *The Links*. I couldn't very well clear the area, because that would make me a public hypocrite. Nor could I accept the offer of a fag and stand there. So what I did was smirk and say, 'I'm supposed to tell you off and report you,' snigger conspiratorially with them all and wander off. Thus I was able to not only show

I was in a position of authority, but also that I would bend the rules as I saw fit.

As I was walking back into the building I heard Old Morris the Deputy Head saying to the Head that she would be paying a visit to smokers' corner because she'd seen several people making their way over there. The Head told her not to worry as Alison had gone to take names.

Short of rushing back to warn them, which would make me look desperate for mates, I sought out Jeremy, who was by himself nibbling crisps in the common room. I told him half the school was in smokers' corner and I was too shit-scared to say anything to them. ('Please don't tell anyone I'm such a coward.') Did he think he could do any better?

It was like watching Clark Kent turn into Superman. He threw his crisps aside, took a deep breath, and boldly marched off. Ten minutes later he returned to the common room a minor hero, having been observed confronting the smokers by the Deputy Head herself, as she sneaked round from a different direction.

[September 1980]

Today's assembly was all about breaking school rules. Following yesterday's incident at smokers' corner, anyone found lighting up on school property (teachers and ground staff not included) will be instantly suspended. I had to read some relevant bible verses about one's body being a temple. I didn't know where to look while the Head ranted. I felt so guilty. If I'd kept my mouth shut, several Links mates wouldn't have had letters sent to their parents.

During lunchtime, while I was reading by myself in the common room, Jeremy sidled up.

'Crisp?' He tentatively held the packet under my nose. I told him I hated cheese and onion and carried on with my reading. Aware of him observing me, I asked him if there was anything else he wanted. He said, 'Not really,' in that pinched, nerdy voice of his, adding, 'Well, I was just wondering if...' Cue what seemed like several minutes of beating-around-the bush. How did I spend my evenings? I lived near the seafront, didn't I? I had a dog, yes? I knew what he wanted from the way he'd been lurking by the careers leaflets, pretending to peruse while really he was building up the courage to come and ask me out.

I interrupted him before he asked me and I had to disappoint him. I said, 'Most evenings I hang out with James.'

This didn't deter him. He'd been making enquiries and had discovered from Anne that I wasn't hitched to James. 'Do you fancy, erm, do you think you'd like to, erm...' His cheeks were on fire, and salivary glands were on meltdown, causing him to punctuate every utterance by swallowing. This was fun to watch.

'There's a good film on at the Regal tonight.'

'Oh yes? Which film's that, then,' I said coolly.

He couldn't remember. Saliva welled under his tongue and had to be cleared away. 'I was, erm, did you fancy, erm, seeing as how we're, erm, you know, Head Boy and, erm, Head, you know Girl, if you fancied, like, erm, going. Erm. To the, you know, the Regal. You like films, don't you.'

'No, thanks. Thanks for asking, though. I prefer foreign-language films.' I always enjoying specifying my interest in Euro Cinema. Maybe I'm just a snob at heart.

Unequipped to discuss Bergman or Rohmer, he excused himself and returned to the careers stand. Like an annoying fly that keeps lapping the room when all the doors and windows are open, he came back.

'The thing is, what I was thinking was, it's like this.' He sat, leaning his cheesy-oniony orifice closer. 'I've not said anything to anyone. About the tip-off.'

'What tip-off? Have you gone and got yourself circumcised?'

'Smokers' corner,' he said. 'No one knows yet that you tipped off me and the Deputy Head.'

I put my book down. 'I did not tip-off the Deputy Head. Or you.'

'Erm, you did. You told me to go and sort them out because you were too scared to. And you told me not to tell anyone. And I won't, if you, erm...'

'Go to the pictures with you.' I saved him the bother of finishing his blackmail threat.

'Well?' He was half smirking, confident he'd got me over a barrel.

'I wouldn't be seen dead going to the pictures with you,' I said. His smirk faltered. 'And I certainly won't be blackmailed into going out with probably the least liked bloke in the school.'

After masticating this unpalatable slice of truth, he said, 'I'll just have to spread it around that you reported the smokers. No one will trust you again.'

'They'll trust me even less if it gets out I hang around with Jeremy Gowan outside school.' He recoiled at this, as if I'd given him a good slap. 'Go on, then. Go and spread it around. I won't stop you. I'll just deny it. I think people are more likely to believe me than the School Twat, don't you?'

He returned to the careers leaflets, his face conspicuously pillar box red. Mobbsy, who had been watching our *tête-à-tête* from the other side of the common room called out: 'I'm afraid it's going to be another romantic night in with the gerbils, Jezza, old mate.' Everyone laughed, and Head Boy snatched a leaflet at random (*Join the Army*) and slumped down in a far corner to read it.

James, the sweetie, has offered to go and put the fear of Pinter into Gowan. He has a few relevant threatening speeches in his repertoire. I've asked him to wait for my signal.

[September 1980]

Dirty look from Gowan as we ascended the stage together.

Has he told, or hasn't he?

Visited smokers' corner during lunch with the intention of lighting up. I figured that to be seen to be smoking would stand me in good stead should my trustworthiness be put to the test. Then, just as I was about to get my ciggies out, I thought: what if someone here would try to blackmail me for breaking the rules?

So I walked away.

[September 1980]

Gowan has apologised for last week! Amazing. Naturally I was suspicious, but I do believe him to be genuinely sorry. Mind you, the fact that I'd not spoken to him for several days might have had something to do with it. Plus there are rumblings coming from the direction of the staff room that if we aren't getting on he will have to relinquish his position to Mobbsy. They won't replace me because the Head and Deputy Head like me too much.

[October 1980]

Half term. No rest for the wicked. Anglo-Saxon translation has taken out most of today. If it wasn't a requirement for entry, would blissfully bury this *boc* where the *sunne* don't shine. Got a little pissed earlier on, but it's worn off now. *The Links* is rapidly becoming my fourth home (my second is the Rudds', my third, Anne's). Dad has just been sitting on the end of my bed offering his unwanted opinion on inebriation. It's all about *face* with him. What'll people think, etc? What'll the neighbours etc?

Who gives a toss what the neighbours etc?

Now I've completely wound myself up.

To wind myself back down, I think I need a damn good etc.

[November 8 1980]

Cooking lessons with Mater after she caught me hard-boiling an egg in the kettle.

Today:

Lesson One. How to boil an egg correctly.

Lesson Two. Perfect toast.

Tomorrow morning:

Lesson Three. Basic scrambled egg.

Lesson Four. Perfectly grilled bacon.

She asked me to go to the butcher in the high street for half a pound of streaky; which is a variety of bacon. Old ginger bonce was serving, a poppy attached to his overall like an extra splash of blood. I find him creepy, I'm not sure why; but all his female customers seem to love him. Maybe the secret's in the repartee. He flatters them. He remembers things they've told him on previous visits. He notices if they're looked tired, or peaky: 'You ought to be careful Mrs Webb, there's a nasty flu doing the rounds.' 'And how's your elbow today, Mrs Wright? Oh much better: you couldn't move it last Wednesday, could you.' 'And how can I help you, Alison?'

'Half a pound of streaky,' I said.

He weighed the slices. '*The Links* tonight?'

'Not sure. Depends on what the others are up to.'

'Well, you know I'll always be propping up the bar until TA,' he said. 'I'd buy you a drink if you didn't have anyone to go with.'

Two woman behind me started cooing and nudging me on the arm. 'You're in there, love,' they said.

Scott turned on them in mock disgust. 'Your minds, ladies! I was just being friendly, that's all.' With a practised flourish he sealed the bacon into a bag. He grinned at me. 'I know full well Alison's already spoken for.'

And I know he knows full well that James is just a good friend. The creep.

Afterwards I caught the bus to Lowestoft to see Nan.

While I was there, some old bloke came round selling poppies for poppy day, which is on Tuesday. 'I refuse to wear one of those things,' Nan said to him, and when the man asked why, she said, 'Because I don't believe in War.'

The man said the poppies were not about war, they were about remembering those who'd died in conflict.

'Alright, let's remember them, shall we,' Nan said. 'The tens of thousands of teenage boys our generals sent to die in the Belgian mud. Did they have a choice? And what exactly where they fighting for? God? For King and Country?' She spoke with such venom as to make For King and Country sound like swearwords.

The man said, 'All right. So next time some Hitler rises up to jackboot his way across Europe, what will you do when he reaches the Channel? Stand to one side and wave him across?'

'We have to use every peaceful means at our disposal to ensure that Hitlers don't happen in the first place.'

'That's easier said than done. Very naïve way of thinking, that.'

Nan made clucking noises of exasperation and slammed the door. The letterbox opened and the poppy seller called through it: 'You know, I've met some short-sighted idiots in my time, but you're... To think I risked my life defending this country. I was in Burma. And Suez.'

'You certainly travel a long way away to defend our little island,' Nan shouted back.

[November 9 1980]

The results of cooking lesson number two were deemed edible by the Mater and Pater, and they were still alive this evening. Next weekend I have promised to subject the Rudds to my newly acquired culinary skills.

As it's Remembrance Sunday, there was the usual parade to

Gorleston Church followed by the usual couple of minutes of silence. Surely it's high time someone came up with a new formula for remembering all those poor sods who sacrificed their lives for this shabby little island.

James and I went to observe the proceedings. We stood on the corner by the library while Army, Navy, Air Force, Scouts, Sea Scouts, Girl Guides, etc traipsed by, and followed the procession towards the church. I picked out Nuclear Scott, although James couldn't. We hung around outside St Andrew's church, and when the all-important silence fell we started a loud conversation based upon the interrogation speech from Pinter's *The Dumb Waiter*. We didn't plan it, it just happened.

James first, after the eleventh clong of the bell: 'I say, I say. Why did the chicken cross the road?'

'Which chicken? Which road?'

'The road that was crossed by the chicken.'

'I say, I say. Road? Chicken?'

James: clucking noise.

Me: 'I say, I say. Which fowl?'

'The foul fowl. The foul terror of this touch-and-go town. It should be obvious.'

'Obvious.'

'Obvious which chicken, which road.'

etc

We were shushed after five seconds but persisted with our nonsense. A couple of stern-looking women bore down on us and ordered us to show some respect or clear off. Other people were beginning to move towards us so we scrammed, whooping and whistling all the way back towards the library.

Phoned Nan from the harbour to tell her what we'd been up to. She was not greatly impressed. In fact, she was downright critical.

'That was a terrible way to behave,' she scolded. I tried to defend what we'd done, but Nan cut in. 'You should know how much Remembrance Day means to a lot of people.'

I said, 'Nobody really uses that two-minute silence to remember. It's just for show, like the prayer in school assembly. They just stand there wondering if they've polished their shoes enough.'

'Oh, but people *do* remember,' Nan insisted. 'You would, if you'd lost a brother, or a loved one.'

I couldn't understand Nan. Railing against poppies and war one moment, while the next, she's going along with it all. I started to wish I'd never phoned up, and couldn't wait for my ten pence to run out. I was so angry I started crying, and as soon as it opened, we went into the *King William IV* for a pint.

[November 1980]

It sounds so pathetic, but what I'd really like is a boyfriend. Someone to go out with. Someone who'll love me, desire me, be obsessed by me. Someone who'll feel ten feet tall because he's with me. Who wouldn't feel intimidated by James. But where is this loving, desiring, obsessing boy to be found? Not at school, not down the pub.

Discussed my love life with Anne in *The Links* while the gang were playing snooker. She recommended I go out with James or simply lower my sights.

[Tuesday November 11 1980]

Gowan and I led assembly with two readings. Gowan quoted from the bible about turning the other cheek, while I read Wilfred Owen's *Strange Meeting*. Thanks to James' seafront tutorial last night, I was able to project my voice nicely towards the back of the hall without making it sound forced. I was really nervous (a wonky-leg moment when I first stood to recite) until I blanked out where I was and concentrated on getting the meaning of the poem across. I have to say my audience remained remarkably attentive. No one shuffled, or coughed.

And when I'd finished, there was a stunned silence five heart-thumps long before the Head said, 'Let us pray.'

Two-minute silence at eleven. I was in English. Bird and Robinson, who really fancy themselves as comedians, started mucking about, making pathetic farty noises and giggling until Dawson glared at them. At least my disruption on Sunday had been politically motivated. This was just puerile.

Interesting discussion in smokers' corner about who would and wouldn't fight for this country in the event of war. Out of ten smokers (I succumbed to the temptation of the weed) only Chris Fenn said he'd volunteer. Anne said if there was a war, we'd all be obliterated anyway. There are quite a few airbases in East Anglia, and it's likely the Soviets have missiles pointing at them. Anne said, 'We'll hear a siren and four minutes later we'll be dead. That's just enough time for a bonk. Or in your case, Chris, eight wanks.'

I wonder what I *would* do if the four-minute warning went off? Ideally I'd have Oliver with me. And James. The three of us would hole up somewhere and wait for the big bang. If James wanted to be inside me, I'd let him, and we'd have a big bang all of our very own. Perhaps the radiation would act a bit like the lava at Pompeii or Herculaneum and perfectly preserve us in the fucking position, and in hundreds of years' time, when we're no longer radioactive, we'd be put into a museum. Sex will have been replaced by test tube babies. 'On your left, ladies and gentlemen, unidentified citizens of the Borough of Gorleston making the two-backed beast. If I shine my torch, you will see how things used to be done by our primitive ancestors.'

Nan came to tea. She agreed with Dad that my cauliflower cheese was more like cauliflower chewing gum. I didn't think it was too bad for a first attempt, although seconds would have been unthinkable. (I can feel it working its way undigested around my gut. I haven't stopped farting since I got into bed.

One spark and there'd be a thermoflatulent explosion big enough to wipe out Gorleston and Yarmouth.)

Nan accompanied me when I walked Oliver down to the seafront. She apologised for being curt on the phone. 'The thing is, you wouldn't attend a funeral and stand there laughing, would you. You'd show decorum. Remembrance Day is a funeral service, and if you attend, you have to behave appropriately.' When I mentioned the poppy seller, she said: 'That's a different thing altogether. I don't need a badge in order to remember the dead. Margaret Thatcher wears one at the cenotaph, and yet she wouldn't think twice about packing the armed forces off to fight, if she was required to. If peace was so important to her, she'd reduce military expenditure and jaw-jaw a lot more. This world is on the brink of a nuclear holocaust and all she does is build more and more weapons. You'd have hoped a woman prime minister would have been more interested in preserving human life than she has been.'

Nan told me about the peace marches she used to go on during the 1950s and 60s. 'Aldermaston was the big one,' she said. 'There was a real feeling that we could make a difference. I'm more cynical these days. That's not to say I wouldn't carry a placard to Downing Street if I believed it would have any effect.' Later we looked through the photo albums. Even in black and white you can see Nan was pretty darn hot when she was younger; long wavy Hollywood hair, sultry eyes and a self-consciously half-open kiss-me-quick mouth. When Mum was out of the room Nan picked out a couple of men in a wartime dance hall she'd 'been particularly friendly with' (= fucked). 'The swinging sixties started a lot earlier than people imagine,' she said.

Dad drove her back after the nine o'clock news. I strolled over to *chez* Rudd. James was already in bed, reading *Under Milk Wood*, which is to be his school production next month. He's learning the part of the first narrator, and is in the process of developing a suitable accent. He wanted me to climb in with him and read the other parts. I wasn't in the mood, so I persuaded him to get dressed and join me for a stroll and a cigarette. The sky was suitably starless and bible black. We ended up walking to Hopton and back along the beach. We hardly spoke, we were so busy enjoying the walk. With anyone else, even Anne, I'd have felt obliged to invent conversation for the hell of it.

And then, just as we were nearing our houses, he went and spoilt the hour-and-a-half of bliss by going all whiney and teary on me: 'Let's both apply to do English in Norwich. I don't think I'll be able to live apart from you.'

a) James would make a crap English student. He's an actor.

b) Why the hell would I want to go to the University of East Anglia when I stand a chance of getting into Oxford?

c) Harsh as it sounds, I think our relationship would benefit from a period of enforced separation. There's nothing stopping us visiting each other while we're away.

[Saturday December 21 1980]
To begin at the beginning.

I write this on Sunday, eleven o'clock in the morning. I am sitting up in my bed with this diary propped on a pillow, and a hot water bottle under the pillow to relieve the toothache in my poor old tum. I feel bleary and hungover even though I haven't been drinking. My parents have been in twice to tell me off for phoning so late, and for not warning them about the 'party'. Mum's gone all KGB because my clothes don't pong of smoke or alcohol. Exactly what sort of party was it. Who was there. Where was it. I didn't know? Then describe the house. Suspecting that I'd been injecting myself with drugs, the old hag checked my arms for punctures. Then she confiscated my clothes for the washing machine. I wonder if she could smell James on my knickers and hanky. She must know about male reproductive fluids. She has had sex – once. (*Yuk*.) Unless I was created in a laboratory.

Yes, folks, I have succumbed to intimacy with my dear James, and I'm not exactly sure how I feel about that. It was hearing him telling me he loved me that did it. It all happened so quickly. He said he loved me. I said I loved him too. Then after a kiss that made the snow melt around us, he *dragged* me like a caveman to find a place to *ravish* me. I could've easily stopped him, as he's extremely obedient, but the truth is, I wanted him to ravish me.

He found a beach hut that would serve as a boudoir. It reeked of paint and putty and was freezing from having no door, but I wasn't backing out now. Anyway, I was too randy to care how cold it was. We stripped quickly in the dark, and lay under our coats warming our hands in our armpits before attempting to touch one another. I had to take charge of the technical side as poor James hadn't a clue. As I'd expected, he'd splurted and shrivelled before my itch had been scratched. Thanks to a good hard Dury snog and some nifty handling, it wasn't long before he was up and running again.

While the sex was lovely, our friendship should really have been above, way above physical pleasure. I felt as though I'd broken a law. Sullied our friendship.

[Sunday December 22 1980]

James wanted to continue our new intimacy. So did I, when I looked up and my love, my life entered the room. But resolved to end this now, however difficult it proves. How to wash away the stain of what we did, though? Hypnotism? 'Ven I count to sree all sexual desire vill cease.'

Sexual desire is not bad per se. Sexual desire between two close friends is [heavily scribbled out]

For one-and-a-half decades we lived almost as brother and sister. *Almost*, because I don't deny there was sexual attraction.

(We confessed in the beach hut how attracted we were to one another.) In the space of one evening we ended years and years of innocent flirting. It was like being thrown out of Eden. Or is that too melodramatic a comparison?

[Wednesday December 25 1980]
[...]

James got into a right strop. I don't blame him. He doesn't deserve the way I've messed him around. We took Oliver for a walk. As soon as we arrived at the beach he ignored me and mooched off with Oliver, throwing pieces of driftwood for him to fetch. Then James found an ancient golf ball, peeled off the casing and started used Oliver as target practice, lobbing it at his flanks. Oliver, assuming this was a new kind of game, yelped when the missile struck and truffled in the sand for it. Except he couldn't get anywhere near it. The ball was self-destructing; threads of rubber were firing off it. James simply picked it up and threw it again. And again and again; each time harder than the last. He was relentless. It was alarming to watch. I called Oliver to me but he wouldn't come. 'Stop being a prick, James,' I said, though not so that he could hear. 'Stop being such a spoilt prick. You can't have everything you want. You want me to change my life to fit in with yours. I refuse to. (Oliver!) I gave you what you wanted in Southwold but you're greedy; you want more. More us. Like your brother wanted more. Oh, I've never told you about your brother, have I. More precisely, your brother and me. (Oliver!)We had an affair, you see. When? Oh, last summer. It was the culmination of weeks of flirting following my birthday party, when, if you remember, he spent the entire day being obsessed with me. He took me down the coast after work and rogered me on the beach at Benacre Ness. My first time. Which explains why I was such an easy lay in Southwold. You could slip straight in there, no worries. (Oliver! Oliver, come here!) How long did it go on for? I like to think it ended after three weeks. He wanted more from me than just plain old me. I mean, what is the deal with nurses' uniforms and French Maid uniforms and stockings? Stockings make legs look ugly. Three times, then. Then we finished the affair, and I stayed away from the house. But I showed I was grown up and went back after he apologised. And then (Olly!) then the screwing started all over again. This time on my terms. He'd insulted me, you see. He'd said I was bad at sex and I was determined to prove him wrong. I wanted to be the best lay he's ever had and is ever likely to get. And I didn't care if I hurt Lizzie after what she'd said about me, that I was basically little more than a posh tart. Oh, we were so discreet, James. So quick and businesslike. Half the fun lay in the planning. The when and where and how of the operations. I planned everything like a battle campaign. I'd make sure I was walking Oliver down such-and-such a road at such-and-such a time so that Martin could drive by and collect me and whisk me away to a lonely spot. Or else I'd let myself into his garage at a particular time for a quick ride on his bonnet. Or, and this is where my whoring becomes most outrageous, we'd be over your brother's and I'd give a secret signal and he'd pop upstairs, and two minutes later I'd go up to the bathroom and he'd be in there all ready for a thirty second knee-trembler up against the bathroom wall. Thirty seconds is a long time when your wife and brother and son are sitting downstairs. I could come in thirty seconds, if I was sufficiently aroused and nervous. Once, we – in the kitchen when I popped through to grab a plate of biscuits. You won't remember. The signal on this occasion is a protracted yawn. I yawn, then, and Martin goes into the kitchen to fill the kettle and ready himself. Precisely two minutes later, and terrified that you, Lizzie or your nephew will catch us, I calmly go into the kitchen, where I lean over the kitchen table and Martin takes me from behind like a good opportunist dog should. Less than twenty seconds, James. And we've both come powerfully while you are two rooms away laughing at

Morecambe and Wise. How long did this affair go on for? Weeks, James. Months. It is still going on. And you know nothing of it. I am his whore and I was your virgin. I gave myself to you as a gift, so our love-making was little more than an early Christmas present. The selfless gift from a whore. (Here, boy!) So do you love me now, because look at you hurting my dog – *our* dog, because he's yours as much as mine – all because you can't get your own way? Well I'm not going to cave in. We're friends, the best friends two friends can get, but we're not lovers. (Oliver! Come here! Here!) We can never be lovers. Same as Martin and I can never be friends.'

Through my tears I made out the blurred shape of James turning to look at me. I wiped my eyes on my coat sleeve and was able to see he had been crying too. We hugged, a long, long hug he took as a cue for greater intimacy. He said he loved me, wanted me, couldn't exist without me, said that I was the only thing he could think of. I kissed him to silence him. A mistake, because I enjoyed it. We would have continued kissing forever if a rambunctious Alsatian hadn't homed in on Oliver.

We must never kiss again.

[January 1981]
Disaster. Discovered trysting at the new pick-up place, in the field behind the lay-by on the A12. Scott unexpectedly emerged from the ground with a torch. M strangely complacent, no doubt because I am such a prized mistress.

[January 1981]
Martin has struck a deal with Scott and acquired a key to the padlock for the listening station hatch. Have missed the first rehearsal of *Oklahoma!* Told James I had a sore throat and couldn't sing. I hate lying to him, but it's rapidly becoming second nature.

Pub followed by night manoeuvres. So-called listening

station is simply a cramped underground hidey-hole containing a bunk bed and a government-issue bucket. I would prefer to be vaporised than be stuck down there with someone I despised.

[January 1981]

That raffish art student showed up again. I made the effort to say hello this time and he came to sit with us. Anne said no way would she ever let him or anyone draw her because she hates to be stared at. Julie offered to pose. I think I would if invited to.

[January 1981]

I am totally, totally pissed, and it's wonderful. I feel like I'm on a Pleasure Beach ride, my head's going round and round even though I'm in bed. Today's Darren's brother's birthday and he came into the pub and bought us all a drink. Everyone got totally pissed and we kept putting *Vienna* on the jukebox and singing along. We got so loud Tim Collins stopped serving drinks and fetched Big Jim, who threatened to chuck us all out and ban us for a week, so we went as quiet as oldies after that. At chucking out time a gang of us went down to the beach and smoked The Weed. There wasn't much to go around, though, and, anyway, I hate the taste of the stuff these days. I really like the look of my girl's bits. Meg Hunt. I've got a mirror between my legs so as to have a good look at myself. I've never really studied me before. It's lovely when you ease the labia aside and see bright bubblegum pink. Like getting a sudden glimpse of an expensive coat lining. A shame I'm alone in appreciating the beauty of Meg Hunt. It's far nicer to look at than blokes' bits. More compact. Tidier. There, I'm all packed away again. Hidden by my little bush. If you came from another planet and knew nothing about human reproduction, you'd never know there's a way in here.

[the following day]

Ouch.

Very ouch.

Never again. Too ill to get up, although I will have to as The Sow is being most insistent. She is easily disgusted by lassitude. And pools of vomit left in kitchen sinks. And knickers and socks discarded in bathrooms. *She* never behaved like this when she was my age. *She* never over-indulged. *She* never made a fool of herself in public. It was only a matter of time before I was sleeping around and getting a reputation. Well I've got news for you, Sow, you're too late. I'm a much-ridden and much-sought after Raleigh.

[January 1981]

James looks and sounds as decidedly camp as a cowboy, like the guy in The Village People. If he's not careful people will start calling this musical *Oklahomo!*

James hates (and I quote) that arrogant, flick-fringed, living forgery. Why? He wouldn't say, but I know it's because he's jealous, which is simultaneously annoying and flattering. He must never get to know about my whoring; it would kill him.

[February 1981]

The whore has been busy. If she were to charge, she would be rich in no time.

[March 1981]

Twice in the same evening not a thing to be proud of. (Five minutes-ish; seven minutes forty-four seconds.)

The main thing is not to get emotionally involved, to remain apart from the activity. When you think about it, all that's wanted anyway is the flesh, not the me that lives in it. No one can winkle that out, however deep they might delve.

[March 1981 (flier for *Oklahoma!* stapled to page)]

Okla... Okla... Homa... Homa...

A fine production. James was brilliant. He really knows how to connect with an audience. The sets were bare but effective. Shame I'd missed so many rehearsals and couldn't take part. A wonderful piss-up afterwards in the *Pier Hotel*. Felt amazingly proud of James, and extremely jealous of the camaraderie of the troupe. I felt such an outsider. Half the time James forgot I was even there. I actually left the pub on my own just before closing time but turned round and went back inside when I saw those vengeful hags who'd chased Anne and me queuing to go into the *Ocean Room*.

[June 1981]
Sunday afternoon tryst and tristesse. Watched poppy heads stirred by the breeze nodding over the hatch-hole. Imagined I was buried looking up from my coffin. Six minutes six seconds, start to finish.

[July 1981]
No love-bites, I tell him, and what does he go and do? Bite me. And now there's a red mark the size of a one p piece below my right collar bone.

[July 1981]
[...]
And so I have been loved for once. Properly loved. Adored and loved. W worships me. *Vidi, vici, veni*! I am now responsible for de-virginating three men. I could advertise in the *Yellow Pages*.

[July 1981]
W kissed every square inch of me in the studio this evening because, he said, every part of me is precious. I made him kiss one particular square inch over and over again. Then we fucked brilliantly until half midnight.

[Editor's note: there are many, many entries similar to the above which I am omitting in the interests of credibility. Suffice it to say, W was a remarkably talented lover.]

[August 1981]

Too pissed to hold the pen hardly. I have the grades! I can go to Oxford!! The joy, the relief!!! I can make a clean start. My lover too wet behind the beers, I've discovered. He's started whining about missing me. He even suggested we get ourselves engaged. I'd never have thought he was so conventional. If only James had an identical twin. I'd keep one of them for friendship, and the other for a full relationship, and they'd be *au fait* with the set-up so there wouldn't be any jealousy between them.

[August 1981]

Very rude pose in watercolours, flaps wide, based on a picture in the *Egon Schiele* book. My last ever pose, I have decided. Raunchy little bonk afterwards. *Veni! Veni!*

[September 1981]

W took me to see *Tess* in Yarmouth. He claims to be a Hardy *aficionado*, yet while he was out of the room, I plucked the paperback from his shelf in order to reacquaint myself with the opening and found a bookmark one third of the way in, where he'd abandoned his attempt to read it. To satisfy my curiosity, when we were on the bus to Yarmouth, I quizzed him on the latter stages of the plot: he started changing the subject, which means he hadn't a clue. Why he has to lie, I don't know. I wouldn't think less of him.

Anyway, the movie was a very pretty-looking adaptation with an annoyingly very pretty Tess played by Klaus Kinski's daughter. (James would have found her German-Mummerset hilarious, though, and had some fun with it.) The Boyfriend was mesmerised by the woman, which made me feel inadequate to say the least. He kept phewing to himself every time her face filled the screen. I refused to hold hands with him for the middle hour. Not that he noticed. I know why he fancies her so much. It's because she resembles Claire. Facially. Same long nose, over-ripe mouth and heavy eyebrows.

Afterwards he was reluctant to quit the cinema and refused to tell me why we were lurking in the foyer while it emptied of traffic. Then he made me go to the counter and distract the girl. When I asked how, he told me to just improvise. So feeling like a complete berk, I went and struck up a conversation about forthcoming presentations until he slunk beside me and dragged me into the night.

He'd pilfered a *Tess* poster.

Imagine if he'd been caught. I'd have been his accomplice. I was furious. As we hurried for the bus stop I said, 'What are you intending to do with that? Wank over it?'

His haughty response: 'Don't be so disgusting. I'm going to put her into a painting. She's sublime.'

He unfurled her in *The Links* for the delectation of the rabble. I was fuming. After all, he'd never thought to take any of *my* portraits to the local in order to show *me* off. (I'd have objected, but that's beside the point.) I wanted to tear that bloody poster to shreds. Needless to say there was no physical intimacy between us tonight.

And no, I do not want to go and see the film again tomorrow.

[September 1981]

Girls' farewell night out. Me, Anne, Julie. *Links*, *Cliff Hotel*, then to Yarmouth and *151*, where we boogied the night away surrounded by Debby Harry-wannabes and ghostly-ghastly Banshees. Brilliant fun. No blokes in tow. All boarders repelled (and there were plenty of offers for all three of us). Tears flowed in the taxi home. Mine and Anne's to start with, then Julie joined in: 'Because when everyone's eventually cleared off to uni, the pub's going to be dead. It's going to be horrible. Just me and Nuclear Scott,' she said.

'One very good reason to become teetotal,' I said.

[September 1981]

Two farewell parties in the same evening although the first, at Anne's, could more accurately be described as a gathering. It was a civilised affair presided over by Anne's parents. Enjoyable, but too prim-and-Pimms for my liking, with triangular sandwiches, ambient Mozart and carefully posed group photos. The second party, in Darren's house, was a drunken riot. Took the boyfriend to one side and informed him we were now officially 'over'. He was surprisingly and gratifyingly sorrowful. Not at all what I'd anticipated. I granted him a valedictory hug (with much kissing) during which he degenerated from morose to uncharacteristic sobby. No boy has shed tears over me. And even though these were ten per cent proof, they were heartfelt and set me wondering if I ought to hang on to him. A short while later, however, I noticed Julie had taken it upon herself to console him, permitting his hands to roam where they wished. I forgave them because she was drunk and Wilson was simply being Wilson. Needless to say, we continue to be 'over'.

James was next in the queue. Very polite and restrained parting in the kitchen of same party. A quick embrace was followed by a closed-lipped bump-kiss on my cheek. After all we've been through, a proper kiss and a few tears wouldn't have gone amiss. It was just: (Me) 'Bye, then.' (James) 'Mind how you go' (exit kitchen and party). Mind how I fucking go?! He might as well have told me to 'Have a Nice Day', the passionless sod! I shut myself in the downstairs loo. Anne found me in mid-misery. She told me I only had myself to blame; I was responsible for elbowing James out of my life. I didn't say so, but the cow was right.

Too late to do anything about it, though. Mind how you go, James.

[October 1981]
Final farewells. Hard pressed to fit them all in. Oliver can sense something's up. He won't leave my side.

[October 1981]
Complete change of venue.

I am little more than a learning robot. At least I have few distractions to impede the inputting of knowledge. My booklist grows daily. It is invigorating to read so much, so intensely. To comprehend in a single reading. I eat words. And I spew words too: from my mouth, my pen. Postcard from my ex described the easely-easy life he leads. Made me very angry. Phoned home for a chat and heard Oliver barking in the background. Miranda found me crying outside the bar. She tidied me up and took me inside for a well-earned vodka. Mirry is a good person. Possibly religious, but thankfully not at all preachy (except when she's talking me out of buying any more cigarettes). She now knows *everything* about me and amazingly still likes me. In fact, she is awed by me. She introduced me to her friend Crispin, who has already had ten poems printed in magazines. He is the only guy I've ever known who wears a suit, waistcoat and bow-tie in everyday life. I rather think he imagines himself to be a latter-day Inkling. His aloofness is affected, but his gentle humour is compensation. Again, possibly religious, because one of his poems was a kind of prayer addressed to 'You, my overseer'. Again, though, not remotely preachy.

[October 1981]
Day out in the countryside with Mirry and Crisp in Crisp's catarrhal old mini. Pootling about the lanes at two miles per

hour we ended up at Burghclere, where we visited the Sandham Memorial Chapel. I found the experience extremely moving. The Stanley Spencer murals that decorate the walls made me giddy with the horror of war. And yet Spencer gives us no conventional depiction of men in battle. Here are soldiers depicted not as warriors but as human beings, scrubbing floors, frying bacon, filling water bottles and tea urns, making towers of sandwiches in the hospital ward. The most astonishing painting is the one behind the altar: *The Resurrection of the Soldiers*. The composition is filled with white crucifixes. In the foreground there is a heap of crucifixes, through which soldiers are emerging, waking up after being killed in battle, shaking hands with one another. In the distance, more soldiers, fully resurrected, each man carrying his own cross, are milling round a white-robed Christ. It is an extraordinary and inspiring vision, devoid of jingoist heroics.

While Crispin disappeared to write a poem, Mirry and I sat outside in the car eating bananas and discussing the chapel. Her brother is in the army, as was her father. 'They're not gung-ho types,' she said, 'but they are fiercely patriotic. They wouldn't be offended by this place, because it's not offering a pacifist point of view.'

'My Nan was a pacifist during World War Two,' I said. 'A conchie. She took part in a famous peace march in the 1950s: Aldermaston.'

'My family would not be impressed if I were to go on a peace march,' Mirry said.

'What's stopping you?' I said.

'Well, I'm not sure if I'm a pacifist. If someone tried to invade us, I'd want to do my bit to keep them out. Someone's got to. If everyone had thought like your Nan, we'd have been born into a Nazi Europe, and one of my best friends at school wouldn't even have been born.'

'You'd kill someone?'

She cocked her partially denuded banana and pointed it at an imaginary enemy. 'If our lives depended on it, I might.'

'Might? Not would?'

'You never know what you might do in a situation like that.' She turned the banana on me. 'So do you think it's wrong to take any person's life? Even if they're a Nazi? Surely you wouldn't give the bad guys a chance to win.'

'To some nations we're the bad guys. We've slaughtered millions of innocent people in order to expand our Empire around the globe.'

'True.' She plunged the firearm into her mouth and distractedly slid it in and out.

I said, 'Someone has to have the guts to stand up and say enough is enough. Wouldn't you prefer it if your brother carried a diplomatic case rather than a gun? I know I would.'

Crispin returned and slumped into the driver's seat. He took out his notebook. 'Bear in mind this is a rough draft,' he said.

> *Two men went to mow,*
> *Went to mow a meadow.*
> *Two armed men with maps*
> *Went to mow a meadow.*

> *The two men face to face*
> *Yelled: 'Get out of my meadow!'*
> *And spread their maps to show,*
> *Who could mow the meadow.*

'In the next two verses they discover their maps are identical except for the fact they're printed in different languages,' he said. 'I've not yet sorted out the last verse. I'll work on it tonight. Maybe some other man with a map shows up to mow them down.' He looked in his mirror and broke into laughter. 'Mirry, what you're doing with that banana is positively obscene.'

Which is exactly what I'd been thinking. But Mirry being Mirry, simply took out the banana, which was still whole, and said with endearing ingenuousness, 'I don't know what you're talking about.'

And she really didn't. Which is why I like her so much.

[...]

Joined CND with Mirry and Crisp.

[...]

I wish I had the wherewithal to paint, or to write poems or novels. The sad truth is, I'm not a creative person. The ex could be ~~an~~ annoying ~~prick~~ at times, but he was a superb painter, creating real art by smearing pigments over a blank rectangle of canvas. Jim had a real flair for acting, turning a paragraph of printed speech into a believable utterance: yes it was a dagger that he saw before him, and we were able to see his hallucination too.

What's Alison Dury's strength? An aptitude for learning? What's the big deal about filling your head with other people's achievements? Isn't that the same as being a living filing cabinet?

[...]

London for the day in order to take part in a peaceful demonstration outside the US embassy. There seemed to be more police than protestors. No violence erupted, in spite of taunting skinheads on the periphery. After speeches had been made and songs sung, the demonstration broke up. I went to the Tate with Mirry in order to look at some art, then we searched out somewhere in Pimlico where we could eat. There was a couple sitting in the café. They seemed very much in love. Sickeningly so. Nothing existed for them save each other. They were staring into one another's eyes, fingers like Celtic knotwork, frequently leaning their heads together to kiss. Long, toungey kisses of the sort I'd not enjoyed since the summer, with the ex, and before that in Southwold and on Gorleston seafront with James. I suddenly felt envious, and lonely and lost and decided I had to see James. Mirry understood. While she went to Victoria to catch the next coach back to Oxford, I trekked to Muswell Hill, and using the A to Z located his house, a rebarbative soot-blackened haunted-house of a house emerging from jungled shrubs. There were no lights on. And when I knocked there was no one at home. The ancient-looking curtains were drawn, so I couldn't see the conditions in which he was living. I sat on the wall of the neighbouring house in order to scribble a note under the orange streetlight. But what to say? The words wouldn't come, in spite of my having written so many words recently. A plain *hello* would not be sufficient, while a more affectionate *hello, I miss you*, would have the same effect as saying *walkies* to an ever-expectant Oliver. After waiting twenty minutes, I came away. I won't even mention it in my next letter.

See, James: we're not as symbiotic as you wanted us to believe, otherwise you'd have been there.

[1 November 1981]
Sunday. Very, very bored. Mirry and Crisp went to church clutching their holy fiction. Even though he knows I'm a committed atheist, Crisp still invited me to join them. Fearing for my soul, I suppose. There is no such thing as a soul. Shoes have soles. The sea floor has sole living on it. Southwold overlooks Sole Bay, and Southwold residents drink at the Sole Bay Inn. But human beings, while having soles on our feet and an arse-soul to poo through, do not have souls. The ghost in the machine is simple electricity, not some supernatural essence which zooms off to an eternal existence once a period of

enforced corporeality is through. You live, you mate and then you die. That's all there is to it. When the electricity is flickering between the synapses, you are said to be alive. When the flickering stops, so you cease to live. The soul is a no more than a concept. It's the cushion you hide behind when watching a horror movie. Throw the cushion away, I say. Confront the horror. See that there is no horror after all, only spooky music, lighting effects, anticipation, shock. BOO! Nothing to be alarmed about.

Stayed in bed reading until half-eleven and then enjoyed a long bath. With my eyes closed, I found I could imagine myself in our bath at home. Could even imagine Oliver sitting patiently on the bathmat, waiting for me to get out so that he can lick my toes. A miracle of simple electricity that such imaginings can be as vivid as actual experience. Like dreams.

Wrapped myself up and went for a very brisk walk around town. Hardly a soul about, to use that particular figure of speech. When I got back, Mirry and Crisp were leaving again, having been invited to lunch with their fellow holy joes. I fixed myself a bowl of tomato soup and then phoned the ex at his hall of residence. I imagined it ringing in the stairwell he described in his last letter, rrring, rrrrrring!

Some Welsh-sounding guy answered and went off to fetch the 'weirdo art student', as he humorously (I assumed) called him.

'Hi, it's me.'

He'd forgotten my voice already. There was a pause while he worked out my identity. 'Oh, wow. Hi, Ally. How's things?'

'I'm bored. It's Sunday.'

'It's Sunday here, too. I'm just back from a walk with Helena and Siobhan.'

'Who're Helena and Siobhan?'

'My mates.'

'Girlie mates.'

'They were last time I looked.' He laughed at his own remark, thus saving me the bother of having to. 'I've just been drawing Siobhan.'

'Nude?' I inquired, feeling oddly jealous of the latest model.

'Nah, I'm keeping my socks on.' His chuckle echoed around the stairwell. 'Seriously, she's fully clothed, and Helena's rolling me a supply of cigarettes. It's not like...' He hesitated. 'You know. Us.'

Mildew and unshiftable odour of frying. Oil paint and turps. Kate Bush and scurrying jazz scales. Wilson undressing reluctantly, and the feel of his bony, girlish limbs, the narrowness of him between my thighs. And light. Light. Skylight light contracting my irises.

'I miss you.' I said it before I could stop myself.

'I miss you too.'

'Sure you do.'

'I do. I keep meaning to write to you.'

A voice beside him in the stairwell. 'Is that your mum?' A Midlands accent.

'Who's that?' I said.

'Helena,' he said.

The girl put her mouth next to the phone. 'Hello Mrs Wilson. Thankyou for the knitting pattern.'

'It's not my mum,' I heard Wilson say. 'It's Alison.'

The phone beeped. I fed another ten pence into it. Helena said, 'Hello Alison. I've been hearing all about you.'

I didn't like that word *all*, or the meaning tone with which she said it.

'Have you,' I replied flatly. 'Is he still there?'

There was some kind of friendly fight, with tickling and giggles. 'Go. Away,' my ex kept saying. 'Do *not* do *that*.' Laughter. And I swear, as the interloper retreated, I heard her remark, though not for me to hear: 'Maybe she'll let you bonk her if you tell her how desperate you are.'

'Sorry about that,' he composed himself with catarrhal throat-clearing.

'Such hilarity,' I said, wishing I'd never phoned. I'd wanted him to be as bored and miserable as I was.

'You sound really posh on the phone,' he said.

'Like the Queen?'

'No, just posh. Extra posh, like someone who reads the news.'

I found myself willing the next beeps so that I could lie about how many ten pences I didn't have left. 'So your mum's been handing out knitting patterns, has she?'

'Helena's knitting me a jumper for Christmas. It's going to be outrageous. Pink and green stripes.'

'What's the matter with an ordinary jumper?'

'Boring,' he said.

The beeps. Saved.

He said, 'I'll write this week. Maybe I could come and visit you for the day. It's not that far, really.'

'We'll see,' I said. 'I don't get much spare time.' But the line went dead after the word much.

[4 November 1981]

Letter from the ex. As dictated to and added to by his 'secretaries' Helena and Siobhan. [Letter stapled to page]

Hello Alison!

My name is Helena and I have been asked to write this letter because your ex is so lazy. He has been drawing Siobhan with his soft one for the past hour (a 6B pencil, he wants me to explain). Siobhan is spread out on his bed revising for a test. Siobhan is an Aquarius. I am a Taurean. What are you?

Mr Wilson wishes me to inform you that you are welcome to visit us here whenever you like, although I must add that these beds are so narrow it'll be a bit of a squeeze. Siobhan's Leonard comes every other Saturday, and he ends up having to sleep on top of her in order to avoid rolling onto the floor. That's what he tells her anyway.

Are there any fit bits in Oxford? I bet they're all really rich. Bring me a spare one when you visit as I'd quite like to see a posh knob close-to.

Hello, this is Siobhan. Helena's just read back what she's written and we've decided it doesn't sound intellectual enough. That's why I've been called in. I may be a Valleys girl, but I know my Balzac from my Blyton. You might have gathered from the state of Helena's handwriting that we're a little bit sozzled. We popped down to the Red Lion earlier on for a swift one. We ended up having a slow several.

Your ex says please could you send him a letter as he wants to hear all about Crippen and Myra. At least, that's what I think he's saying. He says the room's spinning and he might throw up any second. Oh, and do you miss him? (I know he misses you because he's turned a sketch of you into a giant painting which is now hanging on the wall above his bed. The cleaners have asked him to take it down because you can see everything and they think it's rude, but he says it's not rude because it's art.

It'll be lovely if you could visit. I wonder if I'll recognise you with your clothes on?!

Helena here again: did you really pose nude?

To this my ex has added in painstaking scrawl:

We're off now for chips. Will post this on the way. They want me to write that I love you. I won't. Becuause [sic] you won't like it. I do miss you though. An awfully [sic] lot. Please come. Or if not I'll come to you. Bye bye. Love from me. XX

To which has been added:

PS Siobhan's got the biggest lotties out of us three. 40D.

PPS 38C, actually. Helena's are so small, they look like shoulder blades. Yours look like 34B? XX

I was going to tear it up, but have decided to keep it to remind myself about the perils of drinking. It makes Hogarth's Gin Lane look like a street party with Lucozade.

I ought to be furious he's turning me into a pin-up, but I'm actually flattered. It's the thought of him thinking about me that I like. Him remembering my body. Remembering the shape of my arms and breasts, my thighs, the particular pinks of my areolae and the lips of Meg Hunt. Remembering the feel of me. The smell of me. The taste of me.

[11 November 1981]

At two minutes to eleven, during a lecture on Blake, someone asked Hodgson if we were going to respect the silence. Hodgson said that she would be prepared to if the majority wished it and invited us to put up our hands. There wasn't much in it. 'By the time I've finished counting, it'll be too late. Any suggestions? Alison, I see you're sporting a CND badge.' My face burned as sixty pairs of eyes focused on my left tit. 'What would you suggest we do?' I was paralysed. I never speak out in lectures. Far off, bells were already starting to mark the hour. Hodgson prompted. I swallowed: 'If we hold a silence anyway, those people who want to respect the dead can use it for that. The rest of us can use the time to read through our notes.' Hodgson nodded, satisfied by my solution, although I think she had been hoping for a straightforward 'no' to provoke debate. Perhaps I should have said no; been more controversial. After all, mass debating can be very enjoyable.

[November 1981]

Incredible damn cheek turning up in his van like that, posing as my brother, when it's pretty obvious he's not. What am I, some long-distance whore? Claims he had to be in the area anyway, but I know when he's lying because his cheeks go red with the effort of having to use his imagination. I wanted so badly to break with this aspect of my past, and then it comes crashing in on my new life. My CND badge became unhooked at a crucial moment and the pin lodged in his arm. Nice and deep too.

Writing to James made me feel cleaner than all the bathing and showering has. I'd invite him here, only he has a new life now. No room for me in it. Desperate to talk with someone, I phoned the ex's hostel. Pissed. At five in the afternoon.

'We were in the pub with the tutors until three. Then we bought wine from Bejam and carried on drinking in the studio. Everything's spinning,' he said. Loud clunk as he dropped the phone, followed by the sound of applause. Not applause: puke hitting the floor. 'So how's it going?' he continued.

'Fine,' I said. 'Just thought I'd be sociable.'

'I miss you.'

'Sure you do. You're only saying that because you're drunk.' I was disappointed when he failed to contradict me. 'Shouldn't you have been painting and your tutors tutoring? Or would that be too conventional and boring?'

'You said it.'

His apathy makes me indignant. 'You do realise those tutors of yours are being paid a hell of a lot just to sit in a pub. As for you, I thought you lived to paint.'

I hear the tuneful chime of his Zippo. 'I'm taking a break from painting, but I'm still busy. This morning I was slaving on my assemblages,' he just managed to say. 'Schlop –'

'Schlop?'

'Schopen –'

'Shopping? What are you talking about?'

Clunk. Assorted retching noises. Silence. Then: 'I think about you a lot.'

'What about Helena?'

In one breath he said, 'She's not a compatible star sign. I think about you a lot all the time.'

'So you said.' I was curious. 'What exactly do you think about?'

'I think about your lovely –' He interrupts himself. 'Oh shit, I'm going to –' Clunk. Retch.

Silence.

'Are you okay?' I said. My lovely what? I was intrigued. Face? Personality? Furry friend?

Silence.

I shouted his name into the phone. No response. Then I heard approaching footsteps on concrete stairs and a Welsh male voice: 'Hope you're planning on cleaning up this fucking disgusting mess.'

Mutter, groan. I called out his name again. The Welsh guy answered. 'Sorry, love, but baby's gone bye-byes, like. Know him, do you?'

'I'm ashamed to admit that I do,' I said, and hung up.

[November 1981]

Summoned to face the Houyhnhnms. Three of them. Moste anciente they were, and gowned to intimidate. Their solemnity was almost, if not actually, comical as I was hauled over the coals for my numerous sins. Suppressed a smile throughout. Would I promise to –? Yes, I would. In future, would I –? Yes, I would. Do you understand, young lady (sic), that if you don't –? I understand, and I'm very sorry.

One of my three outstanding *Hamlet* essays now completed.

Anne's phone call brief but welcome. I'm not sure if I approve of her dabbling with religion, though. Letter from James saddened me. There was no spontaneity in it. It was as carefully planned as an essay: the polite greeting, his news, the humorous anecdote, the summing up. It could have been a carbon copy mailed out to several people. Dear Mum and Dad. Dear Julie. Dear Martin. Does he write to Martin? Shouldn't think so.

Interestingly, that's the first time I've thought of M for days. I don't miss him, and I certainly don't miss the sex fix I confess

I'd become addicted to. The person I do miss is James. My oldest, closest friend. I stare at his photo when I should be concentrating on my work. I stare at the drawing of our seafront shelter. The hours we've spent in there! It was the throne of our kingdom. I never sat in there with W. I used to insist on using one of the concrete ones below.

Feeling particularly homesick at the moment. I do like it here. But this is not my city. The Jameses, Julies, Annes, Darrens and Simons of Oxford have as much desire to connect with the students as we did with the holidaymakers who passed through Gorleston. I'm looking forward to Christmas, to seeing Oliver, the gang, even my parents. Nervous about seeing James.

Late evening, I was summoned to the payphone downstairs.

'Hello, ex.'

'Hi.' He sounded sober. Sober-ish, anyway. 'Thought I'd give you a quick call. Sorry about the other day. Listen.' He was in a busy pub. I could hear *Japan* playing on the juke box. 'That made me think about you, Ally. *Ghosts*,' he added unnecessarily.

'Funny, but I was only listening to that this morning.'

'Spooky.'

'Hardly.' I refuse to entertain any notion of symbiosis.

'Are you drunk?

'A bit tipsy. The Red Lion.'

'What's with the Welsh accent? You can't have gone native after a few weeks.'

He lowered his voice. 'I'm above average height and fair-haired, right? All the locals are five foot six max, dark-haired and very Welsh. They don't exactly like the students round here. Especially ones from over the border. To them I must sound like –' He thought for a few moments. 'Like that guy Jim played in *Salad Days*. If I stoop a bit as well, I don't stand out quite so much.'

Someone is with him at the phone, interrupting his already

slow train of thought. Helena? Siobhan? 'Who's that with you?'

'Erm. Only Helena.'

I hear a Midlands protest about the use of the word 'only', and my ex apologising. 'She's gone now.'

'Do you like her?'

'Not really,' he lied. 'Listen.' Another snippet of *Ghosts*. 'It's a weird juke box. It's got everything from *Strangers on the Shore* to the latest chart stuff. Siobhan keeps playing Ultravox. Vienna. Makes me think I'm back in *The Links*.'

'Siobhan's there as well?'

'The three of us go everywhere together.'

This was good news. 'I thought you were going out with Helena.'

'We're just mates.' Did I detect a soupçon of regret? I imagined James saying the exactly same thing in exactly the same way to inquisitive housemates when the morning post arrived. 'I can't wait to see you again.'

'That's nice.'

'Do you miss me?'

I do, but it would be dangerous to tell him the truth. 'I miss posing for you.'

Recollection of either my body, or his paintings of it, sent him into a paroxysm of delight. 'Come and visit.'

'Can't. Sorry.'

'I'll come to Oxford, then.'

'I don't have any spare time. Sorry. Hey, it's not long until Christmas.'

The phone beeped. 'Shit. I'm out of change. Maybe... Helena!' he called, forgetting he was supposed to be Welsh. I heard some guy who really *was* Welsh mock his accent. 'Look. Better skedaddle. Love you, Ally.' Just as the line went dead.

Love. Figure of speech, or does the poor guy actually believe he loves me?

[...]

No straight male, however intelligent, however cultured, however highly regarded by his colleagues, is above ogling. I was reading in the library when I looked up to see [ ] tilting his head to peer up my skirt. He continued peering, too. The man has a DPhil. He speaks eleven languages, has published fourteen books, is president of this, chair of that. And yet he still is a slave to basic lust. He came across as he was leaving.

'Hello.'

'Hello.'

He is almost fifty, but his dallying was adolescent-awkward. He tilted the book in my hands so as to read the cover. 'She's a very overrated critic,' he remarked, wrinkling his wrinkles, making his nostrils flare so that the furry inside poked out. 'We had one or two interesting battles when she was my student.'

I was actually a great fan of the book and its author. Did I dare to contradict?

I didn't get the chance to. He leaned confidentially close, and using a raised eyebrow and an unintentionally baleful smile implied, 'You have delightful knees, my dear. Thankyou for letting me see them.' Then he said, 'Perhaps we could arrange to...' His eyebrow continued the sentence, and his thin mouth twisted into another variety of menace to complete it.

I was speechless. I'd been innocently studying, not advertising my wares. I told Miranda, who advised me against reporting him: 'Who would they prefer to believe?' Instead, I've been shopping for trousers. Jeans and cords. I've rarely worn trousers. Mirry helped me to choose. She knows about these things. I'm wearing my new jeans as I write this. They feel like armour. Impenetrable. Mirry bought herself a salmon pink ball gown. I have to admit she looked stunning, even though I should really disapprove of such traditionalist clobber. 'When in Rome,' she said. So I tried on a lustrous, very pale blue gown. The annoying thing was I looked stunning too. I almost cried. Unfortunately it was hideously expensive. Mirry offered to pay half, but I will hire one, should Cinders ever decide to attend a ball.

[...]

Phoned M to warn him about the new me. He sniggered, the sod.

[...]

Demo in Hyde Park. Well attended. Somehow I ended up at the very front with my placard. TV cameras caught my sullen good looks and I was on six o'clock, nine o'clock and ten o'clock news. Phoned Anne's hall of residence. Had to leave a message as she was at a Christian Union meeting. Phoned the ex, but he was not in, probably down the pub, possibly drunk. The parents were in. Nan too.

[...]

I am famous! Several students and the woman in the book shop recognised me. The Houyhnhnms placed a note in my pigeonhole asking me to see them at once. I thought I'd make them wait. Finished an essay first, had my hair cut to make me look less girly, and later walked with Crispin to watch the rowing for an hour.

Houyhnhnms most displeased. Randy Houyhnhnm was clearly disappointed my legs were in retirement. They said they found it hard to believe a young lady (sic) of my potential was so intent on wasting her not inconsiderable abilities on trivial pursuits. Then they produced a copy of the *Daily Mail* and turned to a report of my demo. My photo was plain to see. Except the camera had lied. I had been singing, but here I looked as though I was hurling abuse at a policeman.

'Jolly good thing you've changed your hair,' one of them said. 'This is not acceptable behaviour. You are a representative of this University.'

'WH Auden helped in the general strike of 1926,' I said. 'During his first year at Oxford.'

'So you're WH Auden now, are you?' one smugly remarked.

'What Auden did is neither here nor there,' said another.

'Why isn't it?' I said.

Randy intervened. 'The point is, young lady (sic), you are neglecting your work. If this recklessness continues –'

'Recklessness?' I went to stand.

'Sit! And listen.' He paused for effect. My cheeks were burning. 'You are clearly a young lady (sic) of passionate nature. My advice to you is to sit on those passions. And if possible, channel your energy into your coursework.'

All three of them stared at me. I looked defiantly from one pair of eyes to the next. I had an idea. I said, 'If a member of staff makes an improper suggestion to one of the students, what's the procedure for reporting him?'

Randy smirked. '*We* are the procedure,' he implied in the way he looked at me with one brow raised. 'Is there something you'd like to tell us?'

Pointless. *Pointless*. And now I felt ridiculous for opening my mouth.

'Do you have anything more to say?' Randy Houyhnhnm inquired.

Shaking my head, I stood, and this time was permitted to leave their presence.

[...]

Here's a recipe for a laugh. Take one framed popular print of dogs playing snooker (Oxfam, fifty pence). When no one is looking, steal into the hallowed stable of the Houyhnhnms. Chose a painting of similar size to the print (*A Willow Grows Aslant a Brook* by some minor Victorian will do) and swap them, carefully storing the painting out of sight. Withdraw and allow Houyhnhnms to marinate in their own bile.

Here's a thought. Why not prepare a batch, using a variety of prints? Suggested prints: photo-poster of woman tennis player rubbing tennis ball on her bare arse. Crying child/puppy/Pierrot. Adam and Eve and a giant swan.

[...]
Q: Who am I?
A: I am Alison Dury.
Q: What am I?
A: I am a young woman, a student, a retired whore.
Q: What do you aspire to be?
A: Useful. Perfect. Perfectly happy.
Q: What stands in your way?
A: Men.
A: Me.
A: M.

[December 1981]
Spent the morning in the supermarkets putting No to Apartheid stickers on South African and tinned fruit. A solo mission as Mirry had to see her tutor. The irate manager of [ ] was choking on his own expletives as I legged it through the covered market and to freedom. I was shit-scared and exhilarated at the same time. Just how I'd felt at Benacre.

Parcelled up a dog turd and mailed it to the South African Embassy. I pity the secretary who has to open it, but these things have to be done.

Crisp is a virgin. I think that's sweet. What's even sweeter is he is in no hurry to lose his virginity. He read me some of his published poems, which are about various aspects of sexual innocence. (I wonder if James has been sowing his wild oats? I hope not.) He also unveiled an early draft of a poem about me.

> *Ash eye,*
> *Light collecting*
> *Iris*
> *Sunlight-tightened,*
> *Observes*
> *Nothing, perhaps.*

He's working on the second verse (also acronymic). The provisional title is *Eye/I*. I'm not sure if I like the poem. Probably because I don't know what he's actually saying about me.

[December 1981]

'Viewpoint, Alison, love (sic). There's no viewpoint. This is just –' The Trendy Houyhnhnm shook his head despairingly and tossed my pages into my lap. 'I don't get you at all,' he said. 'You worked like crazy to earn a place here, and for what? So far, *nothing*. And you were one of the students I predicted would excel. I'd have staked money on it.' He paced around his ancient and untidy room while I tore my essay into pieces. 'Are you in some sort of trouble?'

'No.'

'Sure?'

'Everything's AOK,' I said.

'I want you to know you can trust me.'

'I'm fine.'

'If you say so.' He huffed disbelievingly and dropped into his antique chair. 'Well then.'

'Well then,' I echoed. I stared at him across the desk. No stockpile of qualifications can protect a person from the Dury withering look. He cracked in under four antique ticks of his mantelpiece clock.

'Go,' he said.

'Go?'

'Just – clear off.' He flapped his hand effetely towards the door. 'If you can spare the time, and the energy, re-do that essay and drop it in before the holiday.'

I gave a cynical laugh. I decided to shock him. 'I know what you want.' He looked up. 'It's so obvious. You want to have it off with me.'

Trendy jumped up as if something had tried to crawl into his bum. 'I beg your pardon?'

'Come on, I've seen the way you look at me. You're frustrated because I've never given you the come-on.' The man just stared. I continued: 'The thing is, you don't do it for me. You're too old. I like my guys to be able to keep up with me. Stay the course.'

'*Get out*!' At last, a reaction. Apoplexy. He gurned pure fury at me and pointed to the door. I started to say something else but he was suddenly bearing down on me like a disco bouncer. '*Out*!' He bundled me out of his room and threw the door shut.

'See ya,' I called, although I was shaking.

I hid in my room afterwards. Began rewriting that essay but my interest quickly waned and I ended up drafting a letter instead.

[December 1981]
Mirry told me never to post a letter written in anger until I'd read it in a calmer frame of mind. I disobeyed.

[December 1981]
Oxford to Victoria Coach Station to Great Yarmouth. Slept for much of the journey.

Dad collected me from Yarmouth in the car. Greyer sideburns. Eyes baggier. More paunch. Mum older-looking, tired-looking. Gorleston shabbier than I remembered. It reminded me of something ~~that has been left out in the garden the rain~~ left out in the garden ~~that shouldn't have been~~. Oliver went truly berserk at the sight of me. Ditto. Total joy at being reunited. Took him for a brisk walk to the beach and along the upper esplanade as far as the special shelter. I sat in it in the gathering dusk and was visited by the ghosts of me and James.

After a decent soak I went straight to bed and slept right through for the first time in weeks.

[...]

No one is back yet. No one will be back for days. M does not know when my term ends, so I am staying indoors to read and work. I will only venture outside with Oliver when it is dark.

[...]

Reclusion does not suit me. I am going mad. I am climbing the walls. I have fifteen pairs of knickers, ten pairs of socks, twelve pairs of nuclear-blast-proof tights in three colours, four pairs of thin black tights and four bras. Weeded out the least attractive underwear for something to do. I'll work on my wardrobe another day. Dug out my old diaries and read the story of my life.

I can sum up the story of my life in one word. James. Everything I did, every choice I made, every decision, somehow involved James. Open any diary at any page and there he was. It was like slicing through a stick of rock and getting Gorleston-on-Sea every time. Okay, we went to different schools because I was a bit brighter, but being apart made us closer than when we were together.

My favourite time was when his parents had the key cut for me. I'll never forget the thrill of leaving my bed, hurrying down the road with Oliver and letting myself into the Rudd's bungalow, where I settled Oliver in the kitchen before slipping in beside James, who was woozy with sleep, and floppy-limbed and a bit malodorous. Those were the days, my friend. No one would have believed our innocence. Two sexually mature teenagers in bed together like siblings. Or like Morecambe in bed with Wise. Like Mork and Mindy. I admit sometimes I thrilled at the feel of your early morning hard-on, nudging and nuzzling against me while you drifted in and out of sleep. If you hadn't been wearing your Y-fronts, who knows what might have happened, because one morning I felt you pressing against my bum and I instinctively began pressing back. If I hadn't got out of bed I know I just know I would have rolled over and seduced you. I think that was the moment, if such a moment can be so neatly pinpointed, my sexual nature was awakened. After that I was careful how close to you I permitted myself to be. Eventually I decided it would be for the best if I didn't get into your bed at all.

[...]

Christmas card from Crispin:

> *Do such retinas*
> *Unsight hold?*
> *Respectfully*
> *Yours, Me!*

Much to my parents' disapproval, I have now written and sent out my CND Christmas cards. They tried very hard to persuade me to use more conventional cards, but I think it's high time we moved away from our yuletide obsession with robins in the snow and Victorian village scenes. Snow/whiteness = purity/innocence, I suppose. Victoriana = The Past, which people flee to when dissatisfied with The Present. If The Present's so bad, then do something to change it. Don't wallow in some misguided sentimentality. Victorian Britain was no great shakes. In London one in eight females was a prostitute. Poverty was a huge problem. Crime was unbelievably bad. Life was short and brutal if you didn't have money. It's all there in Dickens and Mrs Gaskell etc if you can be bothered to look.

Sing out, folks!

On the twelfth day of Christmas, my true love gave to me, TWELVE shirts for mending, ELEVEN socks for darning, TEN boots for blacking, NINE mats for whacking, EIGHT rats to send packing, SEVEN logs for chopping, SIX days hard labouring –

FIVE mouths to feed! –

FOUR cracked ribs, THREE loose teeth, syphilis and clap, and no vote until next cen-tu-ry!

[...]

Once a guy's had his hands on you he thinks he's entitled to maul you about whenever he pleases. Yes, folks, the ex is back. He was rather more pleased to see me than I'd anticipated. He tried to prolong the greeting hug into a romantic clinch; even managed to get in a micro-second-long feel of my left titty as I extracted myself from his octopus arms. He turned up at the house wearing a candy-pink and pea-green acrylic jumper. I say jumper. The knitting was so loose and holey, it had to have been formed on broomsticks, and the result was no more than a brightly-coloured sack reaching almost to his knees. The sleeves were twice as long as his arms, so that the excess needed to be rolled into extravagant cuffs the size of beach balls. He looked utterly ridiculous. I made him take it off and wear one of Dad's. I lined Oliver's basket with Helena's handiwork.

The ex soft-talked Mum into serving him a giant slice of cake with his coffee, and refused to budge from next to the Christmas tree. In the end I made him take Oliver for a walk with me, intending to ditch him on the return journey. Had to endure him telling me a chain of anecdotes about his getting pissed with his tutors. He bored me, but then he said nice things about me and I felt instantly guilty and sorry for him for not being able to get over me. Ahm jest a girl who caren't say no, and I hate myself, *loathe* myself for being such a pushover, but I let him snog me and frot as we were leaning against the railings. I reminded myself I was in charge. I was the boss. He enjoyed himself in spite of the layers of cloth between us. A proviso: 'One word or hint about this to the gang and I will castrate you with my teeth.' By the time he'd finished scratching his itch and simultaneously grinding my flies into my bits, I was getting in the mood for some, so gave myself a seeing to as soon as I was indoors. Unsatisfactory. Resolved to phone M at work first thing.

[...]

Vigorous rogering. Relief!

[...]

Boredom. Small town. Small minds. Come friendly bombs and rain on Gorleston... I can't wait to get back to Oxford. Next term I'm going to knuckle down and show them what I'm capable of.

[...]

In the not-too-distant past Scott would have been associated with the devil because of his colouring. They would have burnt him as a witch. I can just imagine him trussed to a pole and yelling for mercy as the flames rise to consume. Or better still, skewered from arse to mouth and ROASTED. I would gladly be in charge of the basting, and the carving.

Sausage, anyone?

Chipolata, I mean.

[...]

Ahm jest a girl who caren't say no! (Eight minutes, twenty-three seconds.)

[...]

Christmas shopping in Norwich with Anne. An endurance test

to say the least. Her interest in religion is far more serious than I'd anticipated. She has deliberately reinvented herself and the new her is little more than a boring old cow. No alcohol. No sleeping around. No swearing. No blaspheming. She wears a crucifix, a gift from one of her new Christian Union buddies, Samantha. She mentions Samantha in every other utterance. Samantha says. Samantha always. Samantha never. Anne's wardrobe is 1950s frumpy. (Apparently she even wears a headscarf in church. A headscarf! Even her mum doesn't wear a headscarf.) She attends daily prayer meetings at her hall of residence. She goes to Church twice on Sundays. She now owns her own bible (a gift from Samantha). I didn't feel comfortable with her at all. In fact, she irritated me, banging on about the true meaning of Christmas, and even daring to criticise my godless lifestyle. Could hardly bring myself to speak to her on the train home. Pretended to be asleep. Don't intend to have much to do with her anymore. Boring cow. Boring sanctimonious cow.

[...]

More sympathy frotting. This time in one of the concrete shelters. He took bloody ages to come. My arse was going numb through being ground against the concrete ledge I was perched upon. I was on the verge of withdrawing my hospitality when he roared into my ear that he loved me, and had thought about me every second of every day. Stupid idiot. Why bother loving me? I don't return that love. I made him reach his hand into my jeans, although we soon gave up as he's useless with his fingers. He can't even draw properly anymore. I've had to do the job myself, a few minutes ago in the comfort of my own bed. My fantasy was pathetically embarrassing. James, Anne and I are watching Anne's dad's porn video, side by side on the sofa. We all get turned on and one thing leads to another. Pretty soon James is bonking us; Anne then me then Anne.

Crazy.

Still, it did the trick.

Weird thing is, when I was away I never got randy. Since I've been back, I've had sex on the brain. It must be all this sea air.

[...]

Ode to Meg Hunt

All stand for Meg Hunt!
I know you're really into her.
You seek her out to enjoy her warm welcome,
To wise-crack with her.
She's deep, very deep:
There's much more to her than meets the eye.
And she's lippy, and quite slippery.
She messes with your head, but in a good way.
You feel better for the encounter,
As though a load has been taken from you.
You rarely stay with her for long, though,
And always leave much humbled.
Next time, my friends, aim to linger longer.
All stand for Meg Hunt!

[...]

Half-hearted fall of snow first thing. Put on my wellies and strolled down to the seafront, allowing the snowflakes to melt on my tongue. Bought ten Benson and Hedges from *Mace* on the way and smoked a couple in the glass shelter with Oliver shivering beside me on the bench. Watched Action Man heading along the beach with his dog obediently trotting at heel. I'd forgotten it was early closing today. Good thing I didn't go straight to the beach.

Took off in the opposite direction, down to the harbour and to the end of the pier. I leaned against the railing to observe my home town, remembering James' poem.

If the ex loved me so much, why didn't he write poems about me? Why didn't he worship me with words? Why choose to celebrate me with some wonky, overworked charcoal drawing that made my legs disproportionately long, as if I'd been tortured on a rack?

Brass band carols in the high street. *Away in a Manger*, tenderly played, brought tears to my eyes.

A gloved hand suddenly on my shoulder, as if someone was making a citizen's arrest. I turned to find the Deputy Head, Mrs Morris, beaming at me.

'Very nice to see you,' she said, enthusiastically. 'How was your first term?'

'Busy,' I said. 'Lots of reading, and writing.'

'I don't expect you're having any difficulty with that,' she said, her brow and smile contracting subtly as she noticed the CND badge on my lapel. 'Your name is often mentioned in the staff room. You must pay us a visit one day soon. To inspire others to be brave enough to apply.'

She made it sound like a polar expedition. It's nothing to do with bravery, applying to Oxbridge. It's all about believing in yourself. I did. I don't anymore. But I will again. I really will.

[...]

Official reunion down *The Links*. Got slaughtered. I forget who exactly was there. Simon. Darren. The ex, who was drooling over Darren's cutesy-cuddly little companion, Jennifer, who's a hamster in human shape. Julie was there too, with a loutish hanger-on who tried to chat me up in the lobby outside the Ladies when no one was looking. Bore down on me, he did. Cornered me, he did, looking down my top. I felt scared. I don't know what I'd have done if Action Man hadn't been on his way to the Gents. He saved me. He squared up to the thug like an aggressive Pit Bull; drove him back into the saloon. Of course he expected me to be grateful for protecting me.

Kept out of the way of both the lout and Scott by clinging to the ex, literally, and later accepted his offer to walk me home. Of course he attempted a romantic clinch: on the corner of Buxton Avenue. And was unable to resist the urge to whisper sweet words in my ear on the corner of Hill Avenue. Ahm jest a gal, etc. Kiss followed by heavy snog followed by prolonged grope. Detour to beach. Brisk, stumbling walk along the sand in the pitch dark to the place where we held the birthday beach party. It was too bloody cold to take my jeans off completely, so I pulled them down to my knees and let him enjoy me from behind. Not very romantic, admittedly, but the whore was only doing what was expected of her. And she found she could enjoy it too.

Afterwards the ex was most tender. I allowed him to be tender. I needed to hear that he loved me. Little Ally Pally wants to be loved.

James will be back this week. I'm not sure how I feel about that. He hasn't meant anything to me for so long, when I see him it'll be like meeting a stranger.

[...]

Official letter from Houyhnhnm Central informing me that in the light of my recent behaviour, both in and out of college, and my extremely discourteous letter to the almighty Houyhnhnms of Houyhnhnm Central, my place on the course is regretfully no longer open to me.

I have been sent down.

Fuck.

I'd seen it coming for a long while, although this didn't diminish the impact of reading that letter. I was reduced to a gibbering heap and hid myself in the toilet, tears gushing while everything I've ever eaten poured unstoppably out. One way or another, I used up an entire toilet roll.

I cannot tell them yet. They'll freak. I'm going to act as if nothing is different. Next week I'll go back to Oxford and clear out my room while no one else is around and then I will work out what to do. Transfer to another course? Some shitty polytechnic might have me. One in London, maybe, so I can be nearer to James, or would that be disastrous? We'd get embroiled big-time. Sympathy sex. Followed by guilt, jealousy. I wish James were gay.

Phoned Miranda. When her hag-mother, who needs both barrels of her surname discharging up her snob's arse, realised who her beloved daughter was speaking to, she intervened; grabbed the phone; ordered me never to call again. Ultra-poshly, too, so that she sounded evil, like the Houyhnhnms.

Commiserated with Julie and lots of vodka down *The Links*, the *Cliff Hotel* and the *Ocean Room*. Had an outburst of grief outside the *Cliff Hotel* which I convinced Jules was due to love trouble with my ex. Bless her, she's going to have a word with him on my behalf, to tell him to cease pestering me.

A guy called Adam very appreciative of a bit of seasonal warmth. I told him he'd just met his Christmas Eve.

[...]

M. Three to four minutes.

[...]

Sunny but very cold. The ex and I walked Oliver along the seafront as far as the pier. Sat by the coastguard station enjoying a tipple or two of whisky from the miniature he carried and puffing our way through several cigarettes. While he sketched (badly) some men fishing, he shared his theories on aesthetics with me. Having gone into the subject myself, briefly, I was able to correct him on his Kant and Nietzsche, which irritated him, although he disguised his irritation with sarcasm.

I got him to talk about Helena. They're not an item, although he has had one quick snog with her on the way back from the pub one night. He said she refuses to go out with him because their star signs are not compatible. The woman sounds demented.

Free chips at *My Plaice*. Ate them sitting at one of the window tables, wiping portholes in the condensation in order to look out. Felt truly plebby and so wonderfully *normal* after a term of pretence and ritual and minding ones peas and cucumbers. I was Icarus. I'd flown far higher than my wings had been designed to go.

Afterwards we dossed upstairs in the renovated but untenanted flat. Walls, ceiling and woodwork have been brightly repainted, the carpets have been cleaned and the ragged curtains replaced. All traces of his art have gone. He said he preferred it before, when it was messy.

I consented to sit on a chair at the window for a portrait. The result took the genius maudit under a minute and looked nothing like me. A disastrous combination of flash haste and his choice of a 4H pencil were to blame. Feeling sorry for him, I draped myself over the fusty fuchsia candlewick and slept for an hour while he assiduously scribbled. By the time I opened my eyes, half the sketch book had been torn out and lay scrunched at the artist's feet. Having abandoned the task of drawing me, he was treating himself to a wank instead, using my pose as stimulus. Feeling generous, I asked did he want me to take my jeans off or flash him my tits? No, definitely no. Did he want me to –? No, I was to remain exactly as I was because he *loved* my arse in tight jeans, but could I just – look straight at him? Through my fringe? Perfect. Oh, *perfect*.

He pulled a face. I threw him my hanky just in time.

Now it was my turn, if I wanted. Did I want to? No, I was fine thanks. I wasn't in the mood right now.

After blotting the eruption, he joined me on the bed and we cuddled. I had to remind him this renewal of our former intimacy didn't mean we were an item, just mates.

'You mean, like you and Jim,' he muttered bitterly into my armpit.

'Meaning?' I elbowed him away and sat up.

'You want all your blokes to be just mates. Like you're scared of commitment. I always thought it was us blokes were supposed to be scared of commitment.'

'Friendships are more important than relationships based on physical pleasure,' I said.

'You're not religious, are you? Then why all this Victorian purity bollocks? What's so superior about a relationship that has no sexual pleasure in it? Is it because you equate it with letting go? It's almost as if you want to be computerised.' In the voice of *Star Trek*'s Mr Spock he added, 'Human emotion is illogical, Captain.'

'You don't understand,' I protested.

'Neither do you,' he threw back. 'You're a normal, living, loving eighteen-year-old female who's under the delusion that getting rid of her natural sexual desires will make her a better person. You enjoy sex, don't you? Then why pretend you don't? Do you get some kind of kick out of feeling guilty? Or are you trying to save yourself until Mr Perfect happens to come along?'

To shut him up, I told him about Martin.

His vocal cords took off on holiday. He went over to the window and stared out.

I told him the history of me and Martin. He was suitably horrified.

'You mean, you were screwing him during the summer? While you were going out with me?'

'I stopped seeing him at first,' I said, actually feeling sorry for him.

'Oh, cheers for that! You know what you are, don't you. A plain, old-fashioned hypocrite. Until two minutes ago I thought you were the most wonderful woman on the planet. But now –

Fuck! *Fuck*!' His scoff bloomed on the glass. A gull laughed at him.

'That's your fault for idealising me,' I said, getting up. I stood beside him.

He repelled my attempted embrace. 'I don't understand you,' he said.

'I don't want to be understood,' I said falteringly, beginning to cry. 'I just want to be loved, that's all.' My misery, when I could no longer contain it, was far more wretched than I anticipated. Sobs welled loudly from my core. I could probably be heard by the customers. 'Loved,' I repeated.

'Is this for real, or some kind of act?' He regarded me like a parent assessing a child who falls sick on the day of a school test. He placed his hand on my shoulder. Then his other hand on my other shoulder. Then he drew me against him. Eventually we lay down and I cried for an hour.

[...]

James has returned from his travels. He was in a weird mood from the word go, no doubt unnerved by the presence of my ex, who I can now truthfully admit to loving; although I must stress that I am still not *in love* with him. James sat folded in on himself, like a dead spider. Kept looking at me with sad-dog expectant eyes, like I owed him a beating. I tried, oh I tried, I *tried* to be pleased to be with him again, but he's such a wimp. I beat him and he comes back for more. I don't want to be adored. I don't want to be pedestalled and adored, like the blushing bride, the new mum, the Victorian wife. All I want is for him to respect me as an equal. I'd love him forever if he could do that, but I know he'll never be able to.

The vodka talked. His cheeks burned. I thought: 'Fight me, you idiot. Say something. Tell me to shut up.'

It wasn't him I hated. It was the men who'd turned me into a whore. It was the Houyhnhnms for their closed-mindedness. It was. In fact, it was the whole bloody kit and caboodle of adult life that wasn't me and James cuddled up in bed on a Sunday morning, innocent and safe and together on a mattress that was our Eden.

I raged. He endured it. I raged some more. Then he cracked. He swore at me for the first time ever; told me to fucking shut up, which is what I'd wanted him to say, although as soon as he'd said it, I wished he hadn't. It was like having a door slammed in your face. A door to a bolt-hole you'd used for as long as you could remember.

I cried after he casually left, then ran outside to find him, to fight with him: to the death if necessary. I was in time to glimpse him disappearing over the edge of the upper esplanade. Julie came after me with my coat and we ended up patrolling the seafront looking for him, calling after him. Later, when I was sober, I crept round to his bedroom window and tapped on the glass, lightly enough for him not to hear unless he was listening for it. There was no response. I didn't know if he was in bed or not, asleep or ignoring me. I decided I would keep out of his way. To wait until he made the first move towards reconciliation.

[...]

M can go to hell. I will not be used anymore, by him or anyone. Told him where to go.

[...]

A change of scenery. Nan's house.

'This is no social visit,' she said. 'You're in some sort of trouble. Is it boys?'

I wouldn't (or rather couldn't) say. Instead I told her all about the political interests that had taken precedence over my university work. She didn't tell me off. She understood. She had been a conchie after all. She'd had to endure the barrage of hypothetical questions at a tribunal in Ipswich, after which she was ordered to serve with the Red Cross during the height of the Blitz. 'You won't believe some of things I saw and had to cope with. Terrible things. Made me more determined than ever to stand by my principles.'

Well, now I am more determined than ever to stand by mine. I wish I'd got her onto the subject before. She refused to give me any advice, however. She believes a person should make their own choices, otherwise they'll simply be living someone else's life. 'And there are people who make it their business to boss others around.'

So I phoned M. L answered. I put on a heavy local accent and said, 'Oops sorry, wrong number.' When I phoned back an hour later it was M who spoke. I told him bluntly it was over. He disbelieved me. He laughed. He said I'd called it off before and had gone back to him. I'd do so again.

Shit-for-brains. He thinks he's such a stud.

[...]

M rings using his *nom-de-telephone*, 'Tony'. I'd instructed Nan to say I was out to anyone but James. She knew 'Tony' wasn't the caller's real name. She said it exactly as I've written it, with speech marks around it.

I am fed up with waiting. I have written to James and posted it before I change my mind. Told him how I felt about him. I'm not giving in. I'm in control. I'm the boss.

[...]

'Tony' has phoned twice this evening. I was 'out'. Both times he left the same message to contact him ASAP, or failing that, he'll be waiting for me by the substation between nine and twenty past in the morning. Let him wait. I'm going to cycle straight past him and on to Gorleston, where I shall tell Lizzie everything. The truth will hurt, but it's time for someone to be honest. Bugger the consequences.

Cycled to the beach and ceremonially threw the padlock key into the sea.

Mum has just phoned to say that last night Scott dropped off some meat bits for Oliver. I'm furious. He promised he would never call at the house. I managed to catch him while he was getting ready for work. I pictured him, his white body pink from the shower and freckle-backed, towelling his hair. Where was I? If I didn't tell him the address he'd bribe it out of my Mum with sausages and prime cuts. I called him a wanker and he said that was a pretty accurate description, which was why he needed me to meet him ASAP. I said it's over. I said I don't care who he tells about me and Martin, or me and him. I really, really don't care anymore. I slammed down the phone. Half an hour later Mum rang, wondering if she'd done the right thing. Scott had called round and the stupid cow had given him Nan's address. 'He seemed such a charming young man. He said you'd asked him to deliver some chops to Nan's.'

He's on his way here. Zooming down the A12 as I write. I expect the dog blanket is already spread out for me in the back of the van. Unless he's planning to take me to his burrow.

[...]

James phoned. He knows about me and Martin.

I'm glad.

I'm terrified.

I don't care.

I don't care what he knows. I feel no more for him than I do his wretched brother or Scott the Psycho Sausage.

He was very distressed, and there was no answer when I phoned back to tell him to mind his own business.

I'm going over to see Lizzie now. I've just missed the bus so I'll stick to my original plan and cycle. Plus it'll mean I won't be here when Psycho Sausage shows up. 'Any idea where your lovely granddaughter's gone, missus, or when she'll be back? Don't suppose I could wait here, could I? Cup of tea? That'd be lovely. I've been looking forward to meeting you. Your granddaughter's been telling me a lot of good things.'

It'll be intensely satisfying to completely blank Martin as I fly pass him. I can just imagine his one-cog brain trying to compute why I fail to stop or even acknowledge him. Last thing he'll imagine is that I'm on my way to his house. What'll be brilliant is if he turns up while I'm still there. I'd love to see his face.

When I've blown that sham marriage to smithereens, the next phase of my mission will be to locate my good friend Wilson, who'll probably be doing what he does best, which is tipping beer down his throat like some football hooligan, and tell him that while he's a harmless enough guy, he's wet, thick, embarrassing to be seen with in public and extremely crap at sex. Is this ungenerous of me? I sincerely hope so. Knowing him, though, he'll probably just laugh. He pissed his self-respect into the urinal a long, long time ago.

Finally I'm going to hunt down James, who abandoned me when I needed him most. I've a strong urge to mortally wound him. I know how. By telling him how much I hate him. Because I really do hate him. I do.

www.welovepoole.com

THE REAL INSPECTOR POOLE
An appreciation by
Tim Wilson RA

Gorleston born Tim Wilson studied for an MA in Painting at the Royal Academy and has taught Fine Art at Cardiff and Winchester. The winner of several prizes for his work, he is currently artist in residence at Kettles Yard, Cambridge. Examples of his work are to be found in numerous public collections.

I expect there are a lot of people sharing the same thought, how Sunday evenings will never be the same now that the good Inspector – or more accurately since season two, Chief Inspector – has taken his final bow. True, we have the repeats to satisfy our hunger, and there's a thriving Poole industry to hook into – novelisations, audio tapes, DVDs (they really ought to have remastered the earliest episodes, shot on 16mm film, shame on the manufacturers), fan clubs and fanzines, and websites galore, and guided tours of Poole country (Bournemouth and Poole and the New Forest) – but surely none of these is a substitute for a brand new episode in the eight-to-ten Sunday slot.

The thing I like most – correction, *love* most – about each episode of *Poole* occurs at the very start, while the titles are still rolling and our man strides confidently into the crime scene then stops dead and simply looks. Looks at the corpse, looks at the surroundings, looks at his colleagues and any witnesses there might be. The camera becomes his point of view. Cut to extreme close ups of apparently insignificant details – a coloured thread, an envelope, an odd-looking bruise – these are the vital clues Poole and we the viewers must connect in order to solve the crime. And we have two hours (one hour forty if you watch on DVD) in which to do it. Easier said than done, given all the twists and turns and the trawler-load of trademark very-red herrings we have to negotiate. Personally, I don't have the brain for crime-solving, and I'm far too lazy. I prefer to spectate Poole doing all the work, and gasp in admiration of the man's genius when he identifies the perp in the closing minutes. I have been known to applaud.

In the early days he was frequently compared to Morse. TV audiences took sides. Journalistic sabres were frequently rattled in the name of the preferred detective. For me, there was no doubt whose banner I would fight under. With his passion not for beer and opera, but for Earl Grey tea and his Thelonious Monk LPs, which he never upgraded with the advent of the CD, Poole was my idea of the perfect TV detective (leaving aside the fact he was being played by a good friend of mine). I admit season one looks as though it was filmed by a person with DTs and edited by a butcher's apprentice, but for all its technical shortcomings, it's a classic in the making. It was a *coup* of the original production team to use *Blue Monk* as the theme tune. Quirky and wonky, it's a sort-of-but-not-quite blues that grabs your ear every time. And Poole was more than your average detective. He was younger than standard, and overtly sexy in a way that Morse would never be. He's that species of lover for whom the slow and deliberate folding of his clothes before love-making is part of the foreplay. Picture him if you will, ensuring his trousers retain their blade-sharp creases while his latest woman feverishly rips off her clothes, jamming zips and losing buttons. I cherish a remark Our Hero makes in season three, while his latest conquest, forehead beaded with the sweat of unrequited lust, writhes under the duvet as if her pelvis has been demoniacally possessed. Poole is conscientiously arranging his suit on a hanger: "Got to preserve the real me,' he says calmly. Tum-ti-tum. 'Are you familiar with *Monk's Dream*?"

The real him. Think about it. Who was the real Inspector Poole? The genius detective, the urbane conversationalist, the amiable lover of mid-Century jazz, or the lady-killer? Which leads me to think just how fascinating a biography of Poole might be: his comfortable lower middle class upbringing in Weston-super-Mare, his educational achievements, his brief spell in the TA, his years on the beat, his various promotions, his triumphs as well as the departmental in-fighting that frequently hampers his work. Wouldn't it be fascinating to know the reason he never commits to one woman, and why she'd always be a brunette. Or why, in later episodes, he secretly cherishes the Edwardian flower brooch he retrieved from under the floorboards of his holiday chalet. Whose was it? And whose diaries and letters does he preserve in that safety deposit box in his bank? And why is he never shown reading them, just staring at them as the credits roll? A biographer would get to the bottom of these mysteries, and thus end once and for all the website speculation, which I have to admit I'm starting to find tedious.

My favourite moment? The penultimate episode of the final season, in which Poole learns an ugly truth about his foster sister, that she wasn't all sweetness and light as everyone had supposed. The concluding five minutes had me howling into my hanky. Real moving stuff.

Most hated moment? Easy. Season three, episode nine, in which Poole is framed and has to prove his innocence. Yawn.

All detectives go through this paste gem of a plot, from Morse to the Belgian one. And you just know they'll get themselves off the hook by the end. They should have camped it up a bit; played it for laughs.

Speaking of laughs, surely no one will disagree that the good Inspector's appearance on last year's *Comic Relief* was the highlight of the evening. Anyone who has seen Jim Rudd on stage knows he had a flair for comedy. What a crime, therefore, that Our Hero was never allowed to grin cheesily more often, or stumble into furniture. Perhaps in future episodes, as a consequence of this, he might have been allowed pratfalls and actual jokes.

It's too late, of course, now that the Inspector is no more. Not through retirement, or change of career, or contractual disagreements. He has simply gone. Vanished into the ether.

So what? some people will say. It was just a TV show, like *MASH, Cheers, Friends* – and *Morse*. They were all popular, but when they ended the world continued to revolve. New shows replaced them. Better shows, even. But can there be a better TV detective than Poole? Perhaps we should consult the power stations who braced themselves every Sunday for the eleven million kettles that were switched on at ten o'clock. (I like to imagine a giant red button: 'Post-Poole Booster Supply. Emergency use only'.) Personally, I don't believe any other small-screen detective was as believable or profound. He will never be bettered.

Consider the scripts, ninety-eight per cent were brilliant: clever, literate, witty, generally as unpredictable as the Monk solos Our Man listens to. Two of them won BAFTAs. Remember *Judy* – season five, episode seven? Jim wrote that himself, basing it, I'm proud to say, on the germ of an idea given to him by yours truly (check the credits next time you watch it). For those of you unable to remember, the subplot was a sort-of Vertigo in reverse: Poole becomes obsessed with a blonde – intriguing in itself because of his lack of interest in blondes – and gradually changes her into the dark-haired double of his childhood sweetheart. A shame he didn't sit at the typewriter more often, because that episode is truly powerful and strange and haunts you long afterwards. I must have watched it twenty times. (Not so long ago I met Kelly Temple, the young actress who played Judy so sublimely. I persuaded her to pose in a kimono. The best work I'd done since rehab in the mid-nineties. Check out www.wilsonartzone.)

To get back to the subject of the Inspector's superiority over rival sleuths, Poole was the most enigmatic of them all. Who was he? Why was he? What was his first name? From whence came his formidable sex drive? He was seemingly insatiable. Not that he was disrespectful, or irresponsible, or a heartbreaker, or even heartless. Poole worshipped women. He put the tease into Cartesian: he loved therefore he was. He gave each fresh conquest the definitive bonk and sent her on her merry way perfectly sated. Few ever demanded seconds. And yet his promiscuity was never dirty. It was noble, decent. The women were always classy, independent. No wonder the series has so many female fans (including, I like to imagine, those campus-dwelling sour-pusses who commentate negatively on popular culture, using big words such as hegemony). And gay men worship him too. Remember in season one when Poole's colleague reveals he is gay and madly in love with him? What does the Inspector do? Takes his infatuation seriously and lets him down with tact and humanity. Morse would've tipped a pint over his head. Cracker would've beaten him up.

I've been reading what the press has had to say about both Poole and the actor who breathed life into him. On the whole they admired the series, although the top and bottom end of the gutter were sniffy about it. Elitist? Hardly. Soft porn for women? That's (mass) debatable. I have to agree with the *Evening Standard* on one matter: the final season was too clever for its own good. The plots were far too convoluted. *Tick Tock* was unfathomable. Who was the true bad guy? Beats me. I can't wait for the DVD so that I can have a stab at working it out.

Speaking of the tabloids, there are umpteen lies circulating about Jim.

For the record:

Jim was not gay. All of them referred to this, failing to mention they were responsible for putting out that story in the first place. And why? Because there's nothing the tabloids detest more than asexuality and abstinence. A person buys a tabloid or celebrity gossip magazine not for reasoned observation, but because they have a yen for the prurient. Jim's having no woman automatically meant he was gay. When no same-sex lover was unearthed (I was under suspicion for a time), his apparent lack of sex drive was blamed on defective wedding tackle. The truth was, Jim just didn't fancy anyone enough to want them in his life. He was perfectly content with casual friendships, and he had plenty of those.

As far as I am aware, Jim did not have faulty wedding tackle.

He was not scared of women. He did not hate women.

He was not a transvestite.

He was not a miser. This lie offends me deeply because Jim was one of the most generous people I have ever known. I wouldn't be alive to write this had he not supported me financially during my rehab years. And he never asked for one penny back – just the promise of sobriety.

Jim did not have cancer, or a brain tumour, or AIDS. He did not have a faulty heart. He wasn't mad. He wasn't taken out by an obsessed fan. Jim committed suicide because he was deeply depressed. More deeply depressed than any of us realised. No firearms were involved. He didn't slash his wrists in the bath, or inhale car fumes, or stride into the sea at Southwold, or leap off Gorleston pier with weights in his pockets while his eighty-nine-year-old wheelchair-bound mother screamed for help.

Suicide by sleeping tablets washed down with Scotch. And yes, they were administered by his own hand, not forced down his gullet by a deranged fan. Same old story: the tabloids have been fabricating rumours in order to sell copy. My advice is don't buy the blessed things in the first place. There's more truth in *The Beano*.

Contrary to one of these rumours, there was a suicide note. The police took it very seriously; tweezered it into a plastic bag and whisked it away for analysis. I've read it. It's short and to the point. He doesn't say why he is so depressed (please show some respect and refrain from speculation, web-users), only that he's had enough and goodbye folks. I can report that the writing was uncharacteristically shaky, which I believe was due to his having written it while barely conscious. There was a Will. His money and investments are to go to his parents and nephew, while all his material possessions are passed to yours truly: house and contents, including personal papers to dispose of as I see fit, his holiday beach-hut and contents (fold-up chairs, camp bed, kettle, 11 Co-op own brand tea bags which I'll never have the heart to brew or sell on the internet).

A word of warning: the items of clothing for sale on the internet – shoes, shirts, even underpants – are not Jim's. Do not be fooled into buying them. I personally saw to the disposal of his modest wardrobe, every last thread of it, in a bonfire on Gorleston beach.

Were there any more of Jim's own *Poole* scripts hidden among his papers? Alas no. Sorry, guys. Nor were there any unfinished novels or an autobiography. Surprisingly, there was no intimate journal. There were, however, box loads of letters from friends and fans, and notebooks filled with professional observations. Never one to embark on a theatrical role without proper research, Jim had penned to self innumerable notes regarding the characters he was playing or playing against. This sort of obsessive preparation paid dividends. He was a renowned interpreter of Beckett, and his Pinter had the critics going all bleary-eyed and weak at the knees. His finest Pinter moment? It has to be *Betrayal*, of course. The broadsheet critics have been unanimous: the finest production ever! a must-see! Sold out for months in advance at the time of Jim's passing, it is now, regrettably, a can-never-see. Consider yourselves blessed, those of you who attended Jim's final, note-perfect performances.

Surely our world would've been a poorer place without James Rudd, and not just because of the Grade 1 listed detective he breathed life into, or his theatre work. Not many people appreciate just how sought-after Jim was for his mellifluous voice-overs. Why do so many women hypnotically reach for a particular brand of coffee rather than another, or drive to some way-out-of-town warehouse to check out the sofas when the one they have at home is brand new? And why was that documentary about *The Extremely Tedious History of Hinges* so inexplicably riveting? Keep your eye on the credits; you'll see Jim's name two, three times a week.

I was asked by his mother (who I must point out is sixty-six next birthday, not eighty-nine, a line-dancing exponent with no need for a wheelchair) to speak a few words at the memorial service. How could I refuse? I spent a week composing Jim's eulogy, filling it with clever quotes, over-polished anecdotes and the obligatory poem (one of Jim's own, called *Gorleston* – yes, at one time he had harboured ambitions to be a poet), but as soon as I was facing my fellow mourners, all I wanted to do was tell them what a great guy he was, and how I valued his friendship more than any other. So I left my script in my pocket and improvised. Spoke from the heart. No quotes. No cleverness. Just the plain truth, that you couldn't find a nicer guy, period.

Our Late Friend deserves more than a couple of thousand words dispatched into cyberspace, and if I had the wherewithal,

I'd certainly pen a more fittingly substantial tribute than this. With that in mind, let me end by thanking everyone who attended that service at St Andrew's church in his home town. The turn-out was extraordinary. I've never seen anything like it. Sir This and Dame That rubbing shoulders with gaffers and best boys, and an exaltation of his screen lovers lining up for the paparazzi: forty of our finest and most gorgeous actresses looking nothing like the dark-haired and pasty-faced lovers Poole craved. It was particularly good to see so many of our old Gorleston friends, too, some of whom had travelled hundreds of miles to pay their respects. Shame we didn't have *The Links* to sardine ourselves into afterwards. It would've been like old times; except mine would've been an orange juice.

Cheers, Jim. Hail and farewell!

Biography latest!

In a recent *Bookseller* article, celebrated painter Tim Wilson reveals that since inheriting James Rudd's private papers, he has been assembling them into a biography. 'It's not your usual biog, though,' he says. 'You know: born such-and-such, did this, did that. That would be boring. Jim deserves more than that. He deserves Art. I'm certain he would have given my project his blessing.' Is there sufficient interest to warrant a biography? 'There's a hell of a lot of speculative crap posted on the internet. I feel it's my duty to every Poole fan to let them know what the actor who played him was really like,' Wilson affirms. 'That's potentially a heck of a lot of readers.' Are his intentions for writing a biography entirely altruistic? 'Yes. Definitely. I'm hoping to reinvest all monies earned from the book in a French property my wife Maria and I are currently developing into a residential painting school. Painting was dear to Jim's heart. He would certainly have involved himself in this exciting project, had he been around.'

Full details of courses and fees will be appearing on Tim's website, along with some never-seen-before photos of teenaged Jim at a beach party.

Watch this space for full publication details of Tim Wilson's forthcoming biography of James Rudd, provisionally entitled *The Story of You, Me and Her*.

(Real) author's note

The History of Us[1] is fiction, not autobiography. It was through sheer laziness that I set my novel – the first from my three-decade apprenticeship[2] to be published[3] – in and around my home town of Gorleston[4] and the South Wales of my student years. With the exception of Oliver[5], whose leash I led on several summer evening strolls[6], all characters are invented. The things they do are not based on any real events and are determined by the logic of plot.

[1] Written 2003-2008 and dedicated with love to my partner Pamela. The book is also for the late, great Jan Mark, much missed, who read an early draft.

[2] Many books penned, many rejection letters received, my instruction 'Please Do Not Bend' on the return envelopes always rejected by the Post Office.

[3] Thanks to the efforts of my agent Judith Antell, who helped me turn a typescript into a book. I am eternally grateful for her support, enthusiasm, good taste and professionalism.

[4] Resident 1962-81, partial resident 1981-84, frequent visitor thereafter. *The Links* existed. It was comfortable and popular with locals and tourists (beachwear not permitted). As James mentions, it was demolished at the end of the century. The Art Mouveau building on Trafalgar Road in Great Yarmouth which house the excellent College of Art and Design stood empty for many years before being converted into apartments. Wilson would have been a contemporary of mine there. I wouldn't have liked him. *My Plaice* is imaginary, as is Lake House Clinic, Scott's shop and listening station, Alison's school and Oxford College and James' beach hut. Polanski's

Tess was screened in Yarmouth in September 1981 though I was regrettably unable to attend.

[5] Timourous and taupe, though possibly not terrior.

[6] In 1981, on the beach and along country lanes since engulfed by housing development. All things change (and we change with them).

Legend Press

Independent Book Publisher

This book has been published by vibrant publishing company Legend Press. If you enjoyed reading it then you can help make it a major hit. Just follow these three easy steps:

1. Recommend it
Pass it onto a friend to spread word-of-mouth or, if now you've got your hands on this copy you don't want to let it go, just tell your friend to buy their own or maybe get it for them as a gift. Copies are available with special deals and discounts from our own website and from all good bookshops and online outlets.

2. Review it
It's never been easier to write an online review of a book you love and can be done on Amazon, Waterstones.com, WHSmith.co.uk and many more. You could also talk about it or link to it on your own blog or social networking site.

3. Read another of our great titles
We've got a wide range of diverse modern fiction and it's all waiting to be read by fresh-thinking readers like you! Come to us direct at www.legendpress.co.uk to take advantage of our superb discounts. (Plus, if you email info@legend-paperbooks.co.uk just after placing your order and quote 'WORD OF MOUTH', we will send another book with your order absolutely free!)

Thank you for being part of our word of mouth campaign.

info@legend-paperbooks.co.uk
www.legendpress.co.uk